NIGHT TRAINS

What would you do if you suddenly started seeing lights, people and trains that aren't supposed to be there?

What would you do if you were given a chance to help right the greatest wrong of the last century?

What would you do if the price of the train ticket was your sanity, your life, or even your soul?

ARTHUR CHRENKOFF

ABOUT THE AUTHOR

Arthur Chrenkoff was born in Krakow, Poland. For the past 18 years he has made his home in Brisbane, Australia, where he completed a Doctorate in Law and has been working in national politics. Until recently he wrote an extremely popular and well-regarded international affairs blog (chrenkoff.blogspot.com); his work has appeared in *Opinion Journal* and *The New York Times*. This is his first novel.

NIGHT TRAINS

—◆—

ARTHUR CHRENKOFF

COLD SPRING PRESS

COLD SPRING PRESS

P.O. Box 284, Cold Spring Harbor, NY 11724

For my father Stanislaw Chrenkoff
and my mother Ewa Chrenkoff nee Starzak (1943-2006)

ISBN 1-59360-080-1
Library of Congress Control No. 2006929069
– All Rights Reserved –
Printed in the United States of America

Acknowledgments

While many characters in this book are real, and many incidents described did happen, *Night Trains* is a work of fiction, and as such it takes some liberties, particularly with the geography of night-time Europe.

Getting this project all the way from a germ of an idea almost ten years ago to the book you are now holding in your hands has been a long (though exciting and rewarding) journey. I would like to thank all those who have boarded the night trains over that time to offer suggestions and encouragement: Estelle, Borys, Mark, Karl, Harry-David, Daniel, Sophie Masson, Pip Masson, and Margaret Kennedy. I would also like to thank all of my blogger friends whose help and support made it possible. And most importantly, a big thank you to my publisher, Jonathan Stein – who wanted a book about a different war, but fate intervened – for his faith in *Night Trains* and his encouragement and support.

CONTENTS

———

Before Twilight

I PUT THE gun to the back of the woman's head. The muzzle almost brushes against her bronze hair, once glorious, now matted and lifeless after all the sleepless nights and the long journey on the back of a lorry. Her body quivers and she whimpers something in the incomprehensible gibberish of Yiddish.

It's a beautiful day. The summer is so intense, so warm, so determined to stamp her full glory on the world before she'll wither away in a few weeks' time.

The crisp, fragrant air fills my lungs, and I feel they could burst through my chest and float to the sky like two balloons. Above me, pine treetops spear the deep blue sky. There's hardly any breeze to sway them. I have never felt so alive.

I pull the trigger.

A clap of thunder rings through the forest. And yet there are no storm clouds in the sky.

Blood, brain, and bone splinters rain on me, spray my face, coat the front of my uniform. Again. I'll have to get it washed tomorrow. I wipe my cheeks with a handkerchief. The cloth is no longer white.

The women collapses as if the ground had suddenly disappeared from under her feet. A few short spasms convulse her body and then everything around me is still again. Only other thunders explode among the trees. No other sound intrudes. The birds are long gone, and the flies haven't arrived yet.

The woman is lying a few feet away from a girl, seven, maybe eight years old, and a younger boy. I gave the mother a choice: which one of her children did she want to save? She took too much time deciding, so I shot the boy first, then the girl, and then, finally, her. By that stage, I suppose, her mind was already gone. Next to these three lay an old man, half his face missing, his long white beard matted with blood that has already started drying out in the warm sun. And further away, another woman. She screamed, tried to run, took two bullets.

I weigh the gun in my hand. The magazine is empty. I eject it and slip in a new one. Time for a break. I walk back towards the edge of the clearing.

Werner's there, leaning against a tree, smoking a cigarette. He offers me one from a pack and I take it.

"How's the pest control going?" he asks.

"Good," I say. "Hopefully not many more today. I want to go swimming."

"Yes, a nice day for a little dip, isn't it?" Werner says, looking up to the sky.

Somebody, somewhere out there cries out. The shots keep on ringing.

*   *   *

The night is so peaceful and still that for a brief moment I can almost believe that none of it is real.

But it's no use.

And so here it is, T.J. I made a promise to myself that one day I would tell you. I'm sorry it's so late – too late–but I just couldn't do it before ... Bear with me and you'll know why.

When you're listening to these words I'm probably dead. Or at least away. Far away. I'm sorry if it's not making much sense to you. That's because it all still doesn't make much sense to me. It has destroyed my whole life, yet I still don't know quite what to make of it.

But listen on. Even if you won't understand, at least you'll know, and for whatever it's worth I'm now quite desperate for somebody to know. Having to hold it all inside has been tougher than anything else I've had to go through.

Maybe it's better that I not tell you all this. Maybe it's better if you remembered me like I was before. Maybe.

But the tape is rolling, and it's too late for second thoughts.

So here it is, T.J.

Dusk

IT DIDN'T SEEM like the way my life would start to end. I guess it never does.

Just an ordinary station at midday. Walls of trees muffling the noise from distant roads, a dirty quilt of clouds, promising the rain that would not come. A world of its own, suspended like an insect in a drop of suburban amber.

All the smoothly dressed professionals working in the city were long gone, taking with them their rolled up newspapers, irritating cell ring tones, and bored looks. Schoolchildren were gone, too.

So it was just me, the platform, and three others.

There was a dishevelled schoolboy very late for school, swinging his legs from a bench too high for him, and a few paces away from him an unhealthy looking pensioner, his parchment-like skin tightly wrapped around his head as if his old skull were a precious gift. He was sweating profusely, suffocating inside a woollen coat two sizes too big.

And then there was an old man in a gray tweed suit, sitting on a bench against the wall of the station building.

Later, I would wish that I'd not have paid him any attention and forgotten about him as the train took me away. But now I realize that it wouldn't have mattered. I don't have the luxury of believing in coincidences anymore, and I know that if it hadn't been that day, I'd have met him some other time.

So I can't really curse myself that I suddenly grew tired of standing alone at the end of the platform and came over to sit on the bench next to the old man in a tweed suit.

*   *   *

Night. A different station. There's no moon and no stars, all hidden under the dark shroud of clouds. The only light, a sickly bluish glare, comes from a few lamps swinging underneath the overhanging roof. On the platform, bundles wrapped in blankets and shapeless coats huddle against the wall of the building, barely distinguishable as human beings.

I strike a match and bring it close to my face. I feel the pale shadow of warmth on the palm of my hand as I shelter the flame from sudden gusts of wind. It comes violent and biting, like howling packs of wolves, travelling all the way from the deep bowels of a frozen continent.

The tip of the cigarette starts to glow faintly inches from my face. I inhale slowly and close my eyes. The tobacco is raw, fetid, and priceless. The smoke scratches at my eyes and flows down my throat like a vaporous sand paper. But it kills the stench of fear and burnt onion that hovers over the shapeless forms that share the platform with me. The one next to my feet stirs uneasily in its sleep, perhaps dreaming of home, a lost lover, or maybe just the warm welcoming darkness of death.

In a few minutes a train will slowly roll alongside the platform. An asthmatic steel centipede will exhale great clouds of steam as its wheels grind to a halt, and the station will erupt out of hibernation with a few frenzied moments of scramble and noise.

A man in his early thirties will step out onto the platform, a flowing overcoat with a fur collar hastily thrown on top of a drab olive uniform. He will look around, slowly and deliberately, a copy of yesterday's paper tucked under his right arm as an agreed signal. Our gazes will meet for a moment and I will look into his eyes, burning in the pale lamplight with the sick glow of a morphine addict. He will take in a few deep breaths of the ice cold air, cough perhaps, and disappear back inside the carriage without acknowledging me. After the last drag, the cigarette will die under my boot and I will follow him onto the train, to the third compartment down the corridor.

I'm straining to hear that distant rumble of the steam engine, but there's nothing yet. I turn my back to the wind and try to peer through the black curtain. The light of day, a cloud-covered sky and the rain that doesn't fall are an unthinkably distant memory. So is the old man in a gray tweed suit. I can picture him in my mind as if I'd seen him only a moment ago, but he, the bench he sits on and the station - my station - are so very far away they might as well be somewhere beyond these stars that I can't see tonight.

*   *   *

Although he was sitting down I could see he was small and rather chubby. His clothes were neither new nor fashionable, but they were tidy and well cut. Even the felt hat resting on his lap was color-coordinated with the rest of his outfit. The picture seemed just right; a perfect grandpa from a TV commercial shot in warm autumn colors through a misty lens.

There was a healthy glow about him that made him look at least ten years younger than betrayed by the whisks of white hair behind his ears and at the back of his head. His gaze was fixed on something in the distance, his thick rectangular glasses halfway down his nose, overhanging a snow white, pencil thin, well groomed moustache that went out of vogue a long, long time ago.

I came over to the bench and sat down on the edge. He turned towards me, smiled and nodded. I nodded back, hoping that this would be the extent of our social interaction. I always hated small talk with strangers, with its fake politeness, fake concern and fake interest. No casual conversation with a stranger has ever had any consequences for my life. Until that day, that is.

"I hope it will not rain," he said after a while, breaking the pleasant silence.

I turned and nodded in a non-committal way, but he didn't elaborate and returned to staring into the distance.

I was just about to fall back into my thoughts when he spoke again. "I do not like these trains." He turned towards me and added, "They are not real trains, you know?"

He saw the blank expression on my face and waved his hand impatiently. "They do not have... how should I say it... any soul."

Nothing mundane then. I was expecting a lecture about the perpetual lateness of service, overcrowding, or the schoolkids putting their feet on the dirty-green seat, but his was merely a metaphysical complaint.

"Those suburban trains; they are just glorified trams," the old man went on, unfazed by my silence. "The real trains, now that is something. None of those electric wires, doors that open by themselves, and windows you cannot open at all. Trains were not meant to be like that."

He hesitated for a moment, as if suddenly embarrassed by his exuberance. "But then I think that is what they call progress and I am just an old man who likes to complain, so do not mind me, please," he added and a weak smile played briefly on his lips.

It was difficult to pinpoint his accent on a simpleton's mental map of the Old World. I placed him somewhere in Central Europe, because it reminded me of a neighbor I once had. He was a stern-looking man who kept mostly to himself and listened to crackling foreign stations on his long wave receiver. For some reason he terrified me, though my older brother displayed an unhealthy fascination, imagining him a war criminal, hiding from his blood-soaked past on our quiet suburban street. Only when the man died and his estranged son came up from interstate to take care of his father's affairs, we learned he was Estonian, a slave laborer in Germany during the war; a victim, not a perpetrator. That truth seemed to disappoint my brother. I would wonder whether in some twisted sort of way he really wanted to live next door to a pensioned monster.

"And one other thing; those suburban trains are just that – suburban trains," I realized that the old man was still talking to me. "How far can these trains go? Just to the outskirts and that is it. Trains should be free like horses; go, go, go" he cackled. "Go across the empty fields, through forests, down the valleys..."

He paused suddenly and lowered his eyes, "Gosh, you must be wishing you had not sat next to me." Suddenly he seemed almost bashful. His fingers drummed on the bench next to his leg, yet his face radiated with excitement, as if he had just won a hundred meter sprint.

I didn't quite know what to say. "No," I murmured, but meant yes, even if the old man seemed harmless enough. I glanced at my watch. A few more minutes of waiting.

The old man took a white handkerchief out of a coat pocket and wiped his brow. "You see, I was a stationmaster in Europe, a long time ago, during the war," he went on, but more subdued now. "Do not get me started on trains, I can go on whole day," he chuckled again, but it was a humorless response.

I bet he could. "I won't," I promised.

The train arrived just on time, its rumble breaking slowly like a distant wave above the white noise of the city.

"I–," I stood up and pointed towards the train when it came to a halt in front of us.

The retired station master did not let me finish. "Well, have a nice day," he waved me on. "Who knows, I might see you again some other time soon, young man."

No promises, old man.

II.

He was there again, one Saturday morning, some two weeks later. I forgot about the switch to the weekend timetable and found myself with twenty minutes to spare before my train was to arrive.

I was reclining back on the bench with my eyes closed, mentally undressing a girl I briefly kissed last night before she disappeared leaving me with her phone number. Things were looking good.

"Good afternoon, young man. I see we meet again."

The girl vanished, and he was here instead, a rather poor replacement. He had a different suit on, a black woollen outfit with gray pin-stripes, as elegant but just as out of fashion as his previous choice. His hat was again resting on his lap, his long fingers caressing the felt rim. I didn't hear him come over and sit down next to me.

"Indeed," I forced a weak smile.

"Going to the city?" he asked.

"My car's getting fixed," I said. "Normally I would drive in on the weekend."

He pursed his lips and nodded in apparent sympathy.

"By the way," he said. "It is quite rude of me to chat with you like that all the time without introducing myself." He extended his hand, "My name is Bartok. Franz Bartok. Like the composer." he added with hesitation in his voice, judging me an inhabitant of a cultural desert.

"Martin," I shook his hand. "Any relation? To the composer, I mean."

If he were a maiden, he would have blushed then. "Oh, no. Not that I know, at least. One could hope, of course. It would certainly be exciting."

His father was Hungarian, he explained, his mother Austrian ("God rest their souls."), but he missed out by a few years being born the subject of the Austro-Hungarian Emperor. Seeing the empire didn't quite survive the end of the First World War, that made him what? Pretty old. Hell, time had obviously been very kind to him.

"-drew a new border and my parents decided they would rather take their chances in the new Austria. We had more family there and they wanted to help, so we moved to near Innsbruck. My father used to work for the imperial railways, after the war for the Austrian railways. When I turned fifteen I too-" He paused, "Oh dear, I am boring you very much, no?"

I shrugged. "No, that's fine." I didn't really care.

*　*　*

By the time Hitler had realized his dream of uniting all the German people within his Reich, Bartok was a station master in a small town close to the Swiss border. A year later, when the war broke out, he avoided the draft as his work for the railways was deemed essential to the war effort. He survived years of bombing raids, but his home was hit by a shell in the last months of the war, and his wife and young son were buried under the rubble. There was nothing left for him in his small town, and so one day he walked away and joined the wandering of millions of others to find a new life beyond the ocean. He kept on working for the railways in his new homeland, retired some time ago and now lived alone in a little house on Alicia Street, not very far from the station.

So that was it. Just another pensioner with nothing much to do in what the marketing industry has ironically christened as the golden years. Nothing much to do, except to sit on a bench and let the sun warm your old bones. And talk to strangers about trains.

I didn't remember seeing him at the station before, but he insisted that he'd seen me quite often in the past. I rarely paid much attention to people around me in public places, so he might have been right. I didn't press the point.

The train finally arrived and we said our goodbyes.

"Until the next time," he said as he waved me farewell.

*   *   *

His English was pretty good for a migrant with no more than a primary school education. Those who came off the ships after the war didn't have a lot of time to better themselves. Railway work didn't make one a polyglot either. They lived, played and prayed among their own, and their English remained clumsy and basic, barely overlaying the inflections of their old corners, and betraying them as surely as did their mannerisms and habits.

Bartok's speech was different. Yes, he would never escape the distant echo of his mother tongue, but the way he spoke, his careful grammar and the textbook vocabulary made him sound more like an émigré professor than a railway man. Maybe this determined young man with no family and too many memories keeping him awake had taught himself the new language night after night while his friends slept, felled by the day's back-breaking work. Maybe.

III.

I can't remember what woke me up.

I was a light sleeper; it could have been anything. It probably wasn't.

I pulled the sheets over my head and curled up in the middle of the bed, hoping to catch a lift back to the comforting landscapes of my dream country. But it was no use. My mind was now awake, even if my body still resisted.

After a while I sighed and opened my eyes. Square digital numbers were glowing on the face of the alarm clock, just some red shapes too blurry for me to read. My hand felt around the paper mountain on the desk, searching for my glasses. I finally found them wedged between books and computer keyboard.

It was two thirty. Too early to give up on sleep. It would catch up with me by lunchtime, and I couldn't afford to spend half the day barely conscious. But I couldn't sleep either.

A gust of chilly morning air burst in from outside and gave me a violent shiver. I leaned over and slid the window shut.

The night was dark, cloudy, and moonless. Instead, it was the pinpricks of street lamps scattered along the valley down below that formed their own giant Milky Way, as if the heavens and earth decided to swap places for a while.

Ahead of me and slightly to my right, at the foot of the hill, lay the train yards. A maze of tracks, with a scattering of old sheds and decrepit buildings, spread out over a few dozen acres in the valley. At night the yards formed a rough rectangle of pitch darkness, a black hole surrounded by the lights of suburbia.

All tracks led to the city, and all of them would pass through the yards. Once, when railroads still mattered, the whole wealth of the state would roll through there. That time was long gone. The lines have closed and the economy now bypassed the yards. Property developers salivated over the inner city site, community groups dreamed of a new park, and the transport bureaucracy, the yard's cruel stepmother, sat back and reserved its judgment, as bureaucracies tend to do. A few freight trains would still pass through, and the old rolling stock would come down to their own elephant cemetery, but it was all a pretense. The last night watchman had left years ago, following the realization that there was nothing valuable left to steal, and even the part-time Satanists now preferred the local cemetery.

The yards should have been peacefully asleep now.

It took me a while to realize they weren't.

Somewhere in the middle of the dark expanse a few pinpricks of bluish light shone brightly, teasing the darkness like the eyes of a predator.

I don't know why I paid it any attention. The last man out must have forgotten to switch off the lights. I would have probably collapsed back onto the bed if not for the train.

The only movement I saw with any clarity were the bellows of steam coming out of the chimney. Almost as soon as I realized what I was seeing the train disappeared somewhere behind the line of trees and old warehouses. The muffled metallic tattoo of wheels rolling on the tracks lingered on a bit longer but soon it too receded into the night.

The spectacle lasted maybe ten seconds.

Steam engine, I thought, how quaint. It was almost like seeing a dinosaur, and just as surreal, at two thirty in the morning.

I took a few deep breaths and I felt the sleep descending on me again, gently caressing my back and pulling a curtain over my eyes. I lay back on the bed and let the night close in around me. In my last conscious thought I realized that after the train had gone, the lights have gone out too and darkness claimed the railway yards once again.

I didn't think about the train until breakfast. It then suddenly occurred to me that I haven't actually seen it coming. Suddenly it was just there, running at full speed through the yards, and moment later it had passed and vanished, like a dream. The more I thought about it the less certain I was that I have really seen it.

IV.

I cranked up the air conditioning and wound up the window to escape the summer heat, the bark of mad dogs, and the quintessentially suburban smell of freshly mowed grass, which I despised.

I was driving back from my ex-girlfriend's place. I had to visit and console her on the tragic and unexpected death of her mother. The mother had turned 45 only a few days ago and was returning home after small celebrations with her friends from work when she wrapped her brand-new Toyota around a power pole on a particularly tricky curve about one kilometer up the road from home. She was never a heavy drinker; her friends later said that she wouldn't have had more than two glasses of champagne. There were no other cars involved, and no witnesses. An old lady who lived across the road heard the crash and called the police. It took the firemen two hours to cut the body out of the wreckage. The accident got a fifteen second mention on the nightly news, just before the sports segment.

"They did the autopsy the next day," my ex said, her head resting on my shoulder, half turned away towards the window. I had my arms around her, but it was nothing like it once used to be. "You know what they've found? She had an undetected cervical cancer. The doctor said she would have been dead in twelve months' time. It was too advanced, he said, they wouldn't have been able to do anything for her."

"Double whammy," I said. "Shit."

We were standing in the middle of the living room. The sun filtered softly through the curtains and the dust danced on the rays of light.

"I'm glad you came. I really appreciate it," she sighed. She did not cry, and somehow I didn't think she would while I was with her.

"Don't even mention it," I said rocking her gently in my arms. "I'm sorry it took me so long. I've only heard last night. From Jim."

Sarah was the only one of my relationships that ended without tears and recriminations. We allowed ourselves to slowly drift apart, intuitively satisfied that it simply wasn't to be, but not blaming each other for our disappointment. Later on, we didn't exactly try to keep in touch, but we did not avoid each other either when mutual friends brought us together for an occasional celebration. We exchanged Christmas cards every year and sincerely wished each other all the best.

We talked for a few more minutes about safe and neutral things, and after the obligatory offer of anything I could do, we said goodbye.

I remembered the road works and the line of traffic I passed on the way to Sarah's place, and driving back I took a different route. I didn't realize quite where I was until I felt the jolt of driving over a railway crossing. Then I knew.

I put the indicator on and pulled up on the side of the road. A wave of oppressive heat hit me when I opened the door. I swore under my breath and yanked myself out of the car.

There was another unguarded crossing about fifty meters down the road. The gate was locked and it didn't look like it had been in use recently. A rusty chain link fence separated the grounds from a narrow asphalt sidewalk and the street. Wilted weeds sprouted along its base, adding to the desolate feel.

Twenty meters beyond the fence a row of decrepit warehouses rose up from the ground. Just like the railways they serviced, the warehouses had seen better times, ages ago. The new management had not even bothered to paint over the ghosts of the old writing. On one wall I could still see "Johns & Sons. Grain Merchants," which in its prime must have stood out in bold black against a white background, but now gray was only melting into another shade of gray.

Only two or three out of a dozen warehouses seemed to be still in use. They looked just as decrepit as the others, but their doors were open and a few workers were milling around, attending to old wagons. Further away, a forklift was unloading small containers from a freight train.

A railway worker was standing outside a small gate, about twenty yards from where I parked my car. He was a tall, prematurely balding man in his thirties, turned rich brown from working outdoors. The black oval sunglasses gave him a menacing insectoid look. He was getting the last few drags out of his cigarette and absent-mindedly kicking the dirt with his boot.

"Excuse me," I started walking towards him.

He turned towards me and stared at me like a man caught doing something improper.

"Listen," I said. "Do you still get many steam trains going through here?"

His body relaxed. I wasn't trouble.

"Steam train enthusiast, eh?" he said. It sounded more like an insult than a question.

"Yes, a bit," I lied.

"Not from around here, are we?" he asked. I couldn't see his eyes behind the sunglasses but his expression was pretty blank.

"Why?"

"Well, otherwise you'd probably know that they took all steamers out of action years ago." There was a hint of satisfaction in his voice, as if he was happy to disappoint another sucker. "Too costly to run and too costly to fix," he added, trying to sound like an expert.

I'm not sure what sort of answer I was expecting but this wasn't it. "I could have sworn I've seen one here quite recently," I persevered.

He pressed his lips tightly and shook his head. "Couldn't 'ave been. As I said we don't use 'em any more. Switched to diesel engines completely. There's still some steam ones running, but that would be up north, just for the tourists. None here." He paused for a few seconds as if pondering something. "When did you say you saw one?"

"Oh," I shrugged. "A few days ago. Actually it was at night."

It didn't ring any bells with him. He shook his head again. "There wouldn't 'ave been trains going through here at night. And no steam trains as I said. You must 'ave seen a normal one."

"Yeah, I must have." I hadn't. Normal trains don't blow smoke.

"Yeah," he said, eager to finish the conversation with a budding trainspotter who couldn't tell a steam engine from a diesel one.

I was just about to walk back to my car but I stopped and asked one more question. "Do you fellows do much work on the nightshifts?"

"We don't have any nightshifts," his eyebrows rose betraying impatience.

"So no one does any work around here at night?"

"No. Why?" The suspicious animal stirred again.

I made a vague gesture with my hand. "It used to be busier, eh? The government's not spending much on railways anymore?"

"Too right, mate," he said. "Too right. The bums only look after themselves and this whole place is going to shits."

This time I was leaving. "Well, thanks anyway."

"No worries," he waved his hand, glad to be left alone.

I was staring at my car when I saw a Barman's Express van pull by the gate. The driver stepped out, slid the side door open, took out a carton of beer and passed it onto the railway man. My railway insider exchanged a few words with the driver while fishing in his pocket for some change. It was one o'clock.

Maybe it was all a dream. Otherwise I was stuck with a steam train that wasn't there, going through the yards lit up by workers who weren't working there at that time.

The day seemed to be getting hotter and I already had a splitting headache. I didn't feel like thinking too much anymore.

V.

He waved at me as I was descending the stairs from the overpass onto the platform. Instinctively I waved back, realizing too late that now I would be obliged to go over to him and have a chat. The angel sitting on my right shoulder was taken aback by my antisocial impulse. Get a hold of yourself, he whispered in my ear, he's just an old man, not a child molester.

"I saw a train," I said as I sat down next to him. It was one of those Freudian slips; I meant to say 'Nice day, isn't it?'

"Ah," he smiled. There was a delicate breeze in the air and it levitated a rebellious strand of hair behind his left ear.

"It was a–" I was suddenly lost for words, "–a different train."

I didn't know whether I really wanted to go any further. It felt vaguely embarrassing, as if I had to owe up to still wetting my bed. But who better to confide about trains than a retired station master? Please lay down on the bench and relax, young man, and tell me about your relationship with your mother. And about the trains.

"A different train," he repeated, just when the silence was starting to become uncomfortable. His gaze drifted off. "Every train is different."

I pushed my glasses back. On humid days like this they had an irritating habit of slowly sliding down my nose. "It was a steam train," I explained.

His upper body rotated towards me, as if to make the conversation more intimate. "Ah, a steam train," he repeated. "Not many of those left around. Pity," he sighed wistfully. "They were the real trains."

A sharp staccato noise made me jump and look around. A half crashed can of Coke was rolling down the platform. It lingered motionless for a moment and then drifted, pushed by a sudden gust of wind, over the gray gritty concrete of the ramp, past the yellow "don't cross this line while the train is approaching" line and disappeared over the edge. There was a dull clink as it hit the gravel and then the station was quiet again. I turned back around. Mr. Bartok, no relation to the famous composer, was still looking at me unperturbed.

"You did not tell me before that you were interested in trains," he said. A half-question, half-statement. Of regret, perhaps.

"No, I didn't. I'm not, " I shrugged. "I'm not interested in trains. But this one was different."

"You said that already."

A truck with a broken muffler thundered somewhere close by. This time I resisted the urge to be distracted.

"I know," I said, feeling more self-conscious with every word coming out of my mouth. I was ready to stand up and make up some convenient excuse, then leave. It was silly. "It was in the middle of the night," I heard myself stumbling on instead. "Pretty dark. A moonless night. But I could see it, you know, the smoke–"

He nodded, encouraging me to go on with my confessions. "I looked out the window but I couldn't really see it. As I said, just a movement; a black shape against the black background. And the steam coming out... Then a few days later I was passing by the yards and I started talking to this fellow who works there, and you know what he told me?"

"That there are no steam engines working anymore?"

I opened my mouth but before I could say anything Bartok leaned over towards me and patted my hand with his. "I am a station master – well, a retired stationmaster, remember?" he shrugged. "I know such things."

He was right, of course. But my palms were sweaty and it wasn't just the Queensland summer heat. "So what was it?" I asked.

"It was a train, " he said. "A different train, as you said."

"How different?" I pressed on. "Some kind of tourist train from interstate?"

He took out a white handkerchief out of the blazer pocket and wiped his brow. "You could say that." At that moment I thought I could imagine him like he used to be, almost sixty years ago, the smiling, friendly station master. It's twenty-five past four, madam. I'm afraid there will be a slight delay. Some little problem up the line. Terribly sorry. Say, aren't they lovely children? You must be so proud. "A tourist train from interstate," the retired station master repeated slowly. He was old again and sitting next to me.

"Have you ever been on it?" I had no idea why I asked this question.

"Oh, no. Unfortunately not." he sounded almost apologetic, as if sorry to disappoint me. "Not on this one. I know it well, though. It is the 2:35 to Vienna."

"Why?"

"Why what?"

"Why is it the 2:35 to Vienna?"

"Well," his hand caressed the rim of the hat. "Because it departs the station at 2:35, and it goes to Vienna."

The eyes are supposed to be the mirrors of one's soul and I peered very hard into his to find a glimmer of insanity, or maybe just a senile dementia. But he held my gaze and the only thing I thought I could see was a flicker of amusement. I now expected him to burst out in giggles, wave his hand around and apologize for having fun at my expense. But he didn't. He stood up instead.

"If you excuse me," he put his hat back on and then straightened the wrinkles on his coat with slow and deliberate movements. "It is my tea time. When you get to my age you do not want to miss it." He put two fingers to the brim of his hat in an old-fashioned farewell. "As always, it was nice talking to you, Martin."

I didn't call after him, or try to stop him as he walked away. The metal tip of his umbrella clinked on the concrete with his every step, until the passing traffic drowned it out.

The train to the city was two minutes late. It was only some time after I stepped out into the beehive of the central station that I realized I had left my bag on the seat. I stood on the platform, motionless, long after all the passengers disappeared up the escalators. On the billboard across the track an unnaturally joyful young couple were engaged in a pillow fight, but I wouldn't be able to tell you what they were advertising.

VI.

You're an idiot, I thought to myself, for not having better things to do than worry about your stupid little conversation.

When I was a child I didn't scare easily. Other kids would watch celluloid monsters and squeal with a mixture of fear and excitement; I just sat there wondering what the whole fuss was about. Even then I must have instinctively known that real people could be far more terrifying and revolting than any imagined creatures. Reading history later on in life only made me realize how right I was.

But reading was a mixed blessing. When my friends were growing out of their cartoon world I was starting to grow into my own private world of delusions, where everything I read was true, if only because it had been written down. I never met a conspiracy I didn't like and a revelation I didn't believe to be authentic. I became a sad paranoid little case.

I got over it eventually. Maybe that's why I finally said goodbye to history and gave my all to money. Money was simple, money was clean, there was only one side to it. It was intellectually risk-free, and I loved it.

And yet, some of that old twisted me remained, only buried much deeper, under all the fine layers of rationality. Once a junkie, always a junkie, even if you quit. You might go through life clean but you are always only one stumble away from the abyss.

So after all was said and done people like Bartok could still screw with my head. Whether I thought him harmless but demented or humorous in a malicious sort of way, I simply couldn't get him out of my head. I scanned through never-ending columns of numbers rolling down my computer screen, recommended some good stocks to my friends and clients, made a pile myself, got drunk a few times with friends, screwed some ditzy blonde until my nuts felt like bowling balls, but wherever I was and whatever I did, Mr. Bartok was the delicate itch at the back of my mind. Not all the time, but always ready to pop up like a malicious jack-in-the-box, with his well-tailored tweed suits, apologetic smile and his phantom steam trains.

And so in the dead of night a nagging thought would descend upon me. I would lie on crumpled sweaty sheets, too weak to banish it from my drifting mind: The nagging thought that what I saw maybe *was* the 2:35 to Vienna.

You're an idiot, I thought. You're a real idiot.

* * *

I did not see Mr. Bartok at the station the next day, or the day after that. Nothing too unusual in that, I thought; can't expect him to be there all the time. I did want to bump into him again, though, and hear him laugh at my expense, after the joke went on long enough to satisfy his wicked sense of humor. That, or hear him engage in a public conversation with the spirits of the dearly departed. Either way, any way, I wanted closure.

But Mr. Bartok was not obliging me. The bench on the side of the station building – his bench – remained empty. Two days became a week, then two weeks. Bartok, like the 2:35 to Vienna, remained elusive. It even occurred to me once or twice that maybe I had somehow imagined meeting the retired stationmaster from Austria, just as I had imagined a steam train powering through empty train yards in the middle of the night. Somehow, it was a very comforting thought.

VII.

By the time Julie brought up the train yards I almost managed to forget about Mr. Bartok. It was over three weeks since I woke up that night and looked out the window. No strange lights since then, no steam trains, and no station master. It was all starting to seem inconsequential, like a one-night stand.

A DJ on the morning drive time show was laughing at his own jokes, and the music wasn't much better, either. I was having breakfast when Julie rocked up to the kitchen. She seemed in good shape considering she'd only returned from clubbing some five hours ago. I woke up briefly when she slammed the front door and stumbled through the corridor to her bedroom.

"I've got a petition for you to sign."

She was a true civic-minded spirit, the only one in the house, thank Christ. Always at the forefront of a greening-the-suburbs campaign, celebrating the introduction of recycling bins, regularly attending the irregular Neighborhood Watch meetings. Brad would say she was a typical upper-middle class princess trying to get rid of all the pent-up sexual frustration and upper-middle class guilt by meddling in other people's lives. Julie would call him a fascist. I offered her a room at my place when I was drunk at a party; now Brad and I suffered for my moment of weakness, but at least she didn't bring strange people home with her and paid the rent on time. And she was a living reminder to both of us not to make important decisions in life while drunk.

"I got it last week, but I forgot to give it to you then," she explained in her usual chirpy manner.

"What a pity."

"You're gonna sign it anyway, aren't you?" she leaned over the table and tossed her red hair. "As a favor? I promised that friend of mine, Val, that I would get her a dozen signatures. I'm not sure whether you've met her. You might have, at the party that–"

"OK, OK, what the hell is it?" I cut her off and put down my toast.

She sat down opposite to me and swept aside yesterday's papers. On the front page a grimacing senator was rudely pointing his finger straight at the camera.

"Well," she said putting the piece of paper on the table in front of me, "there is this residents group around here and in Brook Park and Endersly, and they're circulating this petition calling on the state government to close down the train yards."

The train yards. Funny that. Maybe the concerned residents got tired of being woken up at 2:35 in the morning by trains going to Vienna. Or maybe they wanted more connections – put in the Orient Express at least twice a week, please.

"-you're not listening to me," Julie waved her hand in front of my face. She couldn't stand not getting the attention. "They tried to talk to the department and what have you, but it got them nowhere, so now they decided it's time for some direct action."

Which also is going to lead them nowhere, I thought. The next election was still at least a year away, too far off to make it a campaign issue and force the important people to pretend to care.

"They want to collect at least a thousand signatures for starters. Once there is something on paper the department will have to sit up and listen."

"Why would they want to close the yards?" I asked. The radio station was playing an Eagles oldie, as they seemed to do every morning at the same time. I stood up and went over to the bench to turn the volume down.

"Oh, it's an eyesore," she said. "We could use a nice park around here, instead. Besides, people are worried about all the crime."

"What crime?" From this angle it looked like the senator was now pointing at Julie. And with a little imagination he was slowly turning into Brad. Here, little missy, why don't you take up a nice hobby like, I don't know, embroidery or something. In case you haven't noticed there are still some people trying to make a living down there at the yards. What are they going to feed their children with? The grass from the fucking park?

"Just because no one has broken into our house lately, and no one has raped you at knifepoint as you were coming back from work at night," she sneered at me, but not as defensively as if I were a stranger. "There's a lot of vandalism and other stuff."

"So you think the best solution is to turn the yards into our very own Central Park? I'm sure that won't affect the crime rate at all." God, Julie had this amazing ability to bring out the contrarian in me. I was almost willing to argue in favor of bestiality if she'd chosen to speak out against it.

"Oh shit," she winced. She must have finally realized I was stringing her along. "Just say you don't want to sign the petition. It's not like I'm twisting your arm, or something." I could she was readying herself for a dignified exit. "People are just trying to make the area more liveable; it's not as if-"

"Just leave it with me," I waved her off impatiently. No, I probably wouldn't sign it, but I'd be rid of her for the time being, and with not too many hard feelings.

"Thank you for your contribution to making our neighborhood a better place to live," she chuckled with glee, misreading me yet again.

On the radio it was a news break time. An accident on the highway; two lanes blocked. Some second-rate musician overdosed again. A terrorist attack in Thailand. The usual.

"And thank you for your contribution," I said after her. "Why don't you vacuum the house next time?" But she was out the door and I don't think she heard me.

The train yards. How interesting.

* * *

Some things just can't stay buried, as the grisly old farmers in oil-stained overalls and Yankees baseball caps tell naive city clickers in trailers for B-grade horror flicks, just before a cut to a low, gliding camera shot of something moving through the misty forest.

"–and the people are just trying to make the area more liveable; it's not as if–" the same lines, but a different target. Julie should have known better by now.

Brad was sprawled on the couch, in a position designed to deny Julie any room to sit down. While she stood over him holding the petition he was channel surfing the cable, not paying the screen any more attention than he was to Julie. Football, home shopping, cartoons, golf, a black and white movie, football again, country music ...

"–just say that you don't want to sign it, and I won't bother you. God-"

"I've got an idea," Brad suddenly broke his silence without turning away from the TV set. "Why don't you give that petition of yours to Suzanna's old man. I'm sure he'll be happy to sign."

It took a moment for Julie to click. "Very funny, ha ha, Brad," she said, "You're a real comedian, you know that?"

"What's with Suzanna's father?" I found myself entering the conversation almost against my will, yet I couldn't resist it. I knew Suzanna only slightly, a quiet mousy blonde with an intense gaze and an uncomfortable giggle. I once had a brief conversation with her about merits and demerits of post-modernism.

"Oh, there is nothing really with Suzanna's father," Brad turned his head towards me and shrugged. "Nothing that a few years at Betty Ford's clinic, a lobotomy and some shock therapy wouldn't fix."

"You know, I really dislike it intensely when you make jokes about other people's misfortune-"

The petition would now be forgotten, a slanging match was about to commence.

"And the connection is?" I butted in before Brad could deliver one of his witty ripostes that contained one of the permutations of the word 'fuck.'

Julie turned towards me and glared, unhappy at my interruptions of her climb to capture the moral high ground.

Brad shifted on the couch and stretched out his left arm, which must have gone numb under him. "Correct me if I'm wrong, Julie, but I recall that he used to work at the yards some time ago. Then it somehow made him go nuts, and I mean really nuts, and all the other fun things happened to him, like losing his job, his family, his dignity. Or maybe it all happened in a slightly different order, but–"

"I hate you two bastards, ganging up on the only woman in the house," Julie spun around towards me.

I looked at Brad and shook my head. What have I done? I silently mouthed the words.

"You're just a man," said Brad in a poor impersonation of Julie's voice.

She ignored him completely and pointed her finger at me instead. "I told you Martin, to get another girl after Mick moved out."

"We're not into affirmative action here," I said. The novelty of the argument was staring to wear off pretty fast now. "It's not my fault that all the women you want to bring in are into drugs or witchcraft, or both."

"Well, fuck you," Julie waved the petition in front of my face and stormed out of the room.

"Pity she had to leave so quickly," said Brad and switched off the TV. "I should have done more to encourage her to visit the man, have a coffee with him, help him to discover his inner insane child and get him to contribute to making the suburbs that much more liveable." He was really enjoying himself. "By the way, want to join me in a toast to the liveable suburbs?"

*   *   *

Sipping lukewarm beer that Brad forgot to put in the fridge the night before I tried to remember Suzanna's surname. Both Brad and Julie knew, but I couldn't come up with any convincing cover for my curiosity. Johnsons, or Jacksons seemed familiar in the context, but probably weren't it.

Five beers and two hours later, I was about to fall asleep when I finally remembered. For a moment I toyed with the idea of getting up and racing to grab a phonebook, but by that stage I was too tired to move. There would always be tomorrow. The yards could wait.

VIII.

There were only three Jephsons in the phonebook. One of them was an accountant; the other listing was for a couple. That left me with R. S. Jephson, resident of number 21, Ferntree Street in Parkwood, two suburbs down the train line. Of course I couldn't know whether the Jephson I was looking for still had a phone line. Nuts aren't very good at paying their bills. It was such a longshot – not just finding the right Jephson, but also the assumption that there was a common thread running through his insanity and my discomfort. But what was there to lose, except my time, and possibly my dignity?

*   *   *

It took me a few days to get around to visiting Suzanna's old man.

I'm honest enough to admit that crazy people make me feel uncomfortable. Yes, I could have found time earlier to drop by the Jephson residence, but for an image popping into my mind of Jephson, a hopeless wreck of a human being with a five-day growth, haunting his decrepit house in a soiled T-shirt, surviving on a steady diet of beer, until his dole or pension ran out half-way through the week, and on a prayer for the next few days. There would be piles of junk mail, rain-soaked and sun-dried in turn, spilling out of the mailbox onto the front lawn that hadn't been mowed since last September. I would come to the front door and say, Hello, Mr. Jephson. How are you doing? I just dropped by to ask whether you know where I can buy a ticket for the 2:35 to Vienna? And Jephson, depending on the phase of the moon or the latest suggestion from the voices inside his head would giggle and tell me to get lost, or throw a half-empty beer bottle at me, before loosing his Rottweiler on the uninvited guest ... And don't come back!

The real number 21 Ferntree Street didn't have a letterbox at all, and the grass was no taller than next door. Maybe no Rottweilers and confrontations, either? I thought.

I hesitated before opening a low, cast-iron gate. What was I going to say? Your daughter sends her regards. Her friends think you're nuts. You want to sign a petition?

It was probably too late to phone instead.

I walked to the foot of the wooden stairway that led up to the front door. I looked up but all the windows were closed, and heavy curtains hid the interior. Next door, the agonies of a soap opera gave way to a commercial break, and somewhere down the street a dog was barking its head off. There was no sound coming from inside Jephson's house.

I climbed up the stairs, some of the wooden steps squeaking under my boots. There was no bell. I knocked and put my ear to the door. No response. I waited a moment and then knocked again, longer and more persistently. Still nothing.

So that was it. I felt almost relieved to have avoided the encounter. Maybe Suzanna's old man was out, drinking himself stupid at the neighborhood pub. Maybe the authorities had finally decided to lock him up in a place where he would not be of any danger to society or himself. Maybe his slowly decomposing body was dangling from the ceiling beam in the kitchen, an illegible suicide note pinned to the fridge with a banana-shaped magnet. Either way I would not have the pleasure.

I was turning on my heel when I heard the shuffling footsteps moving from somewhere in the back of the house. I stood frozen as they got louder and stopped. There was a grunt, and the door opened.

* * *

I'm walking slowly down a narrow corridor in a second class carriage, trying to navigate between suitcases stacked up under the windows in the passageway. Whatever's left of people's lives is now packed tightly in shells of cracking leather tied around with old belts.

I count the compartments along the corridor. The third one's the one. There are no curtains on the door window. Privacy is a cosmopolitan luxury, too dangerous a temptation for us, weak human vessels. We're all naked outside.

He's alone. That's still one luxury his papers can secure. Naked but alone.

I open the door and step in. He glances at me as I take the seat opposite him. The documents are between the pages of his newspaper, as usual. He hands them over to me without a word, and that's not usual. I can see he's tired. But it's more than that. How does it feel to swim against the tide, and to know that it's getting the better of you, slowly dragging you back, back and down?

How long can you last, my friend?

* * *

Jephson was standing in the doorway, looking at me through the slits that were his eyes, the expression of forced concentration creasing his brow, as if he was trying to recall whether he had seen me before.

He was a lean man of around six feet with a large head and a receding hairline. What was left of his hair was sticking out at odd angles. There were bags under his eyes and a dark brush covered his cheeks and throat. His Adam's apple moved noticeably as he swallowed. He was wearing an old unbuttoned polo shirt that once used to be dark blue, and an old pair of football shorts. To an untrained eye Jephson looked merely like a migraine sufferer.

"What?" he said. His voice was coarse, like that of a man just about to get his very own voice box for Christmas.

"Mr. Jephson?" I inquired.

"Yeah." The look on his face made it obvious he thought he had made a big mistake coming to the door. At best, I was a travelling salesman or a missionary, and at worst a debt collector or a social services nerd. Jephson looked like he hadn't received any good news in a very long time and wasn't expecting some anytime soon.

"Mr. Jephson, I was wondering whether I could take a minute of your time—" I stuttered a bit.

His response was obviously made up in advance. "I'm not interested." He took a step back preparing to close the door.

I wasn't going to put my foot in. "I'm not trying to sell you anything—" I gestured putting my open palms in front of my chest. "I'm just ... doing some research—" That wasn't any better. "—and I would like to ask you a few questions, if I can."

Still, it seemed to have worked. He paused, one hand on the door frame, the other on the knob.

"You see, I'm writing an article, and I would like to get some information from you regarding the work you did at the Fairfield train yards—"

There was a flash in his eyes as if somebody had switched on a light inside his head. "Get out!" he spat out. "Get the fuck out!" His nostrils flared and his hands gripped the wood of the door as if he was preparing to launch himself at me.

"I—" I took a step back, almost too far back.

"Get out!" he cut me off. "Leave me alone!" he screamed. His whole body was trembling now. My heart was pounding as I retreated, walking backwards down the stairs, every step on the verge of losing balance and falling backwards.

"Tell them ... you ... out!" Jephson rasped. "Tell them to leave me alone ... leave me alone ..." He spun around and slammed the door.

I was trembling, too. Brad was right. I was right. Shit, shit, shit, I whispered under my breath. There was still a possibility of a semi-happy ending to all this, unless Jephson decided to sit down on the bathroom floor and slash his throat with a piece of broken mirror. I never thought I had such a therapeutic effect on people.

On the opposite side of the street an old woman in a gray dress that matched her thinning hair was pretending to empty her letterbox while stealing glances in my direction. Next door, an overweight woman with sad remnants of a perm was leaning out of the window. For a brief moment the local scene had trumped the ups and downs of the imaginary rich and beautiful on her TV.

"Don't worry about him, love," she said. I hated when much older women called me 'love.' "He's crazy like a shithouse rat. Doesn't enjoy people visiting him." Her three year old cyclist in the front yard below was also staring at me, open-mouthed, rocking on his bike.

"So I've noticed," I cast a nervous glance towards Jephson's house. There was no sign of movement.

"One day they gonna come in a white van and take him away," the woman giggled. That would really make her afternoon.

"Yeah," I nodded and started walking away. The old woman on the other side of the street disappeared inside her house after assuring herself that nothing more was likely to happen. The dog was still barking.

As I stood on the street outside, the tension slowly drained away, only to be replaced by frustration. And smoldering anger – not at Jephson, or the retired station master, but mostly at myself. I swore under my breath and kicked a small pebble lying on the pavement. It bounced a few times before disappearing into overgrown grass on the side of the walking path. That didn't make me feel any better.

IX.

I should have forgotten about the whole thing. Jephson was a dead end, and Bartok still a no-show.

I forced myself to concentrate on work and it felt good. Making money always had the wonderful side effect of clearing my mind and sharpening my senses. My sleep had also improved. I was going to bed at ten and waking up at six, with a fleeting awareness of epic dreams and a total indifference at not being able to recall any of them.

In the days after Jephson I woke up in the middle of the night only once. I forced myself to sit up and peer out the window at the train yards below me. There were no strange lights. There were no trains to Vienna, either. In fact, no trains at all. I waited about a quarter of an hour before crashing back into the pillow. I think I was smiling to myself as I fell asleep, feeling a strange sense of relief.

Two weeks later I was putting the finishing touches on a business plan for an internet-based export-import business. Some friends of mine intended to put in the initial capital and asked me to prepare the paperwork as my contribution to the scheme. The last few documents would have to wait until Monday, after I had a chance to talk to some people in Hong Kong. By four o'clock in the afternoon I switched off the computer and leaned back in my chair. Outside, on the river, two barges were ferrying coal upstream, and a solitary kayaker huddled the shore, trying to stay away from their wake. The weatherman had forecast rain on the morning news, just before exchanging a few lame jokes with the host. The rain hadn't come yet. I always suspected the weather guy was full of shit.

On the way to the train station I bought the late edition of the newspaper. A young local pianist had won a prestigious competition in Japan, and was now gracing the front page on a twenty-by-ten full color photo. I went straight to the movies section, only to be disappointed yet again by the selection.

Instead, I caught the last train home before the late afternoon office rush. A few people got off at my station, all strangers with the exception of an accountant on the verge of retirement who lived three houses down the street from my place. We exchanged polite nods and then I stole a quick glance at the bench next to the station building. Just in case. It was still empty. The retired station master must have now retired for good, I thought.

I had pizza for dinner and then watched some reality rubbish on TV over two beers before I realized that my mind was wandering and my eyes were glazing over. I switched off the lights and fifteen minutes later I was soundly asleep.

It was the last peaceful night of my life.

X.

"You can crash till the morning."

Inside the house the music was still playing, although on the veranda I could only hear the thumping beat, with all the frills and extras mercifully lost along the way. Explosions of laughter occasionally punctuated the murmur of several conversations going on somewhere inside. When you stand at the edge of darkness the sound of people enjoying themselves at two o'clock in the morning has an unsettling quality.

"You can't drive anyway, so why don't you leave your car here?"

"I'll walk. It sobers me up," I said.

"Why would you want to sober up?"

I grimaced and shrugged, trying not to lose my grip on the railing. I wasn't drunk enough to need support, but I simply couldn't think of anything better to do with my hands. "I want to get up early and feel clean and refreshed." Or was it shining and fresh? I couldn't quite remember the slogan from a recent toilet cleaner campaign.

Kate was standing just outside the door. She had thrown somebody's heavy leather jacket over her shoulders. It offered better protection from the night chill than the little black piece she was wearing. The harder my misty eyes tried to focus on her, the more attractive she was beginning to look.

Definitely time to go. Not her. Not tonight.

"I would ask you why you would want to get up early and feel clean and refreshed on a Sunday morning, but I don't think you know that yourself."

"I do, but it's a secret."

Kate rolled her eyes and gave me that nonchalant 'oh well' look before she turned around and disappeared back inside her house. She was always a bad liar, even when she didn't say anything. I could sense her disappointment.

*   *   *

In the corridor a guy I think I'd met somewhere before was pinning a tall brunette against the wall while laboriously trying to fondle her buttocks. She looked very drunk or very stoned or both, and was floating somewhere a hundred miles above the city, her mouth open and the empty gaze fixed at the ceiling.

"I'll see you around, mate. And good luck with your work," I shouted over the noise as I squeezed between his bulky body and the opposite wall. He turned around and looked at me with glassy eyes. There was no trace of recognition there, not even any annoyance at being interrupted. Suddenly it all struck me as absolutely hilarious, the way really bad jokes can seem funny to you after you've had a few. I burst out laughing and waved to him as I walked off, leaving him alone with the love of his life, or his night, whichever would last longer.

While I was on the veranda with Kate the party has shifted to the backyard. Someone turned off the CD player, but a pale looking, pony-tailed nerd in the armchair was still furiously drumming his fingers on the polished armrests and bopping his head to the rhythm now playing exclusively inside his head. He was the only person left in the living room except for a girl passed out on the couch with a streak of vomit drying out on the corner of her mouth. I hoped that somebody would give a really good wash to the cooking pan on the coffee table.

I didn't feel like saying goodbye to the backyard crowd. I dug out my coat from underneath the pile built out of backpacks, handbags, a woman's shoe and a few empty disposable cups, and then headed off.

A summer storm had passed over the city only an hour ago, disappearing in the west, beyond the mountains. For quite some time, as we swam in the humid air, God played ten pin bowls in the sky, and then finally the rain came over, almost an afterthought. It didn't last for long, but when I walked outside the bitumen was still glistening under the street lights and water was slowly dripping off leaves and branches. It would be cool for another few hours, then the morning sun would be back with a vengeance.

Have you ever noticed how quiet the city is at two in the morning after a storm? Your footsteps resonate on the wet concrete of the footpaths with a sinister echo, and you feel like you're committing a sacrilege just by being there. You glide along, a rubber man gently bouncing off the ground, feeling exhilarated and so very alive. You'd think that the alcohol has dulled your senses, but it's not at all how it feels. You are conscious of every step, conscious of every breath you take, how good it feels, how loud it seems. The dark, silent shapes of the houses, shielded behind tall fences seem no more real than stage decorations. The greenery breathes and reaches out to you. Everything is make-believe, my friend.

* * *

And what the hell are you planning to do? Jump the fence and then stumble around for a while until you fall asleep somewhere on the ground, like a pig in the mud, oblivious to the gravel digging into the back of your head? You were supposed to get home, remember? Clean and refreshed? Ah, you unreliable asshole.

I was standing at the train yards' fence, my fingers hooked on the chain-links and my nose rubbing against the rusty wire. The tangled web of tracks came alive after the rain, glistening in the light of the full moon. It looked like the good fairies have tonight laid down hundreds of silver threads along the ground. Listen very hard and you might still hear their delicate bells trailing off in the distance, the task accomplished.

I couldn't remember how I got here. My internal compass must have gone haywire, all quite easy really, just add vodka'n'orange and mix with some darkness and it's almost a given you'll take a wrong turn and walk the down wrong street. They all look the same in the dark, I chuckled to myself. It was an uncomfortable chuckle.

* * *

At the foot of the fence the good me and the bad me were having a raging argument.

The good me was starting to sweat despite the cold. It brought up visions of painful falls while scaling fences under the influence, or being nabbed for trespass. The bad me kept grinning mischievously. Oh, I'll just drop by, see how everything's going down at the yards, said the same bad me that once got me expelled from school. What's the harm?

You're still not convinced? The good me was getting angry, but somehow its voice was growing fainter. You've had a pretty ordinary time lately; some old confused fellow from Austria or wherever the hell he came from, some lights, a train, and some girl's crazy daddy. One thing led to another, and then it led nowhere. You were ready to forget about it, don't you remember? But now you're trying to prove that madness is indeed contagious. Congratulations.

The bad me didn't bother to reply. It was far too busy pulling off the flap and crawling on all fours through a hole in the fence.

For a moment my belt buckle was caught on the wire and I trashed around in panic, trusting my fingers rather than my eyes. It would have made for a nice story if the cops had chanced upon me, a young foolish vandal trapped by a nasty fence. But there were no cops.

I stood up and instinctively shook the dirt and dust off my clothes. The air was damp, smelling of wet wood and old oily rugs.

I took a few steps, looked around, and then the enchantment suddenly slipped away. The absurdity of the situation finally hit me. This was a post-industrial desert. There would be no amazing adventures tonight, just me and padlocked buildings, kilometers of cold tracks, and rusting hulks of carriages buried standing. I shifted my weight from leg to leg and gravel whispered under my feet. A slight breeze had picked up and the weeds growing between the tracks swayed gently. Go home, fool, the wind was singing, go home.

Then, with a corner of my eye, I saw movement.

It could have been a bat. Or sometimes at night you simply see things. It happens when you're drunk. But not now. There was definitely something moving to my right, between the repair sheds. They were ugly structures with corrugated iron roofs and dirty walls that in the dark mercifully melted in with the background. An obsessive-compulsive five year old had arranged all his toy boxes parallel to each other just before going off for a forty-year long morning tea.

The moonlight illuminated a five yard gap between two of the sheds. And in the gap I saw two figures briskly walking away from me. I caught just a glimpse of them, the taller person with his arm around the smaller one was hurrying the companion along. Maybe one or two seconds before they disappeared behind one of the buildings.

Trespass was bad. Stalking was much nastier.

But no turning back now.

The repair sheds were some hundred and fifty meters from the fence. My brisk walk soon turned into a trot. I made it to the buildings just in time to lose them. I flattened myself against the wall behind steel barrels and listened, but there was nothing. No voices, no footsteps.

The sheds were about fifty meters long. I jogged along the wall sending some small creature scurrying for cover. I stopped just before the end of the building and slowly stuck my head out around the corner. To my left I could see the shorter sides of two other sheds and beyond them a string of cistern wagons with a crane towering over them like an oversized gallows.

To my right the couple were walking away from me, some hundred meters ahead. They too seemed to have picked up their pace. Late for the train, I thought, but it didn't seem funny at all.

Now I could see clearly the taller man, dressed in what looked like a suit and a fedora hat on his head, a suitcase in one hand, the other still gently nudging the woman along. She must have been about a head shorter than him, dressed in a long flowing coat. The clothes didn't seem very appropriate for a summer night.

I huddled against the wall and sprinted, trying not to trip on the rubbish that accumulated against the walls. It wasn't easy trying to keep up with the Joneses.

As they turned yet another corner and disappeared behind a brick warehouse I realized that the night wasn't all silent anymore. Suddenly, as if somebody had turned on the radio in the middle of a show, there was a jumble of voices, then a lonely whistle and slow, forced grunts that drowned out everything else.

Even before I rounded the corner and raced up the steps onto the platform I already knew, with all the sickening inevitability of it.

The couple was gone. So was everyone else I thought I'd heard just a few seconds earlier. The train had pulled away. A dim light, shining through the back window of the last carriage, was getting smaller and smaller underneath a plume of smoke.

My head started spinning and I leaned against the brick wall of the warehouse. When I shut my eyes, the stars showered down and fireworks exploded over my retinas. I sank to my knees and with my head resting against the building I emptied the contents of my stomach onto the dirty concrete of a station that wasn't there.

XI.

The phone kept ringing but nobody was picking up. I waited, almost hoping it would stay that way.

After ten rings I was ready to hang up. Then I heard him pick up the handset.

"Yes?"

"Mr. Jephson?"

A pause.

"Mr. Jephson, I was talking to you some time ago–"

"I don't remember," he cut in.

"I came to your house seeking some possible help you might be able to offer me regarding ... regarding the train yards–"

I was expecting him to explode like he did the first time. Instead I heard him groan and when he spoke his voice sounded very distant and very flat, as if he was talking under water. "Just live me alone, will you? Don't ever, ever bother me again." It wasn't a threat; he was pleading with me.

Click.

* * *

I can't remember how or when I got home. The time between losing the contents of my stomach on the platform and waking up in my bed was irrevocably lost.

I was lying flat on my back in my bed, with my sinuses threatening to explode and my dried-out tongue stuck to the roof of my mouth. I felt as if I had drunk three times as much as I did. And I felt much worse now than I did a few hours ago.

I dragged myself out of the bed around midday and went to the kitchen to make a strong cup of coffee. Brad was sitting at the table completing the cryptic crossword in the Sunday newspaper.

"Box with skill, showing confidence about. Six letters," he greeted me. "Just joking," he added before I even had time to grimace. There was an expression of understanding and empathy on his face; almost respect. "You look like shit. Must have been a pretty good night. Why am I never invited to these things?"

I murmured something under my breath and switched on the kettle. Oh yes, it was a pretty good night. Actually, a pity you weren't there with me; you'd be able to tell me whether it's me who's going insane, or whether it's the world.

* * *

My family does not have a history of insanity, no aunties politely described as eccentric, no cousins kept under the stairs. I had a desperate desire not to be the first.

When I was younger I always wanted to see a ghost or a flying saucer. Neither obliged. And now, long after I had stopped wanting to see anything out of the ordinary, I was finally getting my wish. I was seeing things. Trains. People. The trains were normal. So were the people. They just weren't supposed to be there.

It would have been comforting to think that I'd simply had a much bigger night than I could remember, and having stumbled back home and fallen asleep in my clothes I had a particularly lucid and convincing dream about wandering around the yards. Nothing too far fetched, after all, the trains have been on my mind lately, thanks to the amazing Mr. Bartok. And the good mistress subconscious is such a schizophrenic garbage disposal unit with artistic pretensions of David Lynch and an unlimited budget. It can throw up anything.

If only I hadn't woken up on my bed that Sunday morning with my knees still dirty brown from crawling on all fours through the hole in the fence and my shoes encrusted with dried-up mud. My white bed sheets were smeared with dirt in a modernist style of the Berlin school.

And that wasn't comforting at all.

* * *

It was time for a little chat with Mr. Bartok. If the old fool wouldn't come to me, I would have to make the effort. On a Sunday afternoon somebody on his street would surely be able to point me to the house of the retired station master from Austria.

There were only fourteen numbers on Alicia Street. Two addresses were vacant blocks of land, overgrown with tall grass, one of them for sale.

Nobody answered my knocks at number one, but the woman from the next door assured me it belonged to a young family with small children. Then there were the Dawsons, an old woman with cobalt blue hair who offered me her cookies and a middle aged couple, she pruning the bushes, he washing his old Ford. Between them they were able to save me from visiting an architect whose house was hidden from the street by a row of cypresses, a wheelchair bound woman at number 11, and a house next door, which was just about to go on sale after the old owner recently moved to the Lord's house of many rooms.

I crossed over to the other side of the street. I was getting hungry. My dinner last night at the party was a piece of a disgusting pizza; my breakfast consisted of two cups of coffee and watching ten minutes of golf on TV. The pizza was now drying out in the sun on the concrete platform at the yards, and golf wasn't much to live on. But there would be no meal until I found Mr. Bartok.

Number 8 was in the process of being repainted. Its owner, a hunched-over man in his seventies, was sitting on a foldout chair on the veranda sipping tea. His name was Giulliani and in a broad Italian accent he explained to me that he didn't know anyone named Bartok, although there was a man named Burton who lived next door some years ago but he died of a stroke. Then a childless couple in their thirties moved in.

Number 4 was for sale. That left me with number 2. Just my luck to waste all that time instead of having started from this side of the road. I went up the stairs of the non-descript fibro shack and knocked on the door thinking about my opening line: I think we need to talk.

A grim looking, overweight girl with a prominent diamond stud in her nostril opened the door.

There were two other flatmates living with her, the oldest one twenty five years old. No, she had never met Mr. Bartok and she had no idea who he was. They were renting from some guy who had inherited the house from his uncle. But his name wasn't Bartok. "What was the owner's name, Pat?" the fat girl turned around and screamed at her flatmate over the music blaring from somewhere inside the house. Pat's fluoro-orange head emerged a few seconds later out of a doorway down the corridor to announce the man's name was Irving, or something like that.

I didn't feel like going back home yet. I drove two streets down to the small corner shop run by a Vietnamese family, bought a Coke and a sandwich, sat down on the curb in the shade of a tree and had my late breakfast. The little bastard had lied to me. And the sandwich wasn't very good either. I wrapped half of it back in its paper and put it on the grass next to me and just sat there watching the passing cars.

XII.

Life went on. I couldn't fall asleep that night, tossing and turning, trying to make sense of what had been happening to me the past few weeks. When I finally did manage to nod off, my sleep was restless and I kept waking up what seemed like every hour or so. When the alarm went off at seven o'clock on Monday morning, I dragged myself out of the bed and spent twenty minutes under the shower trying to kick-start my body. I wasn't very successful. But life went on.

There was no line to buy tickets at the station. The man behind the counter was reading the sports section of the newspaper when I interrupted him with a ten dollar bill. He barely gave me a glance from behind his horn-rimmed glasses as he slipped back my ticket and change.

"By the way," I said. "Do you know that old fellow who comes over here and sits on the bench just outside?"

The ticket seller started scratching behind his ear. He seemed uncomfortable handling inquiries not relating to the train timetable.

"The last time I saw him he said he was sick," I lied, "and that was a few weeks ago. I was wondering whether he's all right, whether you might have seen him since then."

"Not sure I know the man–" he said after a long pause.

"He seemed to me to be a bit of a regular–"

"Not many regulars at train stations," he shook his head.

"-just sitting here on the bench," I gestured with my thumb. "He said he was interested in trains. A retired station master from Europe."

I was hoping that might cause something to click in the guy's memory.

The ticket seller sighed and shook his head again. "Sorry, can't help you there. Just doesn't ring any bells."

Wasn't this sort of shit supposed to only happen at night?

XIII.

This time there were four of them.

Four lights; white, going into pale blue. No trains, no movement, no noise, just lights.

Moments before I was in a dream. I was walking up a mountain. The place looked familiar, like an amalgam of all the mountains I ever climbed. I couldn't see the sun but the sky was a very rich and warm shade of orange. Somehow it made me feel very safe and at peace.

Suddenly I realized that my grandfather was walking beside me, talking about the pre-war model Ford he has been trying to restore. We got up to the top of the mountain and I looked down. There was a small village in the valley, a few wooden houses snuggling to a winding road.

I turned around, wanting to say something to my grandfather but he wasn't there anymore. Bartok now stood in his place, hat on his head, hands clasped behind his back. He had the same suit on he wore the last time I saw him. He was smiling and I thought he radiated the very essence of the sky; warm and comforting. I opened my mouth, hundreds of questions fighting to come out all once but he beat me to it.

He simply nodded in the direction of the village and said: "He was born there."

And then I woke up, the bubble of my dream bursting without any warning.

With my eyes closed I groped around the bedside table until my hand closed in on the familiar shape of my glasses. I put them on and sat up. The radio clock was glowing "4:05." Massaging my left hand that went numb when I slept on it, I crawled up to the window and looked outside.

The lights were still there, even after I blinked a few times. They looked like two wolves laying in wait. We're watching you, we know you're watching us. Who's going to blink first?

I heard the floorboards creaking in the corridor. I jumped out of bed and ran out of my room, almost bumping into Brad.

"Jesus," he whispered. "You scared the living shit out of me. If you really want to jump the queue to the crapper, you're out of luck—"

"Come to my room," I said. I was hoping like hell that the lights would still be there.

"Uh, I love when you talk like that to me, honey, but—"

"Now!" I said and grabbed him by his t-shirt and dragged him into my bedroom. He was still half asleep and too startled to resist. "You'll have to wash my pants if I piss myself because of you," he murmured.

"The window," I told him. My wolves were still sitting in wait at the edge of the forest. I felt almost relieved to see them again.

"What about it?"

"The lights. At the train yards," I pushed him forward, towards the window.

He looked out for a moment, then moved closer to the glass, as if a few inches were going to make a difference. "What–" he turned to me.

"Four lights. Whitish, bluish. Four of them, over there," I pointed towards them, feeling even sicker.

Brad looked out, trying to follow the imaginary line extending from the tip of my finger into the night outside. "I don't know what's going on," he shook his head, "but nature calls and I unfortunately have to excuse myself from this episode of *The X Files*."

He shuffled back towards the door and I had no will to hold onto him. "Go and see an eye doctor," he said before disappearing. "Apparently seeing lights can be a symptom of a detached retina."

My retinas were fine, but something else - everything else - was wrong. Pretty seriously wrong. When I turned back towards the window the lights were gone and the yards were dark again. Maybe the wolves got bored. Who knows what goes on inside wolves' heads?

I was lying on my bed, staring at the ceiling, when the dawn arrived an hour and ten minutes later.

*   *   *

I yawned and looked around the platform. I didn't bother to be polite and cover my mouth. Thanks to the railway yards and their amazing light show I slept only five hours. I've survived on less in the past, but at least I could blame myself for feeling like crap the next morning.

I had a buzz in my ear. It was a balding man in his forties, talking on his cell phone next to me. With a strong Scottish accent he was dissecting and analyzing the dissolution of somebody else's relationship. Women standing within the ear-shot were exchanging glances and rolling their eyes.

"Long time no see."

And thus the burning bush spoke to Moses and Moses jumped up startled.

When I whirled around to my right he was standing next to me. So you exist, I thought. I haven't dreamed you up.

"I think we need to talk. Over there," I motioned with my head towards the empty far end of the platform.

"As you wish," he said and followed me. He was wearing a single breasted brown suit with a marching vest. An oversized knot of a dark green velvet tie bulged at his throat. No hat this time.

"You do not look too well, my friend," Bartok said, when we stopped at the station's end.

"Oh please, spare me, " I cut him off. There was no doubt in my mind he knew what was going on, and that only made his friendly chattiness even more irritating. "I want to know what's happening."

"With what?"

He just stood there, looking almost absent-minded, as if he forgot where he was and who he was talking to. I, in turn, didn't quite know if I were angry or scared. Probably both.

"I don't have the time or patience for your stupid little games," I waved my finger in front of his face. "You're not a regular here, and you don't live where you said you live. What the hell-"

He interrupted me. "It does not really matter that you could not find me, as long as I can find you." There was still a smile on his lips, but not in his eyes.

I tried very hard not to raise my voice. An old Russian babushka sitting on a nearby bench already glanced at us a few times. "Am I on a bloody candid camera? What kind of a game is this?"

"No game, young man, no game," he said. "Do I look to you a man who plays games?"

"Good question." No he didn't look like a man who plays games, but he was, wasn't he? "I look out my window at night or maybe even take a stroll through the train yards once in a while, and what do I see? Just some lights, maybe a train or two. Not just any train though, just one that's no longer actually in use and shouldn't really be there. Oh, and there are also some people who also shouldn't be there. My intuition tells me that a retired station master who loves his old trains so much might have some inkling what's going on. Because I don't have a clue-"

I stopped to catch a breath and waited for his reaction. He merely shook his head. The 8:05 service, stopping at all stations, was approaching from the city. It was useless trying to talk over the noise. I waited until the train had stopped.

"Who are you, really? Want do you want from me?"

Suddenly Bartok looked sad and tired, as if he, and not me, hadn't slept well the last few nights. "You think I am some kind of magician, yes? That I make you see things. Lights. Trains. People. I am just an old man, not a magician. You see what you see because you can... because you have to."

The train was now pulling off and for what seemed like ages I waited again for the quiet. It was an excruciating pause, now that we were finally getting somewhere.

"What does it all mean? What are these things? Why am I seeing them?"

"Oh, you will learn that in due course. Now, you are tired and-" he searched for the right word, "-jumpy. You are not ready."

"Of course I'm tired and jumpy," I hissed. Maybe, after all, we weren't getting anywhere. "I'm tired and jumpy because I don't know whether all of a sudden I'm going mad, or-"

He touched me lightly on my forearm. "I have to go now, but we will be seeing each other soon. When it is time."

"And what's that supposed to mean?" I said.

"Have a nice day," Bartok ignored my question and took a step towards the pedestrian overpass. I grabbed him by the arm. "You're not going anywhere, until I know what's going on. I've had enough chasing the trains and chasing you."

He winced but didn't try to break free. "Let me go. This is not going to achieve anything. All in its time, I said."

"Tell me–" I tightened the grip.

"Hey, you there!" I heard someone behind me. I looked over the shoulder without letting Bartok go. A tall man in his twenties, a blond crew cut, steely eyes, and a well-cut suit, was standing some ten yards away, tense and ready to pounce. "Leave the man alone," he barked at me. "Are you all right there, sir?" he inquired of Bartok. It was heartening to see that in our age of apathy there were still some people ready to defend the weak. Christ.

Other curious faces were also turning in our direction. I loosened my grip and Bartok slipped out. "Everything's fine. Nothing's happening," I murmured towards the crowd. The blond guy looked unconvinced. "Everything's fine," I repeated to no one in particular this time.

"We will see each other. Soon," Bartok whispered before walking away.

When the train to the city finally arrived I jumped into the last carriage, as far away from other Fairfield commuters as possible.

*   *   *

Brad did not bring up the incident with the lights. Not that evening, and not the evening after. For that I was very grateful.

XIV.

I was praying that it would work this time.

His voice seemed stronger and deeper than what I remembered from our previous conversations. Maybe I was trying to read too much from that one "Yes?", but I was desperate enough.

"Mr. Jephson, please don't hang up. I need your help. I'm seeing things at the train yards that shouldn't be there–" I sprinted away, wanting to cross that hundred meter line before Jepshon would even realize that a race was on.

There was only silence at the other end of the line but I hardly needed any more encouragement to continue.

"I don't know what's going on, Mr. Jephson, I really don't. I'm seeing small lights, bluish, somewhere inside the yards at night. And I'm seeing trains going through. Steam trains, that aren't supposed to be there. But they still seem to go through the yards and sometimes they even stop to pick up passengers-"

He hadn't hang up yet. A few seconds of silence dragged on like eternity. Then he whispered just one word.

"Jesus."

"Mr. Jephson, I don't know why I'm telling you all this, but I can't think of anyone else who can help me. Is it making any sense to you, or do I sound like a-" I stopped myself just in time.

"Again..."

I waited.

"My God, not again ..."

Again.

So he knows.

"Mr. Jephson-"

"I don't know who you are, and what ... why-" he stuttered. "You obviously know who I am and ... How ...? And the trains?"

"I only know that I'm seeing things, which aren't supposed to be there. And I know that you ... used to work at the yards. I don't know ... I don't know anyone else ..."

I had to strain now to make out the words he was saying. "Jesus ... I really thought I'd never ... You know where I live ... obviously?"

"Yes, I do."

"Then come over."

* * *

He must have shaved before I came for he still smelled of soap and cheap aftershave. But he didn't look better. His eyes never met mine, except in brief passing, and when he gestured me inside his house I noticed his left hand, half buried in the pocket of his shorts, was trembling.

He didn't offer me anything to drink. I sat on the sofa, he on the chair opposite. The curtains remained drawn keeping the living room in a permanent twilight. From the wall, a topless Polynesian beauty rendered in all the early sixties' favorite shades of brown and beige was staring at me provocatively. The ancient wooden giant of a TV set rested on its own short legs in the corner, adorned with an empty Scotch bottle. A vase without flowers, I thought. An oppressive feeling of hopelessness hung in the air, thicker than dust.

It was a struggle for Jephson to talk. He wasn't a born story-teller and lately he didn't get much chance to practice. Particularly about the trains. His voice was a low, monotonous hum and at times I had to lean forward just to catch what he was saying. He would occasionally glance in my direction as if to assure himself that I was still there.

It had all started suddenly, without any warning. He was working the second shift, from noon to eight in the evening. In the summertime it meant finishing just after dusk, in the winter well into the early night.

He worked repairing the old rolling stock. It was the art of postponing the inevitable. As a supervisor he was always the last one of his team to leave, often the last person to leave the yards, locking everything up. Those days there was still a night watchman employed to look after the place until the first shift would roll in just before dawn. On the way out he would say goodnight to fat Alex or good old Con, always troubled by his wife and five kids.

"First it was a light." He was on his way out when he saw it. It was blue, that's the first thing that struck him about it. All the other lights around the yards were white or yellowish. But it was just a light, and he didn't think much about it that night, hurrying home to watch a football game on TV.

The next night there were two lights. They looked like they were suspended in mid air between the warehouses, but who knew, maybe it was just an odd perspective that made the lights somewhere outside look like they were a whole lot closer. Either way, there was no harm in checking. But the lights vanished before he could get anywhere close.

Then he started hearing things. Not seeing yet, just hearing. Seeing would come later.

There were sounds of steam engines straining somewhere in the night, whistles and shrieks, groans of wagons woken up from slumber, and slowly pulled along the cold tracks. There were still a few steam trains in use, so why would he be bothered? He didn't know the answer to that. They just sounded different, and when he would check the freight timetable, the times printed on the sheet would somehow never match with when his trains went past. Alex - he couldn't remember him ever without some sort of food in his hand – would only shrug, "They must be on the western line," while his eyes were asking the question: what's the big deal here?

Then Jephson started hearing voices. Trains were borderline normal; people weren't supposed to be there are all after dusk.

He could hear people speak, but he could never catch the words, a murmur but no meaning. Jephson tried to find the source of the chatter a few times, but the people, whoever they were, eluded him, always maintaining their distance.

By that stage Jephson knew that something was wrong. What he didn't quite yet know was whether it was him or the yards.

Seeing people didn't help. In fact, that kind of crossed the line. Men dressed in suits. Sometimes women. And children. Often hurrying along, walking briskly saddled with their hand luggage. They never reacted to his yelling at them, never stopped, and never looked back. They seemed to be always just far enough away to be able to disappear behind a building or sidelined carriages by the time he got anywhere close. Then, when he finally caught up, they were no longer anywhere in sight.

Jephson raised hell with Alex and Con, sending them on wild goose chases around the yards. They couldn't hear or see anything. Alex, out of breath and sweating like a pig, would swear his head off at him after each unsuccessful pursuit of the elusive trespassers. And Con would just shake his head; he had enough problems of his own, even without Jephson's contribution.

When Jephson went to the management they listened politely, not knowing exactly what to make of his stories. Just to be on the safe side they gave Alex and Con a stern talk and brought in another two men from the railways to patrol the yards.

So now there were four people, instead of just two, who somehow weren't sharing his experiences.

He couldn't concentrate at work, and couldn't relax at home. Complaints were made about the shoddy work he increasingly let slip. Some of his men went to the management too, after he snapped a few times and abused them for no apparent reason. All the respect and good will he had managed to build up over the years as a good boss and a union rep was slipping through his fingers like water, and he couldn't stop it any more than he could catch his phantoms. He found himself staying longer and longer at his local pub on Friday nights. Then other nights as well. Small and insignificant things were turning into arguments, his children started tiptoeing around him and his wife seemed to be on the verge of nervous breakdown. The management finally called him back and gave him an ultimatum: see a doctor or else.

But that was already after he'd seen his first train.

"It all came together that one night. Behind the warehouses, where they unload the trains. The lights first, the whole friggin' Christmas tree. Then the noise started. Like a busy station, you know what I mean? Lots of people, and a train coming to a stop, and... just noises. I ran towards it. Don't know why, I should've given up around that time, shouldn't I? All that running, and all for nothing. But I ran and ran, as if I had to catch that train myself, you know? I was still a fair way away when I heard the train starting off again. All them huffs and puffs, and that. So I kept running and praying; I just wanna see the fucker, just once, please God. And suddenly the thing is coming towards me from behind the buildings, slowly at first but starting to speed up. And I stand there, like somebody'd nailed my boots to the ground. It's different, you know, hearing stuff, 'cos that's just ... hearing. And even seeing these people ... They're just people. But this was it, the big one, just coming towards me, the whole set, black like a baboon's ass but it had a light at the front of the engine and there were lights in all the windows of the carriages. So I could see it alright."

He cleared his throat.

"It was speeding towards me and I was just standing there. Like what else would you do?" he shrugged. "But it didn't run me over. I was standing 'bout two 'yards from the track, and it just whizzed past me. I saw the bastard, and all that wind and the steam hit my face. I could smell the metal, and the grease. I could've almost touched it if I wanted to. There were people inside, but they weren't looking out. And then there was this railway guy standing on that small platform at the end of the last carriage. He sort of looked in my direction and I could swear that he saw me and ... I don't know, I must have passed out 'cos I don't remember nothing else."

Con had found him, maybe half an hour later. He didn't see Jephson leaving the yards that night so he went out to look for him. Con shook him a few times and brought him back, then got him to their watch room. As Jepshon sat there in the corner sipping hot tea, Alex kept pacing around the room, a copy of *Readers Digest* in his hand, lecturing him about the connection between seeing light and epilepsy.

The management had similar ideas, only a different type of doctor. Jephson went to see both. There was nothing wrong with him physically; no *Readers Digest* case of epilepsy, only evidence of great stress and exhaustion. The shrink also couldn't figure it out.

Meanwhile, it didn't get any better. He was warned several times for being drunk on the job. The suspension was just around the corner. The only thing saving him was his union rep position. The management didn't like picking fights with the union, even if they were in the right.

Back at home he excelled at fights. The police started coming around regularly. Then he hit his wife one time too many and she packed up and took off with the kids. "I watched my life going down the toilet and I just couldn't do a thing. It was like the current in the river, just dragging you along. You try to beat against it, but it's stronger, and it just carries you away ..."

Then came his last day on the job.

"I saw a man kill another man. Only it didn't happen." Jephson looked away, and fell silent. I was just about to open my mouth and say something when he resumed his story.

Jephson heard shouting and the sound of feet pouncing on the gravel. He saw an older-looking man running, with another, younger man, running after him. The old man was running as fast as he could, but it was not fast enough and the younger man was catching up. "The younger one was dressed in some dark clothes, like an uniform or something. He was shouting but I couldn't hear what it was. It might have been in some foreign language, or something."

The old man was running out of breath. He tried to look back over his shoulder at his pursuer, but he tripped and fell to the ground. The younger man was fast upon him. He was screaming something at the old man, the old man was saying something back, and trying to get up. "And the younger fellow just kicked him in the guts and the old guy cried out and rolled on the ground. Then the younger fellow pulled out a gun and fired point blank into the old guy's head. Bam, bam, bam. Three times. Just like that ... I was standing some fifty meters away, watching the whole thing. And then I just went apeshit. Just broke down. I spent the next few months in the loony bin ... Don't particularly wanna talk about it."

He paused for a moment. "And that's the whole story. I never went back there to the yards. Wild horses wouldn't 'ave dragged me there. And I didn't have a job to go back to, anyway."

The last few words were barely audible. He looked exhausted, as if he had physically relived his experiences all over again for my benefit. I was hoping he wouldn't faint on me.

*　*　*

We were sitting on the veranda overlooking the back garden. The intricate woven pattern of a wicker chair was digging into my back and I had to shift around all the time to ease the discomfort.

"So what is it?"

He sat stiff and distant for a long while.

"I don't know," he finally said. "I don't know."

He hadn't thought of much else since that time, and if he didn't manage to come up with any answers so far then today wouldn't be the day either.

"I used to think that I was crazy," he shook his head. "There was no other way–"

"–and now you know we're both crazy. There's another way but it doesn't make it any better, does it?" I said.

When I was finally leaving I asked him one last question. "In all that time when you were seeing those things, did you ever meet any person who seemed to have been connected to it all?"

He looked at me puzzled.

"There is this man," I started explaining. "His name is Bartok. He says he is a retired station master. He just keeps popping up once in a while. He knows... He knows about the trains and he knows that I'm seeing them. I don't know who he is, how he knows it, or what he wants ..."

Jephson shook his head. "No. I never met anyone like that."

So Bartok was mine and mine only.

"If that fellow of yours ever tells you what's going on, give me a yell," Jephson said when we exchanged goodbyes. He lingered in the doorway until I drove off but didn't wave at me.

XV.

"I thought I would drop by and see how you live."

He was standing two steps below me on the stairs leading up to the front door. It made him appear even shorter than he was. He wore brown slacks, a white linen shirt with rolled up sleeves and two-tone leather shoes that went out of fashion a quarter of a century ago. Informal, as if the tweed suits were a uniform he was only allowed to wear at the station.

Last night, buried under the sheets, I kept hugging the pillow with grim desperation, yet sleep eluded me. My mind was buzzing with Bartok and Jephson, steam engines and lights, people hurrying off to catch trains and men in uniform killing other people. The more I knew the less I understood. The more I knew the sicker I felt inside.

Sometime after one o'clock I went to the bathroom, took the last few sleeping pills out of the cabinet and washed them down with cold tap water. I looked into the mirror and realized I hadn't shaved for days.

When I finally slept it was a heavy, almost drunken sleep. After I woke up just before dawn, I struggled for a while not to get up because somehow I knew that if I looked out the window I would see something again. But it was no use. Like swimming against the current, I remembered Jephson's words. When I finally gave up and set in my bed, my mouth was dry and the sheets were moist.

The train yards were lit up like a shopping mall during the holiday season. It was a shameless, ostentatious spectacle. Some lights simply hovered in mid-air; others were rocking as though disturbed by the wind. When I was younger, trying to put my head around the concept of the infinity of the universe would make me nauseous. Really nauseous. But the feeling now was much worse.

"May I come in, or do you prefer to conduct conversations over the threshold?" he said.

I hesitated for a moment. Home was my last sanctuary. If I'd let him in now there wouldn't be any place left that was free from him.

"Conversations?" I shook my head, but stepped aside to let him come through. "Doesn't that imply some sort of a two-way exchange of information?"

He squeezed by, taking off his hat at the same time.

"Now, young man, do not fret. There is a time for everything," he stood in the hall, hat in his hands, waiting for a further invitation. I pointed towards the living room and followed a few steps behind him.

"Take a seat," I said. He chose the armchair and fell heavily into it. His fingers started drumming on the arm rests as he waited for me to make the opening move. I didn't oblige him. I was tired of making the opening moves only to get myself into another dead end.

"So," he finally said. "You have met your soul mate, yes?"

"You like to watch, yes?" I mimicked his voice. "Do you also know what I've had for breakfast or whom I've slept with last night?" I was angry but no longer surprised.

"The answer is nothing and no one," he looked at me intently, as if to try to put me back in my place.

"Who are you?" I asked.

"It really does not matter," he shrugged in response. "Maybe I am Franz Bartok, once a station master in Austria, now a pensioner. Maybe I am somebody else. For you I might as well be Bartok."

"Do you work for the government?"

"I am afraid you watch too many movies–"

"Damn it, I'm seeing things that aren't there," I cut in, "and you're telling me that I–"

He silenced me with a wave of his hand. "All this is of no importance, a useless talk. The only important thing is that I am here because you are now ready."

"Ready for what? To become a psychotic drunk like Jephson?"

"What happened to Jephson cannot be undone." There was almost a tinge of sadness in his voice. "He saw but he was not supposed to see. It is unlucky what happened to him. You see because there is a reason why you see."

"I'm listening."

"Work awaits you."

I had the urge to walk out, but instead I started pacing around the room. "I don't want any work. I just want you to make all these bloody things go away," I said.

"I cannot," he said. "You can be as angry as you want, young man. You can swear, you can throw your hands in the air, but it is not going to change anything one bit. I am here to tell you that you will be required to do some things in the near future. *C'est la vie*, as the French would say. It means -"

"I know what it means."

"That is good," he said while lifting himself up from the armchair. "Meet me tomorrow night at the train yards. Midnight. At the hole in the fence."

* * *

Brad got out the *Star Wars* trilogy from the video shop. It was a spiritual experience for our generation that never went to church. We would watch it for the tenth, twentieth, thirtieth time, our lips silently mouthing the dialogue with the same fervor our elders celebrated the Eucharist every Sunday.

When I got home from work, Luke Skywalker was still roaming his home planet; by the time I would have to leave tonight, the evil empire would have fallen and Luke would be reunited with his dead Jedi friends on the forest moon of Endor.

We sat on the couch watching the movie for a while before Brad suddenly said, "On second thought, it might have been a bad idea to suggest to Julie to see Suzanna's father with that petition."

God, I thought.

"I think she might have, and now the guy's dead. The last straw, as they say."

"What happened?" I tried to sound vaguely disinterested, but my voice almost faltered.

"Oh, I don't know the details, just heard it from Ben. I bumped into him after work," Brad sipped his Coke. "Apparently they found him yesterday morning. At the yards."

The lights. The whole show just lit up, I thought.

"God only knows what he was doing in there. Maybe his condition," Brad put down the can and gestured the inverted commas, "took a turn for the worse and the guy decided to go back to his past haunts. I don't know. They say he had a heart attack. Dropped just like that, in the middle of the night."

On the screen Luke was receiving his instructions from Obi-wan.

"I guess I'll have to show up at the funeral," Brad said, "I hate funerals."

I stood up. My head was spinning.

In the bathroom I turned on the tap to full stream and put my head under the cold water.

XVI.

My house was asleep when I snuck out into the night. It was quarter to midnight.

You idiot, I thought, it's all your fault. Jephson wasn't exactly in great shape for the last few years but at least he was surviving from day to day. And then you had to turn up, selfishly looking for your answers. And when all is said and done, you are none the wiser and he is dead. What was it that Bartok said? "He wasn't supposed to see. It is unlucky what happened to him." Very unlucky, in fact. I am supposed to see, so everything is fine. Should I consider myself lucky then?

*   *   *

He was waiting for me on the other side of the fence. I pulled back the flap of wire and as I crawled through the hole I tried to imagine him doing the same only moments ago. I couldn't. Not in one of his immaculate suits, not on all fours, not twisting around to avoid getting caught on a wire.

"This better be good," I said getting up. "I better not be having all these sleepless nights for nothing."

He ignored my comments. "Come with me, we have to be somewhere in five minutes."

I followed him, retracing my steps from not so long ago. For a man who was almost eighty he had a brisk walk. He seemed more animated, more alive tonight than I've ever seen him before.

"What have you done to Jephson?" I asked.

If Bartok was surprised that I knew he didn't show it. "I have not done anything to him. He should not have come back. There was nothing for him here."

But obviously there was, I thought.

We didn't get as far as the warehouses. Fifty yards before, Bartok turned left and we started crossing train tracks.

"So what happened to him?" I wouldn't let go. "Got him scared to death? Heart attack looks nice and inconspicuous on a death certificate." Until now it hadn't quite sank in just how serious all this was, and this realization terrified me. It wasn't just the light and the trains, or even worrying about one's sanity; now somebody was dead.

Bartok didn't slow down, merely turned his head towards me and said "Maybe he fell under one of the trains, yes?" His face was a wax mask in the light of the moon, but his eyes looked like two pools of water. Deep, deep water.

Change the angle, son.

"Why wasn't he supposed to see... whatever that we see... but I am?" The wind picked up out of nowhere and I realized that I was dressed too lightly.

Bartok grunted. "Some people see, because they can. It cannot be helped, but they are not needed, either."

I wasn't sure whether it was the complex nature of the problem, or Bartok's grasp of English that made it so difficult for him to explain anything. Or maybe it was only his mercurial nature. Nothing would be handed to me on a plate; I would have to find out for myself. How very old fashioned.

"Will I also end up in a loony bin or swinging on a rope?" I asked.

"You are in pretty good shape so far, no?"

Everything is relative, I thought.

"You see, because you are supposed to see," he continued. "You are needed–"

"If I'm needed–"

I didn't finish. To our left, a woman was pushing an old-fashioned pram.

I was too busy playing around with Bartok to notice where she had come from. She wore an ankle length heavy coat with a fur collar and her black hair was tied up under a small hat. Bartok tipped his hat and bowed slightly. "Madam," he said.

She acknowledged his greeting with a smile.

"Who is she?" I whispered.

"Oh, I do not know. Probably catching a train like the rest of them."

The rest of them.

I looked around. There was a tall middle-aged man dressed somewhat like Bartok, walking alongside on our right. His large leather valise was not slowing him down and he was overtaking us in long strides. Ahead of us, navigating between the tracks, a small boy was guiding an old man with a walking stick. The boy gave us a quick glance. I couldn't see his face under an oversized flat cap.

Jesus.

"Are they ghosts?"

"Do you want to touch them and find out?" Bartok chuckled.

He led me towards an old grain terminal. Two silos towered over two boxcars. The platform was empty except for some steel drums resting at one end like an unfinished modernist sculpture. Or perhaps a finished modernist sculpture.

"And now what?"

"Now you are going to take a train ride."

The strange thing is I wasn't really surprised. It seemed so logical that it was really the only thing he could have said. And yet ...

"Do not worry," he said. "You will know what to do."

I wasn't so sure. "Can I finally get some straight answers, for God's sake? Where? How? Why? This is totally absolutely crazy." At this stage, I think, the adrenaline was starting to kick in, countenancing the effects of cold and fear. I was shaking, but only a little.

"I said, you will know," he patted me on the back. "Now close your eyes. When you are finished over there you can get off at Augsburg or any station after. Close your eyes again when it is time to come back."

I glanced at my watch. It was eleven past twelve. I clenched my fists and let the eyelids roll down my eyes, like stone slabs over the grave.

*   *   *

The rushing wave of sound came first.

For a moment I was inside a bubble, engulfed by noise of people and things, a roomful of TVs, all tuned to different stations, all muffled and unintelligible. It felt like being underwater. I pushed myself upwards, to the surface.

The bubble burst.

My head spun. I took a slow, deep breath to steady myself. It didn't help.

I opened my eyes and I wasn't in Kansas anymore.

A middle-aged woman leading a small boy and a small girl by their hands. A young man with a briefcase too big and too heavy for him, in a hurry to get somewhere. A laborer carting off a metal container. An old man sitting on a bench reading a newspaper, our eyes meeting for a fraction of a second. A man in a uniform. A wavering hand. A white handkerchief. A kiss. A gust of wind.

Like a film.

A film set in the nineteen thirties, give or take a few years.

Of course.

Women dressed in conservative two piece costumes, men in long heavy trench coats. Fur collars, leather bags, hats for women, hats for men. Workers in grease-stained overalls and skewed caps. And that man in the uniform of an army that no longer existed save on a few old black and white photographs.

Of course.

Oh, and it was still night. I wasn't really surprised. What other time could there be?

Dunnenburg, said the large black letters on the side of the station's main building. The old man on the bench had a copy of the *Berliner Zeitung am Mittag* spread before him. The top headline read "Haarmann's Trial Begins. More Human Remains Dredged From The River." The woman leading the two children was reminding them to be nice and polite to Aunt Hilda. The workman with a metal case constantly slipping off the trolley was cursing under his breath, careful not to be overheard.

I never spoke a word of German in my life. Yet I understood everything.

An older man shuffled past me on crutches. His left leg was missing from the knee down and a rolled-up trouser leg was secured with a pin below the stump. The stench of an unwashed body assaulted my nostrils and I instinctively turned away.

I was standing in front of a four-pane window. I looked at my reflection and saw a stranger. I was no longer wearing a pair of jeans and a T-shirt. Instead I had a heavy brown suit on, with a vest underneath and a wide striped tie tied around my neck. I still had glasses, but the frames were different, rounder. And my hair was now combed flat and greased in a fashion I would otherwise find ridiculous.

Jesus.

Somehow, I was – I seemed to be – in Germany, in the thirties. I didn't know where exactly in Germany, or when exactly in the thirties. But once you got past the well dressed middle aged women and elderly gentlemen reading newspapers on station benches, the chances were that somewhere out there roamed the square-jawed thugs with bristling crew cuts and low, sinister thoughts in their stunted minds. Somewhere out there, their superiors, the bespectacled officials in elegant suits and radicalism bubbling underneath their respectable veneer like hot subterranean springs, were scheming and working to unleash hell on earth.

I felt my head starting to spin. Scared again, like a five year old lost in a Christmas rush at a shopping mall, helpless among the forest of legs, none of them your mother's. I felt like running away but I resisted the urge and merely walked off, hugging the wall of the station building.

Shit, shit, shit, Bartok. Thanks for the ride.

I rounded the corner of the building and froze flat against the wall, the back of my head touching the cold masonry. What seemed like minutes passed when all I could hear was the sound of my racing heart.

The voices brought me back.

I opened my eyes and saw a shimmering yellowish glare coming from behind the building. Shadows were dancing on a picket fence and a conversation meandered towards me on the strands of smoke.

"–and when they went on strike last week in Munich, those bloated bastards in their cushy offices just hired some thugs and sent them in through the gates with pipes and chains. One of our brothers died, and God only knows how many were bloodied."

"What do you expect?" said another deeper and more resonant voice, "That's how they always treat the working man. I remember my father used to tell me–"

"The next thing you're going to tell me is that it was always so, and it will always be so," the first voice cut in. "Your father, you, your son. Damn you, Erich. That's exactly what they want you to do; throw your hands up in despair and accept what they're doing to you–"

"I'm not saying–"

"I've seen another one of them National Socialists again," a third voice, younger and shriller than the other two, interrupted Erich. "He stood up on a wooden box in the square and spoke to people. Quite a crowd he got in the end, you should've seen it."

"They're worse than all the bloodsuckers in top hats," said the first voice. The man coughed, spat and went on. "They say they are with us working people, against the fat pigs, but mark my words, in the end they'll suck us dry and then they'll sell us to the capitalists. Mark my words."

"I don't know, Peter," the young one spoke again. "Lots of what that man was saying made sense. Like the Jews ... He said that all those rich men in their fancy hats, they're all Jews, getting fat on the sweat of the German workers ... you know, like you and me, and ... They're stuck to all of us like leeches. The same people who stabbed our boys in the back when they were fighting in the war, and–"

"Yeah, yeah, yeah," I could almost see Peter waving his arm in impatience. "I tell you now as I always tell you. You can dream on about whatever you like, but the only hope of the working people everywhere is Comrade Stalin. I say ..."

They kept on eating their lard sandwiches wrapped up in waxed brown paper, stealing the fire's warmth under the autumn stars. Soon, work would call them again, and they would be off to another train, spitting on their palms and sweating over another bulging raffia sack. They would think of little else but knock-off time, and maybe of their women, lost in an uneasy sleep in little stuffy rooms with draped-over windows and bad dreams hanging in the air like cigarette smoke. And many of them, like Peter, would think, would dream, of Comrade Stalin, his kind eyes smiling as he looks over the sea of hard, honest faces, his hand showing them the way to the future, another future, under the sun so warm it almost makes you weep with joy, a future full of plenty and of comradeship and hope so strong that you would march off to work with a spring in your step and a song on your lips.

And so Peter kept preaching his proletarian gospel, his voice thunderous and his intentions pure. Yet I didn't - couldn't - listen anymore. Other voices, other visions filled my head, the nameless people dragged from their homes in the middle of a night just like this, bullets in the back of the head, pits in the forest smelling of wet earth and blood, cattle trains ploughing through icy wastelands, bony fingers tilling canals or reaping the hard harvest from the deep bowels of frozen earth until the walking skeletons fell where they stood, into the warm open arms of merciful death, an old hag whispering, come, come, my child, come; and wailing children with swollen bellies and swollen heads, abandoned to die by the roadside somewhere among the desert fields of Ukraine or Kazakhstan stripped bare by the red locust in leather boots and leather coats and leather caps, while mothers, their eyes clouded by madness, dig with their bleeding fingers for last year's roots. And Comrade Stalin, towering above all this like a brass colossus, his kind eyes smiling and strong hand showing the way to the future.

God merciful. There was no future. Peter's dreams were someone else's nightmares, as dark and merciless as those swirling in the mind of the Austrian corporal with a waiter's moustache. You're all damned, I wanted to scream. A pox on both your houses, Peter. Another few lost generations steamrolled by history.

The noise of the approaching train pulled me back, made me open my eyes. A train ride, I remembered Bartok say.

You have to go now.

But why? And where to?

Away. Away from here. This is your only way out.

*   *   *

By the time I emerged back into the dim light, the train had already pulled up at the station. The doors of carriages swung open and passengers began slowly stepping out onto the platform. The ticket inspector was having a friendly chat with the station master, his cap under his arm. The man in the uniform embraced a woman who came out of the last carriage, while the woman with the small children was gently prodding them up the steps, indifferent to her little girl's cheerful blubber.

A train ride.

I came up to the nearest carriage and hoisted myself up the metal steps. The air inside was filled with the smell of wet wood and muffled conversations drifting through the half-closed doors of compartments. In the first, two nuns sat still and silent opposite a homely woman whose long plaits of ash-blonde hair made her look like an overgrown child. In the second compartment, four soldiers were playing cards on a makeshift table. The next one was occupied by a small, jovial-looking man in his fifties, who raised his goateed chin from above the newspaper and looked up at me through his thick round glasses as I slid the door open.

I acknowledged him with a quick nod and sat opposite him. A short whistle sounded and the train jerked forward.

The man put down his newspaper and shook his head. "Horrible stuff about that Haarmann, you know."

I remembered the headline from the *Berliner Zeitung am Mittag* and shook my head with a feigned understanding.

"A quiet fellow, police informer," the man continued. "Such unspeakable acts. All those poor young boys, coming to Hanover, looking for work and this..." he sighed. "Twenty six skeletons dredged out of the Leine. Now they write that he sold the meat on the black market. Imagine that."

"What's the world coming to," I couldn't think of anything else but this cliché.

"I guess there always will be some madmen among us."

Always, indeed.

We fell silent. On the other side of the window the countryside was asleep, maybe tossing and turning with nightmares about that Haarmann fellow. I could only see the darkness and my own reflection staring back at me from the window pane. Soon, there would be other nightmares to compete with those about perverted serial killers. But for now, it was still sometime before 1933, the year of no return.

"I remember this little joke, I'm not sure whether you've heard it."

I stirred. The man was now looking at me, a delicate smile playing on the corners of his mouth. His newspaper was lying next to him on the seat, neatly folded. "A rich businessman and a young man are travelling in the same compartment on a train. After a while the businessman notices that the young man is rather intently staring at the businessman's beautiful new golden watch. So the businessman starts thinking to himself: 'In a minute or so he won't be able to resist it any longer and he'll ask me what time it is. I'll tell him the time and he'll commend me on my taste in watches. Then he'll ask me what business I'm in. I'll feel obliged to tell him what I do for a living and he'll lighten all up because he always wanted to get into the same line of work. We'll talk about professional matters, then a little bit about him and a little bit about me, and before I realize it, we'll be in Berlin. Because the young man doesn't have much money on him and because he doesn't know anyone in Berlin, I'll feel sorry for him and invite him home for dinner. He'll politely decline at first but in the end will come with me. I'll introduce him to my wife and to my three beautiful daughters. Before I know it, my youngest daughter will fall madly in love with him, will break off her engagement to that promising young doctor, and will elope with the penniless young man, leaving me broken hearted.' The businessman is thinking all those things when he sees that the young man is just about to open his mouth to say something to him. So he jumps out of his seat and screams at the young man: 'It's twenty to eight, but if you ever touch my daughter, you've got another thing coming'."

The man chuckled at his joke and I laughed politely, too. I think I might have heard it before. Or after.

"My name is Gottliebson, Baruch Gottliebson," he said.

"Max Strasser." I didn't know where the name had come from. Probably from the same place as my newly acquired fluency in German.

"I don't have a nice new golden watch and my daughters, I hope, are safe. The older one is happily married and the younger one is only ten years old. So you see, I'm not going to bite your head off, young man," he chuckled.

But like his alter ego, Baruch Gottliebson was a businessman, travelling around the south of the country, wholesaling bathtubs and bathroom accessories.

"My first love was always ancient history and here I am selling brass faucets," he mused. His father only agreed to let the young Gottliebson study classics at the university on the condition that Baruch would come back and take care of the family business when the time came. When his father died unexpectedly of a heart attack, Baruch for a little while entertained incurring the old man's posthumous curse and defying his wishes. But only for a little while.

After he finished his story the train had stopped. It wasn't Augsburg yet, but another small provincial town. While we waited to get going again he asked me about myself. I told him a convincing tale of a dull job pushing paper at a government department and the trip to see my seriously ill grandmother. The lies rolled effortlessly off my tongue, and I felt a twinge of sadness at having to deceive this nice older man.

When the conversation eventually drifted towards politics, I was vague but reasonable enough in my responses to put him at ease before he opened up.

"I've read in the papers last week that a group of these thugs from the SA stormed a library in Berlin and removed all the books that foul man Goebbels hates. They piled them all up and set them alight. Freud, Marx, Heine, Mann, Remarque... A funeral pyre of great literature. And the worst thing was nobody stopped them."

The tide of ugliness was already starting to lap at his feet. "They hate me, Herr Strasser, you know?" he said. "One of them spat at me outside my own shop. 'You dirty Jew,' he said. What have I done to them? I'm a German, my family lived here for two centuries. I speak German, I think German, I pay taxes, I served in the army during the Great War. Even won a medal for bravery. 'Go away, Jew,' they say. But this is my fatherland, too. Where shall I go?"

For a moment he felt quiet and turned towards the window. Short of another lie, a gross lie, there was nothing I could have said that would make him feel better.

"Surely it won't last?" he asked, as if nevertheless hoping for some assurance from me. "We are all intelligent people and this is not intelligent, not intelligent at all. They will burn a few more books, spit on a few more people but in the end everyone will see them for what they are. Mad and irrational." He looked at me and added, "This is Europe, after all."

He meant it as a statement of fact, simple and self-explanatory, yet it sounded more like a question or a pleading.

And in that very moment I suddenly knew. Knew everything. I knew that Baruch Gottliebson would go on selling his bathtubs throughout Bavaria, and he would continue to shake his head in disbelief at every slight and inconvenience, every new law and act of discrimination, always hoping that reason and decency would prevail. Hoping that this was Europe, after all. I knew that his shop would be burned down during Kristallnacht, set alight by a rampaging mob of torch-wielding youths in brown uniforms. What remained of his business would be confiscated and taken over by a new, Aryan, owner. By then it would be too late to get out of Germany. I knew that Baruch Gottliebson and his family were on one of the first transports to Treblinka. I knew that he died of maltreatment a few months later. I knew that his wife was also murdered, and so was his older daughter, her husband and their two young children. I knew that his younger daughter, who was only ten when I met Baruch Gottliebson that night on my first night train, had somehow managed to hide and survive. She evaded the net for five long years and when the horror had finally come to an end – when this was Europe, after all, again – she left for Palestine. She fought in the Jewish underground and saw the birth of Israel. I knew that she died five years ago in Haifa, surrounded by her large and loving family.

I knew. I didn't know how I knew, I couldn't even be sure that I really knew, but God, I believed I did. I suddenly felt the weight of the whole Europe that Baruch Gottliebson trusted so implicitly and fervently pinning me down and suffocating me. I could hear the wailing of countless voices, curses, pleas for mercy, prayers for help; I could feet all the last breaths on my skin, together an unbearable gale. I could feel and see and smell all the anger and pain, hatred and sacrifice, heroism and cowardice, the whole dark, bloody tapestry of suffering, woven from millions of single strands, each singing its own story, each talking to me with its own voice, each ...

It was too much.

* * *

When the train arrived at Augsburg I stood up and said my goodbye. I wished Gottliebson all the best for the future, and I felt a steely hand crushing my throat. He smiled back and bade me farewell. I never saw him again.

For a long while I stood alone on the platform, while the crowd slowly ebbed away. The station master was standing in the doorway of the building with a little red flag rolled up under his arm, watching me with some interest, and so I had to make my way around the corner of the building, out of sight, before closing my eyes.

The air around me swirled and the sounds of the Augsburg station rushed off into nothingness.

I opened my eyes and I was standing again on the platform at the railway yards, still in the same spot from where I had first embarked on the journey. Bartok was nowhere in sight. I was alone.

I fell on my knees, and then collapsed completely onto the cold concrete, my head in my hands. The dam finally burst and I was shaking and sobbing uncontrollably for a long time, until I had no more tears left in me. And still I cried some more.

It was twelve past midnight, and it had been the longest minute of my life.

Midnight

I.

HANS-BERND GRAF VON SCHELLENDORFF is alone in his compartment. There is a narrow slit between the glass pane and the top part of the wooden frame where the window is jammed, and cold wind slips inside. The angry gale from the east bites his face with cruel, razor-sharp blasts. If he listens to the wind hard enough he might hear the curses and cries of his comrades-in-arms, who wallow and bleed in never-ending snowdrifts, hundreds of miles away. The wind is singing: go away, German. Go away.

He could change the compartments with just one word. A train attendant would quickly shuffle out a travelling salesman or a family on the way to their own lebensraum to make room for him. But Hans-Bernd von Schellendorff doesn't care about the wind. His eyes sting after two sleepless nights and eyelids flutter like a pair of wounded butterflies. His mind is burning, too tired to think properly, too feverish to let him drift away.

The wheels of the train beat the familiar tattoo on the joints of the tracks. Ta-tat, ta-tat, ta-tat. He tries to remember how he fell in love with that sound the first time he ever travelled on a train. His Uncle Dietrich took his nine-year old nephew first to Potsdam, and then all the way to Berlin. It seems like an eternity ago. No matter. That world doesn't exist anymore. Sometimes he wonders whether it ever did.

* * *

What Emperor Barbarossa granted to his ancestors almost a thousand years before, the faithful and prudent generations have multiplied manyfold for the greater glory of God and of the family name. And now he's the last one.

Elizabeth, Hans-Bernd's mother, dies when he was only five years old. He doesn't really remember her, except a fleeting impression of a graceful, willowy figure, pale and delicate, melancholic and almost constantly ill. Sometimes, he is not even sure if the woman he recalls sitting in a garden

59

chair underneath a giant oak tree is his mother or Aunt Gertrud. This thought saddens him.

Then, another memory; a glimpse of a mahogany bed in the big bedroom, the door closing silently, forever. His uncle is squeezing his shoulder, absent-minded. He doesn't even realize he's hurting the boy. It's all right Hannie, it's all right. Hans-Bernd is sobbing but he doesn't quite yet understand why. Why the hushed voices, meaningful glances, and pregnant silences? Who's that tense small man with a heavy leather bag whose footsteps recede down the hallway? The house has never been so quiet in springtime.

A few months later the Great War comes. His father and uncle receive their commissions and on a languid day of a dying summer ride off to serve the Kaiser and the country. While the men are away Aunt Gertrud takes care of little Hannie, the son she has always prayed for but never received. But the Lord's ways are not there to be questioned.

Hans-Bernd will never see his father again. A telegram arrives one cloudy afternoon in the summer of 1916, delivered by a young bespectacled angel of death. The angel wears a dark blue uniform a few sizes too big, but rides his postman's bike with the quiet determination and dignity of a child who's had to grow up too quickly.

The Fatherland mourns with you, the telegram says. Ludwig von Schellendorff had fought the Asiatic hordes of the Tsar with strength and courage that brought honor to his name. He died a hero's death, leading his men into attack in the marshes of Ukraine. You should be proud of him.

Hannie's uncle and aunt will be good parents. By God, they will do their best.

* * *

Uncle Dietrich is not a rabblerouser, God forbid. He is a patriot, yes, but first and foremost a nobleman and an officer. It's not the base instincts that animate him, but the sense of honor, duty, and obligation. How can he remain unmoved now?

The victors have humiliated the Fatherland. There is no empire anymore, merely a republic. Germany has been condemned as a warmonger by the little men with top hats and *pince-nezes* who four years earlier had pushed the continent to the edge of an abyss, only to later discover morality growing out of the barrel of a gun. The country stands humiliated, disarmed and bankrupted by reparations. She can keep ten divisions only, a hundred thousand men, and four thousand officers. With more she cannot be trusted.

Dietrich's former comrades-in-arms are much more outspoken than he is. Germany's honor cannot be violated forever, treason has to be avenged, the country purged, with blood if necessary. Should he join them in agitation, or is there some other way? And what is he to think of that neurotic little demagogue from Vienna? Such a bundle of contradictions, isn't he, the little corporal? One moment he sounds like one of those Bolshevik radicals he claims to despise, the next moment he seems more like a prophet out of the primordial Teutonic forest.

And so Dietrich von Schellendorff sits quietly at home, smoking his pipe and reading newspapers, the sixty-year-old Hamlet in a redwood rocking chair. Von Schellendorffs have served princes and emperors for centuries. Hitler will come and go, but Germany will remain. Let's hope.

In 1927, when Hans-Bernd enters Berlin University to study Slavic languages, all the worst choices are still in the future, unimagined and unimaginable. Uncle and aunt do not in all honesty approve of his studies, but they love him and indulge him, for he will carry on the family name. Maybe the military calling will come in the future. Give Hans-Bernd time, let him see the big city, let him experience the soul-eating emptiness of the capital, let him slowly come to understand and appreciate his roots. He's still young, he's got time to listen to the whispering of his blood, to find out his true future.

The modern world is dying all around Hans-Berndt, impotent in its decadence, rotting from within, its promise wasted away or, worse, betrayed. Yet, by God, it's good to be young at this time, to carry in one's heart the spark of renewal, the imagination of a god, who will make the world anew, better, brighter, truer. Or so Hans-Bernd is told by his fellow students, all seemingly consumed with messianic longings. While Hans-Bernd sits quietly at his desk, memorizing the tongue-twisting vocabulary of strange languages, his friends dream of fire that will cleanse the land of all that is foreign, imposed, unclean. Un-German.

Hans-Bernd, buried between the dusty pages of books no one else reads anymore, doesn't care very much for the fire. But the sparks are already flying and the air is charged, electric. When the conflagration comes no one will be able to escape.

* * *

In Paris people still tango and rivers of champagne flow through the continent's capitals, and even Berlin whirls and dances to the latest tunes from across the Atlantic. Then Depression comes, with Depression despair, with despair darkness. One morning Hans-Bernd wakes up and Weimar is no more; there is now the Reich.

Soon, the Reich is calling on Hans-Bernd.

The nation is awakening and the nation is mobilizing. Abwehr, military intelligence, is the eyes and the ears of the soon to be mightiest armed forces in Europe. It needs people like Hans-Bernd and their skills. While the French deceive themselves and the British dither, the Fuhrer is fixing his gaze on the East; the vast open spaces inhabited by the barbarous Slavs, unkempt and uncouth *untermenchen*, the subhumans. And the Fuhrer needs people, many people, talented people, who can take the delirious ramblings of his badly written autobiography and with blood and iron translate it into a historic reality. Know thine enemy, because the time of reckoning is near. The final showdown, to extinguish for all times the bacilli that infest the tepid plains of the East.

Hans-Bernd speaks Polish and Russian quite well; he can easily brush up on the smattering of Slovak and Bulgarian he had also picked up at the university. He, who only a year ago let Mickiewicz and Dostoyevski, Prus and Tolstoy, lead him to the beauty of form and substance that so often defies translation, now collates numbers and tries to make sense of the puffed-up prose of yellow rag sheets and meaningless language of official pronouncements.

Is that what his education was for? And to what end? he asks himself in the middle of sleepless nights. But is he courageous enough – foolhardy enough – to just say no?

Hans-Bernd von Schellendorff's first desk is at Ausland, the foreign information division, Group I, army espionage. He liaises with the Foreign Ministry, evaluates foreign press, compiles briefings for the chiefs of staff. The work is numbing and tedious, but his output is exemplary and it gets noticed.

One Monday morning he is called into his superior's office and after a few minutes of small talk Hans-Bernd receives a transfer to a new assignment. He is to be the new assistant to the military attaché at the German embassy in Warsaw.

*   *   *

I don't know Hans-Bernd von Schellendorff yet. I will meet him soon.

II.

"Why?"

We were sitting on the same bench where it had all started, an eternity ago, yet not so long ago. The sky was clouded, too, like the first time.

"Why?" I repeated.

"Why what?" asked the old man. "Why you? Or why here? Why now? Why the old Germany? Why the old bathtub salesman who had to die?" He paused between each question.

"Why ... everything?"

He started caressing his moustache, almost absentmindedly. "I am not God, you know. I do not have all the answers."

He certainly didn't seem like God to me, not even a god.

"At this point in time I'll settle just for some answers."

Bartok smiled.

"So you took a train ride with Mr. Gottliebson. Nice man, no?" he started again.

"Nice man."

"Pity he had to die."

"Pity six million had to die. And then some more."

The wind now started driving the rain under the overhanging roof and we were no longer out of its reach. Bartok got up and we walked inside the building. The only other person there was a ticket seller who sat alone in his cubicle.

"You cannot do anything for Mr. Gottliebson now," he said.

"If Mr. Gottliebson ever existed."

"You spoke to him," he pointed out in a matter of fact way.

"Yeah, but I also took a ride on a train that doesn't exist."

"Maybe it did exist."

How does one argue with that? I thought.

"As I said," Bartok resumed his train of thoughts, "you cannot do anything for Mr. Gottliebson. But you can help many others."

The rain's steady drumbeat on the iron roof was starting to drown out Bartok's voice. I shook my head seeking clarification and he obliged, repeating the last sentence.

It didn't help. "I have no idea what you mean."

"Oh, but I think you do," said Bartok. "Mr. Geottliebson will die because he did not get out while he could, and later on did not try to go into hiding. But there are millions of others. All over Europe, not just in Germany. Many of them do not need to die –"

It was too much.

"They are already dead," I cut him off. "They've been dead for decades."

Bartok pressed on. "Many of them need not die, if someone can help them to get out. There are people who are already doing that, but they need your help."

"Believe me," I sighed. "If I were alive ... then ... I –"

Bartok ignored my protestations. "Think about it. It is your choice. You can go on the night trains and help save those people. One, ten, a hundred, a thousand lives, who knows. Or you can do nothing. Pretend that they are all ... phantoms. And let them die."

*   *   *

I did think about it.

It made as much sense as the rest of it; the lights over the railway yards that only I could see, the steam trains that weren't really there, ghost people catching a ghost train ... God, *me* catching a ghost train. To a country far away and long ago, where I could converse in the native tongue of a Jewish bathtub salesman.

And now the proposal: helping the dead to escape from the past using phantom trains.

I would laugh at the absurdity of it all, but I didn't really feel like laughing anymore.

*   *   *

"Why?" It always comes back to the why. When the what and the how are too damned difficult to figure out, you at least hope for the why, because in the end you can survive without the what and the how, but how can you go on without the why? "To pacify my conscience? To show the world what a good, virtuous man I am? What good is there in helping phantoms?"

"It is all about you, is it not?" Bartok shook his head. "Do you know they are phantoms?"

"What else can they be?"

He winced. "Can you be sure? Can you ever be sure?"

No. I couldn't. All I wanted was certainty, all I got was a possibility. "Next Tuesday night, then, at eleven," he said before he left.

III.

Polish spring arrives with hesitation, apprehensive of the latent bite of winter. As the old hag retreats back into the vastness of the Eurasian landmass she leaves behind dying patches of snow that linger scattered on the barren fields like torn pieces of shroud. The thaw turns the earth into a moist rug and breathes life into languid, icy rivers and streams.

In the spring of 1935 Captain Hans-Bernd von Schellendorff arrived to take his new posting at the Reich embassy in Warsaw.

This is how Abwehr places most of its operatives abroad. And the Foreign Ministry officials resent every moment of it. Spies come and go, often in disgrace, but the diplomats have to stay behind to soothe the inflammations and try to rebuild relationships carefully constructed over the years.

The ambassador refuses to talk to Hans-Bernd, save for cold greetings hastily and insincerely exchanged in corridors. The military attaché, the man who should be his mentor and protector here among strangers, cools off too, only a few days into Hans-Bernd's new assignment. A committed National Socialist who actually made an effort to read *Mein Kampf* from cover to cover, Colonel Eisner quickly learns to distrust his protégé. Von Schellendorff is an intellectual, and intellectuals are soft. Eisner fervently believes in the coming racial war. Then there will be a need for ruthless – and remorseless – warriors. Eisner fears that his assistant, with his incomprehensible attachment to this worthless, barbaric culture will simply not be up to the historic task. What could drive a good German officer to stoop himself to the level of his future subjects? Some mental infirmity, perhaps. God help us, maybe a few drops of Jewish blood.

You should see how Eisner rages: Warsaw is full of Jews; wherever one turns one is bound to encounter those filthy creatures. Doctors, lawyers, tailors, peddlers, artists, journalists, shopkeepers, they make up a fifth of the capital's population. The long-robbed, black-clad orthodox Hasidim with their bizarre fur hats and long beards mix with the supposedly emancipated ones who dress and behave like Poles, not Jewish anymore for the orthodox, not Polish yet for their neighbors. But they are all the same for Eisner. It's a disease, and before the German people take over this land and civilize it, it will have to be disinfected. Thoroughly.

"Berlin, von Schellendorff, Berlin," Eisner says, nervously tapping his fingers on the mahogany desk. "My home town, von Schellendorff. You know how many Jews there are? Not many, von Schellendorff, not many at all. Maybe a few thousand. Yet so insidious, so powerful. And what was done about it before the Fuhrer came? Nothing. All the Weimar politicians were either Jews or in Jewish pockets. Thank God for Hitler, von Schellendorff. Germany first, then this filthy country." He bangs his fist on the desk and goes on. Oh, how he rages.

*   *   *

If he ever fears that his work might involve too much cloak and dagger, Von Schellendorff quickly discovers how much one can learn just from reading newspapers and chatting at cocktail parties instead. He rarely has a chance to dirty his hands. No, he dresses up in a well cut, freshly pressed uniform and attended military parades, watching the spectacle from high up on the official stand, while white-clad waiters navigate in between with their silver trays of wine glasses.

It is at one such social call that Hans-Bernd meets *pan* Karol, professor of philology at the capital's university. A tall, bearded man, looking like the vengeful God himself, *pan* Karol now spends most of his time in Sejm, the parliament, where he sits and orates as a deputy for the Radical Nationalists, the latest faction to splinter off the National Democrats. Harassed by the ruling junta and marginalized by their own internal squabbling, Radical Nationalists make for an irrelevant sideshow. But even in a deck full of jokers, *pan* Karol stands out as somewhat of an eccentric, one of the very few politicians willing to overcome one thousand years of hatred and talk to Germans.

Pan Karol corners von Schellendorff under the shadow of a large potted palm, in a quiet laguna that slowly gathers the flotsom of the party. He speaks passionately, aided by his hands, yet the champagne manages to defy gravity.

"Such a painful history of relations between our two nations, Herr von Schellendorff," he seems almost apologetic, as if all that history was really weighing heavily on his shoulders. "I'm afraid our stubborn compatriots will not see eye to eye until such time that necessity will throw us in together to face the Bolshevik menace. It's a great pity it will take an apocalyptic conflagration before everyone sees the light."

His glass is now empty, but there is no waiter in sight. "I want to renew Poland as much as your Chancellor wants to renew Germany. Unshackle her from the chains that the international financiers and capitalists bound her with, breathe new life into our national culture, make the nation and the state one, you understand? But that would require the lessening of the ...," he clears his throat, "alien influences."

He pauses to wave to an acquaintance at the other end of the room.

"Disappropriate them and send them packing," he adds. "They can live in America if America wants them, but Poland should be for the Poles. I know you understand," he squeezes von Schellendorff's elbow in a gesture that is meant to be half endearing and half conspiratorial.

Von Schellendorff nods politely in a non-committal way. Politics, politics, everywhere. He would rather talk about Slavic languages with the professor.

But *pan* Karol is impressed with this German officer. A pleasant young man, cultured and refined, and speaks Polish so fluently. With an accent, of course, but certain things can't be helped.

*   *   *

Pan Karol has a daughter, Helena, and Hans-Bernd is in love, madly and at first sight, in a way that in the past had always struck him as rather silly and fanciful when extolled by the Romantic poets he read in the lyceum.

Helena is a few years younger, a talented pianist with a brilliant future ahead of her, so everyone agrees. She is a shy nymph with long auburn hair and big brown eyes like enchanted pools, where men's souls inevitably drown.

Discreet and casual liaisons with the locals are tolerated for the embassy staff with an air of worldly understanding, serious entanglements discouraged. Anything that distracts form the assigned responsibilities is a temptation to be avoided. Anything that has a potential to compromise personnel and operations even more so. But Hans-Bernd doesn't care.

They go on long walks down the city boulevards and through parks, while the evenings away at cafes and restaurants, are seen at the opera and concerts, drive off in one of the embassy's Mercedes limousines for a day in the country. An engagement is not mentioned yet but even casual observers can draw their own conclusions.

One Sunday afternoon in early autumn, Hans-Bernd and Helena are returning from a day trip to Zelazowa Wola, the birthplace of Chopin. It had only stopped raining moments before, and now a miserable dusk chases them home.

A few kilometers from the city outskirts, where the road curves along a stream, they are about to overtake a horse-drawn cart filled with freshly cut hay. As they are about to pass by, the horse suddenly bolts and drags the cart onto the other lane.

There is nowhere to go yet Hans-Bernd still swerves. The car leaves the road and slams into a tree. It will be an hour before help arrives to rush Hans-Bernd von Schellendorff to the hospital and to cut Helena's body out of the wreckage. The last thing he can remember is lying on his back, watching as the sky darkens. That, and the smell of wet hay.

* * *

Hans-Bernd will spend the next month in an army hospital on the outskirts of Berlin. There, the most talented and dedicated team of doctors that the country can offer to its warriors will work hard to mend his broken body. Fractured skull, broken ribs and femur, injured spleen and kidney, it all takes time to heal. But Hand-Bernd has got time. In fact, time is the only thing he's got. Long days blur into one another, as he lies in his hospital bed, then weeks of walking the cold corridors of a sanatorium in the Bavarian Alps where he is sent to convalesce.

Morphine takes care of the physical pain. But it's got other benefits, too, that Hans-Bernd slowly discovers and learns to appreciate. There is, after all, a worse, deeper pain that no doctor can make go away. But morphine ... Compared to the goddess, the most talented physicians are mere hacks and butchers.

The physical pain eventually leaves him, but that welcome departure will be a secret he will keep from his doctors, so that morphine can keep on flowing. If it comes to the worst, he can beg or steal or make a lonely nurse fall in love with him. Morphine doesn't make him forget – nothing can, and by God, he wouldn't want to even if he could. Yet it does – it does, doesn't it? yes? – soothe just a little, and without that he would surely go insane.

Under the cold watchful eye of glaciers, Hans-Bernd meets a fellow lost soul. Dietrich von Goth is convalescing from shrapnel wounds he has brought back home from the fields of Catalonia. He is an imposing, athletic man, only a few years older than Hans-Bernd, but this great runner and a fencing champion will for the rest of his life walk with a cane. A farewell gift from the Spanish anarchists, he says.

As they share walks in a pine forest they start to talk. Inconsequential, harmless things at first, but as the walks grow longer the chance confidences slowly erode the walls they had both constructed around themselves for protection and preservation. They ponder the burden of nobility, and of honor and responsibility; to oneself, to family, to the people, and to history. They talk about the rot at the heart of Germany, about the opportunistic scavengers eating at the soul of their country. And they talk about the difference between *Hochverrat* and *Landesverrat*; the treason against the government and the treason against the country, and how the time is fast approaching when one will have to choose which one to commit, because there will not be a third choice left for decent people.

When Dietrich von Goth leaves the sanatorium to resume his duties he will open a secret channel of communication with the Vatican, using his brother Erhard, a Dominican monk. He will also whisper about von Schellendorff into the ear of his close personal friend, Admiral Wilhelm Franz Canaris, the head of Abwehr.

* * *

When Hans-Bernd returns to work it is as an adjutant to Canaris.

The Silver Fox. With his thinning, fine white hair, pink cheeks and a drawn, serious face he would look more at home in a white coat of a pharmacist or an old suit of a small-town school headmaster. Instead he insists on wearing his favorite navy blue mufti with a simple German eagle engraved on his right breast. All his shiny military decorations are buried at the bottom of his desk drawer together with sleeping tablets and countless pills to assuage his hypochondria.

To Hans-Bernd he appears weary and depressed. His conscience is contested every day between the growing hatred of his new masters and his warrior's code of loyalty. Neither side will ever triumph over the other, and when at the end he will walk to his death down the corridor of the Flossenburg prison, only one month before the guns fall silent across Europe, he will be able to think of himself as an innocent condemned. His sins, if any, were only of omission. For he understood that only a great conflagration could cleanse his country's soul of all the madness, yet the most he could do was to merely look away while others under him, stronger and more determined, tried to kindle the sparks.

Von Schellendorff will get to meet most of them, even if the meetings will be brief and inconsequential. There will be Mueller and von Dohnanyi, working from the Munich station to open their own channels of communication with the Vatican. There will be Canaris's deputy Oster, who forbade people to give the Nazi salute in his office and never wore his army uniform because he believed the Nazis tainted and dishonored it. There will be others outside of Abwehr; the Army Chief of Staff Beck, the diplomat von Trott zu Solt, and Gisevius at the Gestapo. Once he will even get a chance to discuss poetry with von Stauffenberg, the man who will come closest to killing the beast.

On September 1st, 1939, as German divisions roll through the Polish borders and the grand assault on the Slavs begins, so does Hans-Bernd commence his own private war. He has spent too much time studying them to believe they are barbarians, only destined for slavery or extermination. It's an obscenity, a crime against living people, a crime against history.

So he will spend every minute of his time working to save whatever – and whoever – he can. Every life he manages to snatch back from the jaws of death is a small victory.

*　　*　　*

Canaris is sitting behind his heavy oak desk. He is barricaded behind piles of papers that threaten to topple over any minute and spill on the worn-down Persian carpet.

"Nothing makes sense anymore, von Schellendorff," he pats his favorite dachshund, Seppl. "In this world dogs won't betray you; it's the people who will. Isn't that sad?" his voice drifts off.

Von Schellendorff nods in silent agreement.

Canaris will spend the last night before his execution reading a biography of Frederick II. He will recall what the Holy Roman Emperor known as the Wonder of the World had once said: "Now that I know men, I prefer dogs." His mind will then wander back to that day at the office, with his dachshund on his lap, and von Schellendorff across the desk. Life is but a series of circles; no beginnings and no ends, only coming back.

But that's still far in the future. For now, as long as Canaris continues his unnatural friendship with Himmler's number two, Heydrich, life will travel along its curve. Abwehr will maintain its independence, its actions will escape too close a scrutiny. Abwehr's own passport office, run by von Dohnanyi and von Schellendorff, will continue to send Jews into the safety of neutral countries under the guise of Abwehr agents. Little private wars will rage on.

But you can never see what's beyond the curve. And there's always something beyond the curve. So after Heydrich will die, assassinated by the Czech underground in Prague, all bets will be off.

IV.

You've found the right person, haven't you, you bastard?

I kept wandering aimlessly, trying to put all the pieces together, see the pattern, and in the pattern see the reason why. Meals have become a chore, sleep a luxury commodity. My work now seemed no more real to me than some fantastic pursuits of my childhood.

I am not a hero, I just can't live with too much doubt in my life. You see, the trains were real, at least real enough for me. I've seen them, I've ridden them. I could be, of course, going insane, but what would that fact change? And if the trains were real, on what basis could I deny everything else?

I could have conceivably said no. Maybe some others did. Maybe as time went on I would be able to convince myself more and more that somehow this was just one big cosmic joke. But I would never be able to convince myself wholly and completely of that, and doubt would eat at me every day: what if Bartok had been telling the truth, after all? What if people were dying because I refused to help?

I wasn't having any peace now, but the truth is, I wouldn't have any peace no matter what. Everything had changed. That's why, on Tuesday night, I watched the red numbers of my digital alarm clock make their tortoise race to eleven. I then put on a heavy woollen jumper and quietly snuck out like a thief from my own house and into the yards, to play my part in this grand enterprise I didn't quite comprehend. To ride the night trains and save the Jews of Europe I've never been to – I've never been to until now.

V.

As I crawled through the hole in the fence I felt like I was travelling through a wormhole between two universes. The yards' physical manifestation could still deceive others, but I – I knew better. Even the air felt different on my skin on the other side of the fence. Funny, isn't it, how your mind can sometimes transform feelings of mental discomfort into a full-blown sensory experience.

Bartok was already there, waiting for me just inside the fence. The guardian spirit of the railways was wearing the same dark cream linen suit he had on the last I saw him, almost a week ago. Maybe time had stood still for him, as it seemed to have stood still for me.

He didn't greet or acknowledge me, merely turned and started walking. I stood up and followed, catching up with him after a few paces.

"You will go on a train," he said. "A train from Strasbourg to Lyons. A man will be waiting for you on the train, the last carriage. I do not know which compartment, but you will find that out for yourself. He will be alone."

Even if I'd somehow gotten lost in the darkness, Bartok's suit would guide me like a beacon with its eerie luminescence.

"His name is Hans-Bernd von Schellendorff, he's an officer in Abwehr. German military intelligence," he added obviously for my benefit. "He works with us."

Us? Congratulations, son, you'll be a part of our new crack unit. We thought that combining the skills of a flesh-and-blood wheeler-dealer with some highly experienced German ghosts will make for a quite unbeatable combination.

"He will give you the documents. Not for you, mind you," Bartok cleared his throat. We were heading towards the repair sheds, away from where I had embarked on my first trip. If the yards were just one big station somewhere in Europe then it didn't matter where exactly I would catch my train from, did it? God, the whole yards were Europe. What a way to travel.

"Your papers you will find on you." No surprises there, not any more. I would descend on some French station wearing something comfortably contemporary, speaking the language, holding in my pocket a complete set of identification papers certifying that I'm a travelling salesman from Bruge or some such.

"I suggest you familiarize yourself with your current identity," Bartok continued. "The documents you have to take from von Schellendorff are for a group of French Jews. The documents are fake, of course, but good enough to get them across the border to Switzerland. That is your next task. You will catch a train from Lyons to Grenoble. At the Saint Lambert station a woman will be waiting for you in the station's cafeteria. Baroness Molodyi. She will be reading a book, bound in red leather."

I felt like I was back at university, minutes before an exam, trying to cram everything in one last surge before the bell would go off.

"You will follow her and our friends onto the train. As an escort. She will know all the details. Any questions?"

Thousands, but are you really going to answer any of them?

"How long will it take?"

"Do not worry, you will get home in time."

"Good," I murmured. In time for what?

"Anything else?" he asked.

I thought about it a moment. Just like one of those jokes with a fairy godmother and three questions. "Why night? Why do I have to travel at night?"

He seemed to have been expecting this question, if not then, then some other time.

"You see," he said slowly. "Night is like a different country with its own laws ..."

And if a tree falls in the forest does anybody hear it? "But why?"

"Most people fear darkness. They think: mystery, danger, or evil, yes? But the darkness is like your ... best friend. Sometimes your only friend. She is your safety, a place to hide. The night is your ally. Treasure her." He tipped his hat towards me. "Godspeed, my dear Martin."

Just before I closed my eyes, a realization dawned on me that this time it wouldn't be the thirties anymore, the coiled spring of history, tense but still calm. When I open my eyes again, I will be inside a country defeated and occupied. A violent shiver shook my body. But it was too late for second thoughts.

*   *   *

It was hot. Before there was anything else, there was the heat, the stillness of air, and the oppressive humidity. And the scent of wet rot. I wasn't expecting that. In truth I don't know what I was expecting. Snowdrifts? A bone-soaking rain? Welcome to the Europe of my limited imagination. The old world had summers too, hadn't it? My first ride must have been in spring. How deceitful.

I opened my eyes.

This was worse then the unexpected heat.

I wasn't at the Strasbourg train station.

My knowledge of French geography was limited to occasionally following their football league. This was a little village train station. Little villages don't have premier league teams.

Jesus.

A screw-up.

I'm not where I should be.

How ...?

Then – just as suddenly – another flash. For every panic, counter-panic. Strasbourg was only supposed to be the commencing station for the service. Bartok didn't say that I was supposed to catch my train from there. Little village station was fine, after all.

Still, if not now, what if sometime in the future? What if I arrive at the wrong station? Or at the wrong time? Toto, I don't think we're in Munich anymore. Would I be able to click my heels together three times and reappear at my proper destination?

Another question for Bartok not to answer.

There was no window in front of me this time, and I had to look down to see my clothes. I was dressed lightly, fine wool, I think, but tonight it didn't seem light enough. Dark slacks, a white shirt with rolled-up sleeves and dark patches of sweat under my arms, a loosened-up tie hanging limply around my neck as if I had won a last minute reprieve from the executioner. A useless coat in my hand.

"Papers."

The voice came from behind me. A bored, barking voice of somebody too used to speaking in commands, but with the novelty wearing off.

I turned around very slowly.

There were two of them, a corporal and a private in their pale olive Wehrmacht uniforms, with Mausser sub-machine guns casually slung over their shoulders. They looked similar, in a plain, non-descript sort of way; two nineteen year olds from some small hamlet, seeing more of the world than they would have ever expected. And seeing it with guns in their hand. Boys who have spent their whole short lives being told what to do by their elders, and now they in turn have finally found someone else to order around. Whole nations, in fact.

"Just a second," I raised my hand and let the coat hang loose. There was a breast pocket, inside, on the left, and when I reached there, the comforting touch of paper under my fingers.

The corporal was eyeing me with suspicion. Maybe I was too well dressed, maybe too out of place here, in the middle of the French nowhere. I couldn't be allowed to pass by unchallenged.

I took out my documents and handed them over. The corporal raised the papers close to his face to compensate for the meager light. He looked up at my face, comparing it to the photograph, and then handed them back to me.

"Thank you, sir," he said without much zest. "Have a nice trip."

"Heil Hitler," I replied. The soldiers stiffened for a second, and responded with an instinctive military salute. They walked away and a half a minute later I heard them ask for documents of some other waiting traveller.

It took a lot longer to realize what I had just said.

* * *

That night my name was Heike Gauth, an official from Goebbels' Ministry of Public Enlightenment and Propaganda. Travelling through the Reich's latest acquisitions on a work assignment. To enlighten the public, perhaps.

Sometime later, I told Bartok to try to get me better documents for the future; the Gestapo, or top level Party. A better amulet to protect me at night.

Bartok said that the documents were a lottery, nothing more.

"C'mon," I chided him. "You can send me to the other side of the world and sixty years back, but you can't give me good papers?"

"Be happy you have documents at all," he shrugged. Then he wagged his finger at me; an afterthought.

* * *

The moment I first saw him I knew he was ill. Not the faint and die any minute now aura, but there was a distinct feeling about him that something wasn't quite right.

He had naturally fair skin, but tonight it looked even paler and more bloodless. His straight blond hair was neatly combed to the right and kept in place with pomade. He had a long, thin nose and full lips that remained slightly parted, as if in expectation of a conversation that never came. And then there were his eyes, feverish but piercing at the same time, steel gray.

I sat down and faced him. He was looking at me but didn't speak. This was the last carriage and the only compartment with a lone officer in it. It must be it. So I waited.

"Well, well, well," he finally said. He had a pleasant voice, slightly nasal, but melodic like a wind instrument. Soft for a German.

"Herr von Schellendorff," I couldn't think of anything else to say.

He snorted and quickly pulled out a gray handkerchief out of his trouser pocket. "Herr Bittmann."

I wondered what Bartok told him about me. Obviously not my real name, not even my other name for the night.

"Herr Bartok sent me," I said.

He nodded in an absentminded way, which I still took for an acknowledgment.

His eyes had left me by now and I felt relieved. His gaze was disconcerting, intense yet strangely dispassionate, as if he were looking at an object and not a person.

"Yes," he finally said, "I know." Outside our window the sprinkling of light broke through the darkness and vanished like spent fireworks. A small town, perhaps.

He knew Bartok as Bartok. But who was Bartok? And who was I? Surely, von Schellendorff did not know that his fellow conspirator is sending him a helping ghost from the future? Surely, as far as Von Schellendorff was concerned, I was just another good German, like him, an all-too-rare creature drifting on a sea of indifference.

"It's a beautiful night."

He startled me again. But these were his last words that first night. He didn't explain why the night seemed beautiful to him, didn't try to find out anything about me or the mission we shared. We sat in silence and I watched him, looking out the window, lost in thought. Nothing there to see, only his pale reflection staring back at him from the darkened window pane.

When the time came, he undid two buttons on his shirt, reached inside and pulled out a light brown envelope. He weighed it in his hand for a moment and then handed it over to me. He opened his mouth as if he had finally made up his mind to tell me something, but then seemed to change his mind and turned his head back towards the window. I left him sitting like that, still and absent.

*   *   *

There were fifteen sheets of paper in the envelope, fifteen sets of travelling papers, stamped, signed and folded in half. Underneath the black eagle sketched with runic harshness someone had already filled in all the personal details on a typewriter whose letter "s" was slightly raised above others.

The names of people who never existed but who in a few hours' time would cross the border to safety. It all seemed absurd – the whole set-up, and my role in it. Why couldn't von Schellendorff simply pass the documents straight to the woman in the cafeteria? Why the intermediary? I think I know the answer now, or at lest a part of it. I wish I didn't.

I stuffed the envelope under my shirt, behind the belt of my trousers and stood in the corridor, rocking gently on the balls of my feet as the train sped through the night.

I never thought I would eventually travel through Europe but not see any of it.

*   *   *

The night seemed to go on forever. Maybe it did; maybe in the middle of the last century, unbeknownst to all observers, the Earth's axis had shifted and the North Pole crawled down from the frozen wastelands of the Arctic to somewhere over Lorraine, plunging Europe in a six-year polar night.

Just as well I didn't have a watch. It probably wouldn't be able to tell me anything. Instead, I listened to the train. Tu-tut, tu-tut. Tick tock. It was the only clock I needed.

*   *   *

"Come now, sit down," she said. "Have coffee with me."

Her voice was a strange blend of melodies, like the voice of somebody

75

born on a borderland, physical, or at least of the mind, blending many accents into an angelic melange of smooth sounds.

When I saw her that first time, she was sitting alone at the table in the far corner of the station cafeteria. She noticed me and put down the little red book she was reading.

A lethargic looking barman behind the counter – what time was it really? – was polishing glasses, putting them up to a meager light to check on the quality of his work. An old man was eating his meal at a table next to the bar, a newspaper spread out in front of him though he didn't appear to be reading at the moment. Next to the door two German officers were drinking tea and conversing in unusually soft voices.

"They tried to chat me up and sit at my table," she must have caught my quick glance as I came in through the door. "I told them I'm waiting for my fiancée. They were very polite after that."

"Not in the mood to ravish a local women tonight," I said.

Those were my first words to her. I can remember it so well. That and the fact that she didn't appear to be taken aback by my remark.

"Now they're looking at us. Kiss me, my fiancée," she whispered instead. "On the cheek," she added.

I leaned over and brushed my lips against her cheek. Her fragrance was strong yet at the same time strangely delicate, like the memory of last year's bloom or last year's love.

I discreetly stole a glance over my shoulder. The German officers returned to their conversation. Talking of love, perhaps. Or of France herself, which fell into their hands like an overripe fruit, beautiful and tempting with its promises of women with azure eyes and cherry lips, champagne for everyone, even the lowliest, and the lights of Paris shimmering in the conquerors' gaze. It must have been a beautiful dream for their Germany after decades of waiting. A dream so enchanted they must have been afraid to stir, for fear of waking up. That time would come later when the Panzers were grinding to a halt outside of Moscow. But that night it must have seemed as if the dream would last forever, a fairytale of blood and iron.

"My name is Molodyi." Just Molodyi, unpretentious, not the Baroness. That air of latent restlessness borne of never having to hear the word "no," of walking on air, of living in an almost different world, in the end it all didn't matter. And probably because of that, it didn't matter.

She raised the cup of coffee to her mouth, balancing it on her fingertips, and smiled at me from behind the porcelain rim. "And what is my fiancée's name, I pray?"

"Bittmann," I said and leaned back on the seat, allowing myself to relax for the first time in what seemed like hours.

"Is that your real name?" she asked and before I could open my mouth to speak she waived me down. "Nothing. No need to answer that, Herr Bittmann."

There was something striking about her. The regular if somewhat sharp features were set on a triangular face. Her dark brown hair was pulled back and fastened with a pin, exposing a high forehead. Underneath, distinct crescents of eyebrows arched over large brown eyes. Swimming in the shadow of long eyelashes they looked almost feline, yet too innocent-looking to appear quite that predatory.

Yes, she was striking, but not in a way I was used to. Underneath all the distant air of reservation, a fire was burning quietly in her eyes, and the corners of her lips curled slightly upwards in a half-mocking smile of a younger Mona Lisa. She could have been a few years older than me, but just as easily she could have been a few years younger. She was dressed in a well-cut dark brown two piece costume with wide lapels adorned with a silver brooch in the shape of butterfly. Timeless elegant maturity existed in her side by side with something very childish and sweetly innocent, as if deep down life for her was merely an amusing pastime and a playful distraction from something far more important.

"Mr. Bartok has described you to me," she said.

"Was he accurate?"

"Not quite."

"Thank God, then," I said. "I think."

She laughed and instinctively brushed her hand against mine. The cigarette in the ashtray burned up to the tip of the ivory holder, but she took a last slow drag before extinguishing it and lighting up another.

"Dear man," she said.

Later, the barman made his way from behind the counter to our table. He carried his faithful piece of white cloth slung over his shoulder, as well as the weight of the world. I ordered coffee.

"So what do you do, Herr Bittmann?" she asked after barman disappeared behind the coffee machine.

"Call me Martin," I said. "I'm helping Mr. Bartok."

"Good answer." But she didn't reciprocate with her first name.

"What about you, Miss Molodyi?" A large moth spiraled onto the edge of our table and kept sliding in circles on the polished wooden surface, its wings trembling feverishly. I swept it onto the floor. "What do you do?"

"Oh, I keep company with certain men, Martin." She called me by my first name but on her lips it sounded like a surname. "Which means that I can go wherever I want to and no questions will be asked." She swept a strand of hair back behind her ear. "Did you know that sleeping with a Spanish ambassador confers one diplomatic immunity?" she laughed. "It's like a venereal disease. Except a good one."

Her forthrightness was unexpected and suddenly I felt self-conscious and almost embarrassed. The barman rescued me by bringing my coffee. It smelled rich, the way you want to remember something before the shortages set in. I put sugar in and stirred without looking up at her.

"I'm travelling all over Europe collecting artwork for my ambassador," she took the last sip of her coffee and pushed the empty cup back towards the center of the table. "It's really easy right now. Mr. Goering does it and so do thousands of others. Everything flows, everything changes hands. Such are the times we are living in."

C'est la vie. C'est la guerre.

"Pity the owners," I murmured.

The red leather-bound book lying on the table next to her left elbow was Proust. She started absent-mindedly tracing with her finger the black impressions of the title. "I sometimes think of it this way: one painting for a possibility of saving a life. Or ten paintings for a life, perhaps. What is a fair ratio?" she pinned me down with her gaze.

It felt cooler, as if the dawn was nearing. Somewhere away – years away – under a different night sky, Brad and Julie were turning in their sleep, blissfully unaware of my absence.

Discretely I undid two lower buttons on my shirt and reached for the envelope. Her eyes did not betray curiosity. I pushed the documents towards her over the table and she slid the envelope between the pages of her Proust. She smiled and put the book in her travelling bag.

"And how is dear von Schellendorff?" she asked.

"A man of few words."

"A moody Teuton," she said. "They rain death on Slavs in the morning and contemplate Hegel in the afternoon." She bit her lip. "Not Hans, though. He's only courting his own death, and she stares right back at him through a needle."

A melancholic Abwehr officer with a habit, then.

"But before that time comes we can still help each other," she said. It's all about supply and demand, even in war. Or maybe particularly in war.

The old man finished eating his very late supper or a very early breakfast and went up to the counter to pay his bill.

"It's time for us to go, too," Molodyi whispered.

On our way to the door we passed by the table with the two German officers; they interrupted their conversation and one of them smiled and acknowledged the Baroness with a courteous nod.

*   *   *

We waited at the back of the station under an old oak. The tree towered majestically over a picket fence and a cast-iron gate opening to the street beyond. A faint glow of platform lights was seeping through around the edges of the station building, illuminating its contour against the night sky. The air smelled of mildew. It mixed with her perfumes in a strange, primordial fragrance.

"The train will arrive in fifteen minutes," she announced.

Shadows began scurrying across the street a minute or two later. The gate didn't squeak when she let them in. People crowded in around us, tightly holding onto their bags. The whole of their lives, carefully distilled in few painful moments of hurry and tightly packed to go. Nothing else to declare.

Someone to my left stifled a cough and I felt a man next to me brush against my arm. He looked about my father's age, with an elegant trimmed beard and round, wire-rimmed glasses.

The old man from the cafeteria was here, too. "There are only ten," he whispered to the Baroness.

She said something back that I didn't catch.

"We had a problem with the people from Castelnandary," the old man was explaining. "We haven't made contact. I don't know what happened."

"They'll have to go the next time," she said.

The old man shrugged. "If there is a next time. And if they're still alive."

"That's not anything we can worry about tonight," she squeezed his hand. Not in front of the children.

The old man nodded slowly. In the distant glow of the station lights his face looked like a wax mask. I half expected it to start melting and slowly drip down onto his shirt collar.

I realized I was trembling. I took a step back from the circle to make more room as the Baroness took the envelope out her bag and started handing out the papers. "We'll have to divide ourselves into smaller groups," the old man was meanwhile explaining to the gathered. "Don't get onto the train all at once. It's a small country station. Do you understand what I'm saying?" A few of the figures nodded in silent acknowledgment.

I dug my clenched fists deeper into my pockets. It was difficult to believe it was so hot only a few hours ago.

Molodyi, a young couple and I were the last ones to go back to the station. She put her hand under my arm and leaned against me as we walked out from the shadows towards the platform. In my other hand I carried her travel bag. A nice young pair on holidays, perhaps. Pity the whole world has gone mad all around us. But it had gone mad so many times before, hadn't it, and life would have to go on. Life, such a delicate thing, yet so persistent, like lichen on an arctic rock.

The couple walking in front of us looked about our age. Another pair of lovers in the summer countryside. When we stood on the platform and could hear the rumble coming closer, the woman turned her head towards me and gave me a weak smile. Then it slipped off her face as suddenly as it appeared. She looked like she had been crying not long ago.

Suddenly I thought of Baruch Gottliebson's older daughter who would soon go on another train journey. And I prayed in my heart that this woman standing a few feet away from me would make it safely over the border, that this somebody else's daughter would live to have her own daughters look back at her with their big, melancholic eyes.

We were the last to get onboard. I scanned the empty platform one more time, and as the station master's whistle sounded, I gripped the handrail and pulled myself up onto the lowest step of the carriage.

The old man was leaning against the building, half hidden in the shadow of the awning. His part of the mission was completed. I never saw him again and I never learned his name.

*　　*　　*

The man with an elegantly trimmed beard and wire-rimmed glasses, the man about my father's age, leaned forward from his seat and showed me a photograph.

A woman with short straight hair framing her face was kneeling down and hugging a small girl. Both were laughing as they faced the camera on some cobbled plaza with pigeons flocking all around them. Black and white, slightly out of focus, I was looking at an old photo that was still new.

"They told me not to take anything from my past," the man said. "But I couldn't help it. That's my wife with my daughter. She left me two years ago."

He was playing absentmindedly with a signet on his finger.

"I don't know where they are now," he added. "That's all I have left. An image." He took the photograph back from my hands and put it back inside his wallet.

When I stood up to leave, he was lost in thought, probably travelling back to that time when life seemed so perfect. "I'm praying to the god of my ancestors," he awoke. "I haven't prayed in a long time."

He shook his head and looked to the floor. "I am a journalist, I should pray to progress, to humanity, to the brotherhood of men. Isn't it funny?"

He hunched forward with his hands between his knees. "I have to get out. For whatever my life's worth, I have to get out. Somewhere where I can write, let the world know. I can't carry a gun in these hands but I can carry a pen ..."

I hope that the god of his ancestors had mercy on his soul, for the next and last time I saw him he was dead.

*   *   *

I wouldn't have heard anything but for the fact that the train came to a halt.

Only a little while before we left another station along the way. A familiar hiss of decompression, followed by a grunt of an awakened engine and the metallic cling of buffers coming together. Then a loud, drunken song, a disharmonious chorus of three or four voices singing in German something about Hilda and a barrel of beer. Stuporous laughter, and the sound of a door sliding open.

The stern looking matron sitting opposite me raised her eyes towards heaven. The man travelling with her stirred uneasily but he, too, dared not speak the words on the tip of his tongue. The Huns. Barbarians. Yet ... better keep quiet; nothing can be done.

Then the sound of the moving train again.

And moments later, shouting.

Nothing jovial about it now, a hoarse barking of an awakened baritone, a woman's shriek and a loud crack. It took me a few seconds to realize it sounded like a gunshot.

In the past I would have never thought that my first reaction would be to jump out of my seat and run into the corridor. In the past I would not have thought many things.

Two compartments down the carriage corridor the door was wide open. A woman was standing just inside the doorway, her whole body convulsed with uncontrollable shrieks, stuck on "Oh my God, oh my God, oh my God." A man, her husband perhaps, was clutching her tightly, too stunned to whisper some calming words into her ear.

Inside the compartment, two German soldiers, young, fresh-faced, their rosy cheeks made even redder by drink. Their mouths open in an expression of intense surprise and confusion, quickly displacing drunken exuberance.

The same compartment where I spoke with my journalist.

Jesus, where was he?

The train had by now come to a complete halt. Maybe somebody had pulled on the emergency break. Maybe it was just a coincidence.

The third soldier was standing inside the compartment, with his back to the door, his legs slightly astride as if he were trying desperately to keep his balance. He was holding a gun in his outstretched, unsteady hand. My journalist was slumped over the foldout table, his upper body twisted sideways so that he continued to face the doorway. His eyes were wide open but unseeing behind the skewed glasses, and his mouth parted slightly as though he were trying to say something before he was cut off by the German. The bloody red flower was in full bloom on his white shirt.

"Jesus and Mary ... oh ... they ... sweet Lord Jesus ... he wouldn't move so that Karl could put his feet on the seat ... What will they do to us ...?" one of the soldiers suddenly snapped out of his shock and started babbling, as if trying to make sense for himself of what just happened. With the corner of my eye I could see people venturing out into the corridor, intrigued but cautious, ready to pull back into the deceptive safety of their compartment at the first sign of new trouble.

"Put the gun down. Put the gun down really slowly," I heard somebody say. It took me a few seconds to realize it was me. God, what am I doing here? Why am I looking at a dead man with a hole in his chest, and more importantly, why am I talking a to a drunken killer who's still holding a gun in his hand?

The soldier didn't seem to have heard me.

"Put down the gun," I repeated, this time louder. "I am from the government."

"I knew it, I just knew it," the other soldier kept whimpering. "We shouldn't have let him drink so much. He hasn't been himself lately ... God, Karl, don't do this to us ... Mother, what is mother going to think? Oh, God –"

Delicately I put a hand on the gunman's shoulder.

"Please, nothing –"

His speed stunned me. I imagine a few people must have gasped.

The soldier, Karl, swirled around. His left hand shot out like an ugly Jack in the Box and grabbed my shoulder in a steel vice, while the other brought the gun to my head. I could feel the metal of the muzzle pressing at the base of my nose, still warm from its last discharge. I think that at that moment I lost control of my bladder.

"Are you one of them?" he shouted, while his hand squeezed my shoulder even harder. "Are you one of them, too, you dirty little swine?"

"Oh, Jesus," his comrade wailed. "Karl, don't –"

"Shut up, Schwartz, just shut the fuck up!" Karl hissed back at his comrade without taking his eyes off me. His face was only inches away from mine and droplets of his saliva exploded on my face.

"Where did you get the gun, Karl ... God ... you weren't supposed to take it with you on leave ... They're gonna court-martial us. Jesus ..." Schwartz hid his face in his hands and started sobbing. Now that all the spectators pulled back into their compartments he was the only one still rooted to his spot.

"No respect for the man in uniform, that's the problem," Karl was panting. "That's right, no respect."

"I –" am an official of the Reich government, I tried to say, as if it this magic incantation would make any difference. Nothing came out of my mouth and this was just as well.

"You're going with me for a walk, mister civilian swine," Karl growled and his face contorted into a hideous caricature of the caricature he already was. Tiny beads of sweat erupted on his forehead and his face turned an even richer shade of red, as if he was about to be struck down by apoplexy.

Without letting go of my arm Karl slowly circled behind me. His Mauser also moved and was now touching my temple.

"Come on," he nudged me forward. "You won't refuse a polite request by the member of Reichswehr's elite fighting force, won't you? That would be soooo impolite."

We brushed past Schwartz and his other, silent companion. Neither of them moved. Schwartz's eyes were now closed, and his mouth was mouthing silent words. The corridor was empty as we stumbled towards the exit. From the compartments, eyes followed our journey, too terrified to look, yet too spellbound not to.

With the gun still pressed against my temple Karl released the grip on my shoulder and pushed on the doorknob. The door flung open. A cool wave hit us without warning. My mind was completely blank.

"Gertrud, you bitch. You had to go with ... them, didn't you?" Karl growled. His voice sounded like it was about to break. "Oh, Gertrud ..."

There was a drop between the lowest step and the ground. He pushed me forward and I stumbled down two feet onto the grass. He and his gun followed behind.

"We'll walk, Gertrud, you and me, like we used to –"

Jesus, I thought, he's completely, totally lost it.

"– we'll walk in the forest, won't we? You'll pick some flowers and start making a wreath, I'll sing you a song ..."

We walked down the embankment, the weeds brushing against our knees. With every step I took the train receded a thousand miles.

Karl started singing a song, a melancholic folk tune. I couldn't catch the words, nor did I try to. He was sobbing by now, too, but he persevered, in turn losing and then finding the melody and the pace.

Why didn't I do it before, way before? Maybe back in the compartment, after we all heard the shot, or maybe when Karl was still standing with his back towards me, staring at the dead civilian swine – one of them – them who screwed his girl while he was dodging bullets at the front. Why didn't I do it before? Everyone – not just the three drunken German soldiers – would see a man disappear into thin air right before their eyes. But so what? As if I cared right now.

The song has broken off in mid-note. The snot must have choked Karl, for he swallowed noisily and mumbled something under his breath. The muzzle rubbed against my ear and dug into my temple.

I bit my lip and closed my eyes wishing like I never wished before that I would wake up.

VI.

Sometimes, I still tried to think what it would be like to simply ignore the things going on around me. The trains, Bartok, the rescue missions, the whole lot. Turn my eyes away, pretend they're not there. Go on with my life. Get back to work, get back to life, go to somebody's birthday, get drunk, flirt with some sweet little thing, try the "if I followed you home would you take me in" line, see what happens. Live. Live again.

The trains would still be there, I thought. The lights would flicker too, or maybe they would dissolve in a Prozac haze. The people would be the hardest to ignore, but – well, no walks in the yards, no people.

Would I go insane or would it all just become a part of my life, like short sightedness? A dark secret, too embarrassing to share with anyone, a condition I could never get rid off, irritating beyond endurance, but one that in the end I would learn to live with; a kind of paranormal ringing in my ear.

Maybe all the others went nuts because they simply could not accept the trains. I would. I would accept it, all right, but I would ignore it. Fuck you, keep on riding through the night. See if I care.

*   *   *

We were sitting across the table from each other, Bartok and me, two chess masters pondering our next moves with invisible pieces. I tried to appear at ease, leaning back in the chair, my legs stretched out under the table. Yet I was careful that my feet should not to touch Bartok, as if that was some sort of bad luck. Too late, I thought then, the black Austrian tomcat had already run across my life.

He always knew to time his visits when I was alone. This time, too, he knocked on the front door an hour after Julie went out to have coffee with a friend and five minutes after Brad left for work, saving me from the charade of introducing him as my granduncle. I could live without more deception in my life.

After I let him in, Bartok asked me if he could have something to drink. As if to tease me; hey, look my dear young Martin; see? I drink your coffee, I am flesh and blood, I am not a ghost. Now he was stirring his cup with a precise, deliberate movement.

"You didn't tell me that ... something might happen to me," I said. "That I might get killed, for God's sake."

He kept on stirring. "What did you expect? It is a war out there."

I didn't find the truth funny.

"If I wanted to play a humanitarian hero I would go to some godforsaken place in Africa. I don't need to go on some Flying Dutchman train for that."

"It is life, my dear Martin," he took a sip out of a cup. No one in my house possessed a proper coffee set and the old man was drinking out of Brad's 'Fuck me, I'm Irish' cup. Something I had only noticed after it was too late. Bartok didn't, or if he did, he didn't care. "A very risky business this living. Tomorrow you could fall under a truck. Or discover you have cancer –"

"Tomorrow I could be hit by a meteorite," I said. "I think the odds of me dying tomorrow night in France are much better. How's that for a risky life?"

"Yes, but that would be a heroic death, no? Saving people's lives," he sounded like a traveling salesman whose living depended on commissions. Commissions from selling glory here, or death.

"I don't want to die a heroic death. I don't want to die any death." I hunched over and my legs contracted back under the chair, as if I were subconsciously trying to collapse into a pseudo-fetal position. "What's going happen to me? Will they find my body at the yards like they did Jephson's? Or will I just disappear like that?" I snapped my fingers.

All along I assumed that death there, wherever there was, would also make me dead here. It was not necessarily a logical assumption, but the longer Bartok kept not correcting me the sicker I felt in my stomach.

"And what does it matter to you?" he said calmly as I if had asked him about the likelihood of the dollar losing a cent to the euro on the exchange rate.

"I don't want to do it," I burst out.

He waved me down. "Let us say you decide that the yards are no good for you, had enough of the trains and even the people. So you pack your bags and move. You find your new home somewhere else, some nice suburb, as far away from the trains as possible, yes? But who is to say that the trains need any normal" – he accented the word – "tracks?"

Like surrealist mafia. You fuck with us and you'll wake up with a burning giraffe's head in your bed and your clock melting on the bedside table. But what Bartok said was just a matter of fact statement, unsentimental, no bullshit. Here, sonny, there's no escape for you; wherever you go, the trains will follow to remind you that the longer you resist the call the more people are dying needlessly. You could hide in the Amazonian jungle, but the trains would still come after you, tearing through the dense undergrowth, gliding on the piranha-infested waters. Huffing and puffing: leaving in two minutes, all onboard.

"It's not fair," I blurted out. It sounded petulant.

"Life is not fair, my dear Martin."

No, it's not.

But ... "Will it ever ... end?"

I half-expected him to repeat: 'nothing ever truly finishes', but he only shook his head. "When it is over it is over. But there are many things you must do before."

I didn't waste my breath inquiring what those things were. I would learn, but not now, not yet. That much I have already been conditioned to expect.

It seemed like Bartok was readying himself to leave, but he still lingered. There was some unfinished business.

"You did not even ask how they were," he said, sounding disappointed. "Baroness Molodyi, all the people you were helping to get out."

No, I haven't forgotten. I was thinking about it every waking second since my return. But my own self-preservation was also high up there on the list. That's what I wanted to say.

Instead I just asked "How did things go?"

"They got through," Bartok said. "They got through. Just."

I thought of the man who could have been my father, the woman who could have been Baruch Gottliebson's daughter. Somebody's father, somebody's daughter. Some got through, some didn't.

"What happened to the ... soldiers?"

"I don't know," Bartok shrugged.

* * *

Choices. It always comes down to choices, doesn't it?

The people then, in the world at war, under the occupier's boot, also had their choices. Restricted by circumstances, and not very appealing, but choices nevertheless. To make the best of it all, to give yourself freely because you believed in your new overlords, or to sell yourself freely because it did not really matter in the end who you sold yourself to. Or to resist, with thoughts and words, and better still, deeds, to pull a trigger, hide some papers, rescue the imperilled. Or to keep your head down, try to make yourself invisible, unobtrusive and unprovoking, and hope to somehow last through the storm. And then, so many shades in between. A few chose the first road, some the second, and most, being human beings, chose the shades.

The trains would be my companions if I made one choice, or a constant reminder and regret if I made another. It was up to me. But one way or another they would always be there. I could rage about it, the way I imagine people decades ago raged about the war around them. Why? Why, oh Lord? Except that for them, the whole world was in it together, whereas I could only wonder why I had been singled out. Now. I was born so much later, in a world so different, with no inkling that I would ever be called to make choices – those choices. And no, I was not the type to go to some godforsaken place in Africa of my own free will. But this time, it was a godforsaken place in Africa that came to me, and said: so?

Just before he left my house that day, Bartok hesitated for a moment as he was about to put his hat back on, and said, "Think about it, Martin. Von Schellendorff, Baroness Molodyi, all the people you are helping. They cannot close their eyes. Ever. Think about it."

So, in a way, lucky me.

*   *   *

I tried to follow him. I already knew where he didn't live, and for whatever it's worth I wanted to find out where he did.

I watched him slowly descend down the wooden steps and cross the path through the front lawn. He went through the open gate onto the street and didn't look back. I waited until I thought it would be safe and then I ran down the stairs.

He was about a hundred and fifty yards down the street strolling ahead, unhurried. I crept behind him, from tree to tree, in a way kids imagine spies do. A middle-aged woman walking on the other side of the street gave me a strange look but shrugged and walked on. Not worth getting involved in.

He turned the corner into Brownback Street, which climbed up the hill for about half a click to the main road. The street had recently become treeless after the local authority realized what the roots were doing to the footpaths and sewage pipes. Save for a few cars parked by the curb there wasn't anything I could hide behind. When I reached the corner, Bartok was climbing up the street, a solitary figure ascending to the sky. I could only hope he would not look over his shoulder.

"Hey mister."

The voice startled me for a second, just as I was about to rise from behind an old, yellowish Ford with dozens of peeling radio station stickers on its rear bumper. A boy, about seven or eight years old, with ruffled blond hair and dirty smudges on his face stared back at me, gripping tightly the handle bar of his BMX bike. He was dressed in oversized basketball gear, probably passed on from his older brother.

"Mister, d'ya have fifty cents?"

"No," I barked and waved him off. The boy just stood there, unperturbed.

I waved my hand again, and looked up the street.

Bartok wasn't there anymore.

The last time I saw him he was about halfway up the hill, with about a minute or two of walking still ahead of him until he made it to the crest. He could have walked into one of the houses, of course. There was no reason why he could not have lived on the next street from my place. But I still should have managed to catch him opening his front gate and fumbling with the keys.

As I was walking down Brownback Street back to my place the boy raced past on his bike at breakneck speed. For a few seconds he pried his hand off the handlebar to give me the finger.

VII.

"Tell me about yourself, Baroness."

"Oh, how formal. Call me Katrina. Baroness sounds pretentious when you say it like that."

"Like what?"

"Oh, like the way you say it."

"OK. Katrina."

"What do you want to know, Martin?"

"Everything."

"Ah ... My mother was a Jew, my father was a nobleman. Great misalliance, that one, particularly in Hungary. Then again, I guess it would be the same in most other places, really, wouldn't it? My father used to travel quite extensively. I believe he had a whole string of affairs. This was the one his wife found out about; she slashed her wrists and painted 'I'll see you in hell' with her blood on the wall of the dining hall."

"Jesus."

"At least that what my father's faithful old butler told me one night when I was old enough to get him drunk. Dear old man, told me a few dark family secrets that time ... Quite fascinating, well worth all that old port."

"What about your mother?"

"Oh, I don't really know. When I was a few months old she'd left me on the front steps of my father's mansion in Budapest and disappeared. When I was older, and after I'd learned the truth about who my real mother was, I tried to find her but everywhere I went I seemed to be a few steps behind and a few years too late. I know that she was an actress. Not a very successful one. I don't even know how she and my father ever met in first place, he never said anything. I met her parents – my grandparents – about five years ago. I keep in touch with them whenever I can."

"Aren't you worried about them? I mean with the situation –"

"Oh, it's still pretty safe. There's some harassment, of course, and all the weird laws ... I moved them anyway, and arranged new identities for them. Proper, Gentile identities. That's all I can do. I wanted to send them overseas, America, perhaps. They didn't want to go. You don't replant old trees, that's what they told me. They're not orthodox Jews, you know, they don't stand out in the crowd. So they're in a much better position than most others."

"Which is not saying much."

"It's not as bad as some other places. But yes, it's a fool's paradise. All the Hungarian Jews think they're so Magyarised, so much a part of society that nothing can ever happen to them. A massacre takes place somewhere on the border. That's nothing, they say, an unfortunate incident, an inquiry has now been established, after all. Discriminatory laws are enacted. Not really applied that strictly, they say, we'll survive. They just keep shrugging ... But I've been around Europe, I know how things are everywhere else. I know it can't last ... Anyway, my grandparents couldn't tell me much about my mother. Apparently she was always a free spirit, left home when she was very young, didn't keep in touch with them after that."

"They must have been surprised to find out they have a granddaughter ..."

"... who's a goyim aristocrat. Yes, they were."

*　*　*

It's now November, but it's really October. The only point of intersection between the two places is night. Night is here, and it's there, it's everywhere. Maybe it's not even night. Maybe the lights are out in the theater. Sometimes I think I can feel the eyes of the invisible audience on me, watching my every move.

Tonight my name is Aloise Fouche. I am – or rather my documents say I am – a French laborer, tempted by good wages into coming to work for a German factory in occupied Poland. Now I am returning back to my hometown for a brief holiday. I can tell my life story to anyone who will ask me, though I'm pretty certain no one will. The whole train is full of men like me, each with similar tales to tell, so what's the point of exchanging them? Instead we'll talk of our bastard foremen, of the women we're coming back to see, and if we're feeling indiscreet and boisterous, of the women we've left behind. We can almost smell the air of home, we can almost taste the wine, the good wine, for the horrid vodka of this country still burns in our throats.

What a prominent skull, I think of the man sitting opposite. His eyes are sad, intense and watchful, set under inquisitive eyebrows, and flanking a large nose. His lower face is swollen and he's holding a handkerchief to it, content to travel in silence.

"He will travel under the name of Jean-Baptiste Descourt," I can still hear Bartok's voice as he gives me the instructions. "We have convinced the real Monsieur Descourt to spend his holiday in Poland, in a little village where he will be looked after while we use his documents to get our man out of Poland. His real name is Jan Karski, and he works for the Polish underground. He is a courier and it is essential that the information he is carrying reaches the Allies in the West. You will shadow him for part of the journey from Warsaw to Paris to make sure nothing happens to him. We know you can only stay one night with him. Others will take over when you leave. Meanwhile, just be there and watch. Remember, it is very important."

Karski hasn't spoken to me so far. To everyone else he mumbles incoherently and points at his swollen jaw, eliciting nods of sympathy from his fellow travellers. Karski knows French well enough but fears his accent might give him away. A friendly and discreet dentist has injected him with something that produced the convenient infection and a convenient excuse to stay mum.

The journey is painfully slow. It seems like every dozen miles we get shunted to give way to priority trains. Just about anything now takes priority over French laborers going back home; troops, food, material, equipment, fuel, thousands of ammunition cases and barrels of oil, cans of pickled pork and condoms, rims of forms and pink-faced recruits from Swabia and Saxony, typewriters, howitzers, spare engines and leather boots. The beast is constantly hungry and its arteries have to be kept free of congestion.

So we try to make do in the meantime. No compartments here, only rows of plain, worn-down benches with a narrow aisle running down the length of the carriage. The constant murmur of hushed conversations and the aroma of onions, cheap tobacco and sweat mix in the air. Many try to sleep with their heads on folded-up coats, pressed against the windows. Behind me a few men are playing cards religiously, winning and losing imaginary fortunes in a contemplative silence.

Karski sits with his eyes closed but he's not asleep. Behind the shut eyelids lies a secret.

*   *   *

"My father had always been a very distant man, cold really, not interested in others. Not even in his family. But when his maid brought in the bundle that my mother had left him, he took me in. Maybe he felt something for my mother that he never felt for any of his other women. Or maybe it's because his only other child died of typhoid fever in the Great War. Still, it was all a bit of a hush hush story. Most people knew I wasn't his wife's daughter and I'm sure many things were said behind our backs. Hardly anyone knew, though, who my real mother was. Her Jewishness, not so much the illegitimacy itself, would have been embarrassing to him. He certainly liked to think of himself as better than others, above it all. A lord in the old mold."

"Is he still alive?"

"No. He died a few years ago. Hunting accident. At least that was the official story. He was out hunting with his friends on our family estates in the east. The Scythe Cross used to have a large following there before they were suppressed by the government –"

"I –"

"Sorry, I forget. They were a peasant movement. Hated their overlords, the Jews, the communists; hated pretty much everyone. They wanted to march on Budapest, raze the sinful city to the ground and, I guess, build their heaven on earth. Who knows what they really wanted. There was a stray shot. Who fired it I will never know, and I guess it doesn't matter."

"I'm sorry."

"So am I. I never really got to know him very well. He was as absent in parenthood as he was in marriage. He showed me his love by buying things. When he died he left me everything."

* * *

"I have seen with my own eyes. That's what I have to tell them," he says. The words emerge muffled from his swollen mouth and I have to concentrate to make out what he is saying. What he's seen – the secret, the truth – burns inside him like a little ember. If only he'd kindle it against others and set their consciences alight, it might make his pain worthwhile.

"I've dressed like a Jew, worn the star of David, and walked the streets of the Warsaw ghetto," he says and I listen over the rattle of the train. "The ghetto is dying, and its people are dying with it. People go mad and run through the streets screaming. No one cares. There are naked bodies lying in the gutters. Passers-by only take the clothes off the dead, because why waste? But no one buries them because they would have to pay the burial tax to the Germans. I've seen *Hitlerjugend* boys, twelve, thirteen years old, walk around and shoot people. At random. Just like that. *Judenjag*, they call it. The Jew hunt. And then they walk away, as if nothing happened."

They are hunting Jews and the whole world is walking away, as if nothing happened.

We are standing in a narrow corridor, just outside the toilet, the only place on the whole train that offers some privacy. Even here we have to be careful. When a short, balding man comes towards us I start talking about everything and nothing. The man's got a sly look about him. A badly healed scar runs from his left temple, across the cheek, all the way to the corner of his mouth. He mumbles something to us and locks himself in the toilet. Karski only resumes his story after the man finishes his business and walks back to his seat.

"I've seen the camps, too. I've dressed as a Ukrainian guard and walked right inside it. It was just an open field with a barbed wire fence around it, three meters tall. Inside there were hundreds, maybe thousands of people. The noise, the stench –"

He pauses, as if even the memory itself was suffocating him.

"Do you know what they do? I've seen them do it. They take the boxcars and put the quicklime on the floor. Then they herd the Jews into the wagons, like cattle, until there are so many inside that there is no room to move. Then they put the trains away at some disused siding. The quicklime burns the flesh, and when they urinate on the floor, it gives out chlorine gas that chokes them. So they die, for days, standing, starving, burning. If they're lucky they go insane before it's over."

Karski is a courier. He is the bearer of news so horrible that people will rather choose to disbelieve, because to accept it, one also has to accept there's nothing left to believe in. Or at least not in humanity, anyway. Or the Enlightenment. From the land of Goethe and Schiller and Beethoven comes darkness. It's all around us now, like a poisonous gas drifting over the Somme battlefield twenty-odd years before. Can you smell it?

"I've had Jewish friends at school, you know. I don't know if they're still alive," Karski says. I do not know, either. Probably not.

He can't talk much more. His mouth is dry and his gums start to bleed again. But he has already said what he wanted to say. I watch him go down the aisle to his seat, and then it's time for me to slip into the night.

*   *   *

"I met von Schellendorff in Berlin, about a year before the war started. The time of perpetual motion. Springtime in Paris, champagne on the Riviera, a car rally in Belgium, a masquerade ball with friends in Italy. Life was so beautiful then. The worse it looked on the outside, the murkier the crystal balls, the more we shut ourselves in our world, and the faster we lived, the deeper we breathed, the more stars we saw before our eyes. As if we were trying to make up for the future, store as much heat and radiance inside us to last us through the long winter. I guess somehow we all knew ... Anyway, a friend of mine, the daughter of a German industrialist, had introduced us. Then we kept running into each other by accident. A ball, an air show, a coffee shop on Potsdamer Strasse. He was always pleasant, a real gentleman. I found it easy to talk to him, to gossip with him."

"He doesn't strike me to as a great conversationalist."

"He always found it easier to relate to women –"

"Must be his softer side."

"There was an ulterior motive for him, of course. I was moving in interesting circles: senior officers, diplomats, government officials, all that. You always kept hearing things, people confided in you, most of all in bed. Men always try to impress you in so many different ways, the lovers and the world shakers ... Are you uncomfortable?"

"No. Nothing really makes me uncomfortable anymore. Particularly not that."

"The world around us has turned too obscene to care about such petty sensibilities ... I knew who von Schellendorff was working for, but for some time I didn't know about his other work. One night the whole group of us got drunk and when the two of us were finally alone we started talking. It was not long after Poland, you know. So it was easy for one thing to lead to another. I think it was me who started throwing him bait but he was taking it and then throwing it back to me. We were scared because we were honest but as we sobered up towards the dawn there was no retreat, no embarrassing conspiracies of silence. It was too late anyway, all the bridges were burned. It would have been dishonest to think otherwise. So we went on and life went on, too. And we would assist each other. That was the arrangement that came out of that night."

"And so it goes."

"And so it goes. Tomorrow I can become poor, or an American, a Bolshevik, or a blond, but I can never become a non-Jew. I wasn't raised as a Jew, and until I was seventeen I didn't know I had any Jewish blood in me. God, until I was seventeen I don't think I really knew any Jews at all. Now with every life I can help to save it's like I'm saving a part of myself. Do you understand?"

* * *

It's an enigma.

Why is it so important that Karski reaches England? What does it really matter? If the whole night world is just an elaborate illusion playing in my mind, then surely it doesn't. But if I am – somehow – going back; can anything, will anything, actually turn out any different? A single life can be saved, maybe; that's what I do every night after all. But the whole world?

Or am I travelling somewhere else entirely, to a place where the past stretches out infinitely into an eternal today – tonight – and the bloody bitch history is playing herself over and over again, and we, the poor shmucks, get another go, another chance to get things right?

So maybe it does matter that Jan Karski reaches Paris safely, crosses the Pyrenees into Spain and is smuggled out to England by the British intelligence services. Maybe this time they will listen; listen and believe; believe and act. Maybe it can all turn out differently. Maybe.

But I don't know. I just don't know.

* * *

She didn't tell me the whole story then. Maybe not even in one conversation. But you might as well know it all now.

VIII.

The carriage was almost empty at this time of the day. Only two old women at the other end were engaged in a quiet conversation, and closer to the door a teenager with Down's Syndrome was kneeling on his seat, facing the window. "A car ... trees ... a tall building ... a blue car, blue car ..." The

world passing by filled him with a sense of infinite wonder and so he was
providing a running commentary on the sights outside.

All the information was there before – Jephson, Bartok's hints, then
finally, Karl's gun – but sometimes it takes a long time to ask a question.
Particularly if a meaningful answer is unlikely. Or if you do not really want
to get the answer. Still, you try.

"The trains ... they've being riding for a long time, haven't they?"

Bartok didn't answer. His head tilted slightly to the side as he was
waiting for more information.

"Jephson's seen them way before me. Way before. There were others,
weren't there? Others before me? What happened to them?"

"I think this is one question that you know the answer to already,"
Bartok said slowly. He sounded tired, genuinely tired, like a biblical
patriarch nearing a millennium of life, a millennium of answering the same
questions over and over again. From me and from others before me, I now
suspected.

"Jesus," I gasped. "That's why you need me now. You've run out of all
the others. They're dead, aren't they? Died honorable deaths saving lives.
Unlucky bastards. They were also given a choice, eh? Either help us and it
might all end one day or else you'll see the bloody trains until the day you die
or finally snap, whichever comes first. So they went on and died, one by one.
Gestapo here, a trigger-happy soldier there, an accident, a shoot-out. And
now I'm the new cannon-fodder. That's why you need me, isn't it?"

"The answer to your question is yes and no, my young friend."

I opened my mouth to speak but Bartok cut in, "You will understand.
Not yet. But soon."

The shot echoing through the carriage, the gun pushing at my temple.
The only time in my life when I had come so close to –

"Why did those people get killed at all?" I said. "Why couldn't they just
close their eyes ... and be back ... just as I did?"

Bartok frowned and rubbed the base of his nose with his knuckles. "You
see, it is not as easy as that ..."

Good God.

"So you've lied to me?"

"I never said you can always come back just like that," impatience rose
up in his voice. "It works most of the time –"

"– but not always."

"What do you want from me?" he spread his arms. "I did not make the
rules and I cannot change them."

Some sucker – like me – over there, one night, gets unlucky. Some
Gestapo man gets suspicious, the sucker bolts, runs and closes his eyes, and
closes them again. But this time it's not working, is it? The shots ring out,
bang, bang, bang, and down he goes. And the last thing on his mind is: why?

"What do you want me to say?" Bartok said after a while. "Fifty million people died in the war. Maybe sixty. Just in Europe. Do two, three more lives really make a difference?"

That depends. On whether they do make a difference.

"Did you warn them, at least?" I asked. The words had difficulty getting out through my dry throat.

"I did. Some of them. As for others ...," he paused, "As for others, they were not ready yet. Would you go, right from the start, if I told you that one night, any night, you might not return?"

I bit my lip. "I preferred the old game. Nothing there about dying."

"This is not a game. Not some computer game. You do not get three lives and the stop button to get out when you get bored with the whole thing. That is the problem with you young people now. You always had it so easy, you expect to get everything without any risk, without paying the price. There is always a price."

I didn't expect to get this – everything. I didn't ask for it, so why still pay? Crucify me for the sins of my generation, why don't you.

We fell silent.

"Some die, some do not," he whispered suddenly.

It dawned on me, like a flash of lightning cutting through the clouds. Jesus, I never thought about it either. "They blink and blink ... and nothing happens," I said. "What happens to them if they don't get shot and manage to escape?"

"They keep on riding. On the night trains."

*　　*　　*

Sometimes I couldn't help but to blame Bartok. For getting me into this, for not answering my questions, for being an obstinate old fool, for behaving towards me like a god but then washing his hands of all the responsibility. But on a deeper level, for being a symbol, the one tangible representation and constant remainder of what my life had become. It was all too easy to think, however fleetingly and guiltily, that if I could only get rid of Bartok everything would return to normal and my life would be whole again. He was the link between the worlds, the bridge I had to cross over every night. If only I could sever the link, pull the bridge down.

But it wouldn't work that way, of course. He was merely a messenger, an instrument, just like me, only slightly higher up the food chain. I was not getting all the answers out of him – maybe not because he didn't want to give them to me, but because he didn't know them himself.

Then I would start feeling sorry for him, whoever he was, a phantom or a man like me, somehow dragged onboard the night trains by forces much greater than him. Did he also have his own private Bartok against whom he raged and swore at? Where did the buck stop?

How tired he must have felt, on his own private mission, having to deal with me, and with others before me. All of them – us – restless, resentful, confused, angry, questioning, doubting, going mad. How tired he must have felt.

*　　*　　*

Sometimes there would be a plain white envelope in the mailbox; no stamp, just my name scribbled on the front in handwriting they don't teach at schools anymore. Inside the envelope a folded sheet of paper with all the instructions written in blue ink. No signature. No need.

Or he would simply call or drop by when I was alone in the house. Or bump into me at the train station. No pleasantries; he would simply tell me what I was expected to do that night. Then he would walk away.

I could tell you about all the places I think I've been to. I've seen the darkness over Russia, darkness over France, darkness over Norway, Poland, Germany, Holland, Italy, and Yugoslavia. I could tell you about all the trains, and all the people. I still remember some names, life stories, scraps of conversations, whispered, mingling with the music of rolling wheels, clashing buffers, rasping engines. How many of these people survived? I don't know. I have seen them but for a few hours, taken them from somebody's hands, then passed them on to somebody else. For all I know it might have all been in vain, but now I choose to hope otherwise.

I could tell you so much, but it would only be an indulgence I can't now afford. Time is running out, as are the tapes, and I still have so much that I need to tell you.

IX.

I was dreaming again.

It was the same place, but now we were coming down the mountain to the village below. I couldn't quite see, but I sensed that it was Bartok who was now walking beside me, and not my grandfather.

The sky was deep orange and seemed as warm as I remembered it from the last time. I felt safe and at peace, as if nothing bad could ever happen to me while I bathed in the orange glow. This was my haven, my anti-night.

We followed a narrow path that wound down the side of the mountain. I don't think either of us said anything during our descent. At the foot of the hill the path merged into a country lane, three or four yards wide, leading straight through the village.

As we approached the first cottages a peasant woman passed us by, going the other way, burdened with a bale of twigs she carried on her back. Bartok greeted her but she did not reply and did not appear to have noticed us at all.

In the middle of the village there was a small common, a mere meadow, through which the road cut across. Ducks paraded on the grass and an old dog was resting in the shade of a fence. I couldn't see anyone, any sign of activity at all, except for a little boy, seven or eight years old. He was standing in the middle of the field, looking straight at us. He was barefoot and his torn trousers reached only to his mid-calves. His hair was unruly, the color of straw, and he would brush it off as it kept falling over his eyes. The boy did not seem to be perturbed by our presence and there was a glimmer of curiosity in his eyes.

Bartok came over to me so that we were now standing shoulder to shoulder.

"It is him," he whispered in my ear.

Then I woke up.

* * *

My life has become an empty shell, a façade that could fool some people some of the time. There was hardly anything left of the life I used to live, no work, no friends, no meaningful human contact, no interest in anything around me – just a few hurried and tasteless meals coming after hours of restless sleep that dragged well into the day. My night trains world was now starting to seem more real to me than this world.

One day, after he returned from work, Brad took me aside in the kitchen, pulled out a chair and sat me down. He looked uncomfortable and kept pacing around the table, avoiding eye contact.

"Martin, if there is any problem ... if you're in trouble ... man, you know what I mean ..." he stuttered.

I did know what he meant. And if he ever intended to become a parent he should learn to be more forthright.

"Brad, do you think I am that stupid?" I said. "You know I don't do that shit."

He didn't seem to be satisfied with my answer.

"You don't believe me?" I asked him.

He didn't know what to do with his hands. "As a good friend of yours that I hope you'll agree I am, Martin, I have to say ... I'm not sure."

There was an uncomfortable silence. The rain started drumming against the garage roof. We didn't notice how quickly it had turned dark outside. Brad walked to the wall and turned on the light.

"You've got some problem, don't you?" he asked.

"I'm fine." For the first time it didn't seem like the most blatant untruth I ever uttered. I surprised myself.

"Listen," he collapsed into a chair on the other side of the table. His eyes still avoided mine. "You don't seem to be doing much work lately ... or anything for that matter. You sleep whole nights and then some. You don't go out, you don't even talk much –"

It was a strange feeling to be less uncomfortable in this conversation than he was. I relished it for all that it was worth.

"Brad, I know that it all may seem a bit weird to you, but everything's fine. I know it's going to sound wanky but I'm going through that phase when I'm reevaluating my life – what I'm doing, what I want to do, how to get there. All that."

The lies rolled off my tongue effortlessly. It felt good. I was good.

Brad pondered it for a while.

"Besides," I added. "I'm doing more work now with overseas clients and I work odd hours and often from home. Welcome to globalization," I cracked a smile.

"I'm still worried," he shook his head. The man who went through life as if it were a non-stop comedy routine had not uttered even a single one-liner during our entire conversation. He was serious.

"I'm still worried," he repeated, more to himself than to me. It sounded like surrender. "If you need anything you know where to find me." That was the only time that evening when our eyes met for longer than a second. Then he stood up and walked to the fridge, took out a carton of milk and disappeared into the living room.

Brad was right. I slept nights and I slept days. My night trips would last anywhere from only one minute up to a few hours of real time, but my body wasn't buying it. The nights over there seemed to go on forever. I was coming back so drained, so trainlagged, that I would just fall on my bed still wearing my clothes and I would sleep hours and hours of restless sleep that brought hardly any relief. Even back home I dreamed about that other world. There was no escape.

And I kept wondering how much longer I would be able to go on.

*   *   *

I can't be quite sure whether it was the first time I saw him but it was the first time that I took note.

He was average height, medium built, with regular features and short, neatly kept hair. An inconspicuous everyman. But this time the everyman stood out from the crowd, a Nordic on a train from Saloniki to Athens.

The man sat at the other end of the carriage, by the door. Once in a while he would put down his newspaper and look out the window and then, disappointed by the darkness outside, he would look around the carriage. When our eyes met, there was no recognition or acknowledgment.

"See that man over there?" I said to von Schellendorff.

He slowly scanned the carriage like a bored traveler.

"I've seen him before," he said after a while. "On occasion."

"Is he following you?"

"Might be."

The man folded his newspaper, and stood up.

"Do you know who he is?"

"I don't know," he shrugged. "Everyone's spying on everyone else."

"Maybe it's just a coincidence?" I mused. "Would they be so obvious?"

I glanced towards the door but the man had already disappeared into the next carriage.

Von Schellendorff shrugged again. "My dear Bittmann, I think it's safe to say that we are nearing the endgame. They are closing in on us; it's only a matter of time. Schellenberg, Himmler, Kaltenbrunner, they can afford to toy with us, if that's what they feel like doing."

So blasé. I didn't know whether it was sheer, foolhardy courage or whether he had simply stopped caring by that stage.

"God," I murmured under my breath. "They can't prove anything, can they?"

Von Schellendorff blew his nose, unperturbed and unselfconscious. Several passengers shot glances, but none of them lingered for too long. One had to be careful how one looked at others these days. "My dear Bittmann, for all your good work, sometimes you seem to be very naive about the current realities."

He was whispering to me even though no one was sitting within earshot. In the last week alone, the partisans have ambushed two trains. Our service, normally bursting at the seams, was almost empty. Special units of Waffen-SS in tandem with detachments from von Klaustroff's Fifth Divisions were combing the countryside, trying to make travel safe again, yet for all the bloody reprisals the tracks were still getting blown up and the trains attacked in the dead of the night. When the price of the ticket was likely to also include a coffin, only those who absolutely had to travel did so.

"They don't need to prove anything," von Schellendorff said. "They can get anyone they want, anytime they want. If they wait, it's only because they have their own reasons."

He took out his handkerchief again. Morphine gave him a release of sorts, but also a never-ending cold. Some days – nights – were worse than others.

"We all know the risks, but we take them because we deem what we do to be more important that the price we might ultimately pay. Otherwise we wouldn't be here."

I said nothing. We were traveling on the same train but we'd come from different worlds.

*   *   *

When it came, the explosion ripped through the length of the train, derailing the engine and the first three carriages, and setting the front one on fire.

It threw me out of my seat onto von Schellendorff's lap. My elbow traced an arc in the air and caught him on the cheek. He flew towards the window, as I rebounded to the floor. All in a second or two, in a deafening roar as a flash of brilliant light raced past the windows.

My forehead hit the wooden edge of the seat, opening a two-inch cut from my right temple to above the eyebrow. My body went limp and collapsed between the seats. For a moment I thought I lost my sight, before I realized it was only my blood getting into my eyes.

It was only then, I think, that I heard screams. And gunfire.

Whatever window glass didn't shatter on impact now flew inwards and showered our carriage. Instinctively I rolled into a ball with my head between my knees. I didn't have time to crawl under the seat before the shards rained down on me, bouncing off my back like a heavy hail.

Von Schellendorff was now crouching on the floor next to me.

"Let's get out of here!" I shouted to him. "Crawl to the door!" The barrage almost drowned out my voice.

"Like hell!" von Schellendorff shouted back. "They'll pick us out on the outside. Perfect targets against the fire."

Another burst of gunfire rattled against the side of our carriage and a few rounds whizzed above us through shattered windows.

"Just stay put!" von Schellendorff shouted. "We're safer where we are."

A roar of guns was deafening. Someone on the train was now returning fire. I tried to remember whether there were many soldiers onboard when we left Saloniki. There must have been a hell of a lot more than I could remember.

The noise erupted in the next carriage; short bursts of automatic weapons, pops of handguns, shouts, cries of pain. The fighting was already here.

"To hell with it!" I shouted to von Schellendorff. My ears were still ringing from the explosion but at least I couldn't hear the pounding of my arteries. "To hell with it! They're already here. This carriage is next." I wiped the blood off my forehead. The bleeding just wouldn't stop.

"Where are you going, you cretin?" von Schellendorff screamed back at me as I crouched down close to the floor, ready to sprint to the nearest exit. "They'll kill us as we get out of the fucking train. There's nowhere to run!"

"And there is nowhere not to run," I said, but he didn't hear me. I sprung up from between the seats and in a few leaps reached the door. Someone was praying aloud in Greek, in a voice choking with tears.

"Follow me," I shouted to von Schellendorff and pushed the door open.

There was another explosion as I got onto the platform in a no-man's land between the carriages. I grabbed onto rubber flaps in time to steady myself.

I heard von Schellendorff shuffling behind me.

"You –" he started saying something but I didn't listen. I stood up and flung open the door to the next carriage.

There was a man standing in the aisle, halfway down the carriage. He was tall and broad in the shoulders. The fleece vest he was wearing over a white shirt made him look even bulkier, a wolf bursting out of sheep's clothing. His head was bare and balding, but the beard, black and prodigious, compensated for the receding hairline.

I froze, with my arms outstretched in front of me as if I were trying to grasp and hold on to air. An ancient rifle in the man's hands was pointed straight at me.

There was a brief flash of emotions on his face, a surprise perhaps, but nothing now, save maybe for a quick calculation.

My brain shut down. Time had stopped.

And then the shot rang out. And another.

I opened my mouth to scream, but I didn't feel anything. It wasn't supposed to be that way.

Then I saw a spasm crawl through the partisan's face. His hands shook, and the rifle wavered, its tip tracing a zigzag in the air. Then his left hand lost the grip and the rifle he still held at the butt fell down in an arc. The red stain bloomed on the man's white shirt, right in the middle of his chest. His head fell forward as he looked down on himself, and he haltingly reached with his left hand to wipe the blood away.

The rifle hit the ground a fraction of a second before he did.

Von Schellendorff squeezed past me. He went a few steps down the aisle, his gun in front of him, pointing just in case, at the body.

"Either you or him," he turned to me.

I realized I had stopped breathing. My legs felt rubbery. I wanted to lean against something, but there was no time. Von Schellendorff was already running ahead towards the other exit. I followed him along the empty carriage. Whoever was travelling here must have tried to take their chance outside. The door at the end of the aisle was flung open in an unspoken invitation and the rectangle of darkness stared back at us. I stepped around the body of the partisan, desperately trying not to touch it – him. Von Schellendorff waited just inside the door, listening. I crouched behind him.

It was only then that we both heard a new noise coming through the gunfire. Hissing breaks of a train grinding to a halt. I peered over von Schellendorff's shoulder into the darkness. A familiar black shape was sitting on the tracks some hundred yards down the line, its silhouette only barely standing out against the night sky. Hurried on by barked commands, small shadows were detaching themselves from the body of the train, jumping down and hurrying forward, little sparks of light exploding from the tips of their submachine guns.

*   *   *

It took a few minutes for the firefight to die down. The sounds of ricochets and bullets whistling over our heads receded as the outgunned partisans pulled back one by one. Then I could only hear the German Sten guns rattling their monotonous monologue. After a while they, too, had stopped and an eerie silence fell over the night.

Von Schellendorff jumped out of the door and onto the ground between the tracks. I followed after him.

The fire was still raging at the front of the train, the orange glare illuminating the landscape. Soldiers were milling around us, still cautious of the lull. Some crouched facing out, their guns ready to resume and reply, while others kept moving from one body to another, checking for signs of life.

Three corpses lay on the ground not very far from where we were standing. They must have been the passengers riding in the last carriage, the unlucky and the unwise ones who decided to risk breaking out. They were cut down before they could roll down the escarpment into the safety of a gully. Two of them were soldiers, one lying flat on his back across the tracks like a bound heroine in a black and white movie where Rudolph Valentino didn't make it on time. It could have been me, I thought, if I hadn't in the end listened to von Schellendorff.

To our right somebody was moaning in pain, calling for his mother and Jesus. Two soldiers were carrying another casualty on a stretcher towards the other train.

The other train. An ambush on an ambush. Some soldiers were sent on our train, enough to tie the partisans down in a fire-fight until relief arrived. The other train must have been shadowing us right from the start, following some five minutes behind, just far enough back not to get noticed by those who had set the trap. Until it was too late.

So it wasn't an accident that there were so few of us, travellers, on the train tonight. We were the bait, the cover to make it all look ordinary. Not too many though to get in the way. Now those who survived were wandering aimlessly alongside the train, shaken and dazed. A small group gathered around a German officer. Their hands flew around wildly as they chattered to him in their rapid-fire Greek. The officer remained impassive, repeating over and over something I couldn't quite catch. He kept looking around for an opportunity to disengage himself.

Von Schellendorff walked towards the front of the train, where the engine with its tender and three carriages were strewn astride the tracks. The first wagon decoupled from the tender and was now burning fiercely near the bottom of the escarpment. The second one was lying on its side, its one end dragged down where the first carriage had taken it. The soldiers crowded around it like ants, carrying out the dead and the still alive through the broken windows that now opened skywards.

Neither of us said anything the whole time. I didn't have to close my eyes to still see the muzzle of the gun, the second before it was going to erupt with a flame, the last thing I was ever going to see. I was still shaking, from the memory, from the cold, from everything.

We were watching the inferno when a voice broke over the tumult. "Stop, you idiot! Not before he talks!"

We both turned at the same instant towards the crisp German.

Some fifty meters from us, at the bottom of a gully, a partisan was lying in the grass with his head thrown backwards and limbs strewn around at uncomfortable angles like a puppet whose strings were cruelly and unexpectedly cut. He must have been still alive. Barely.

A young soldier, his helmet missing and hair dishevelled, was standing over the wounded Greek with his submachine gun aimed at the partisan's head, ready to pull the trigger and finish him off.

The man who shouted at the soldier towered above the whole scene from midway up the slope. His back was towards us, but I recognized him instantly.

"Haven't they taught you anything, private?" he admonished the soldier, more in a tone of a disappointed teacher than a drill sergeant. "You take prisoners, not use them for target practice."

The private lowered his gun, still not quite woken up from the sleepwalk of the last few minutes. He opened his mouth to defend himself but he was cut off again.

"What the hell is going on?" an officer was now hurrying towards the commotion. Two other soldiers followed in his tow.

The man – the teacher – turned towards them. "Your boy over here was just about to let his emotions get the better of him –"

"And who the hell are you?" the officer stopped at arm's length from the interloper. The soldiers tensed and swung their guns into ready position, but he stepped forward and whispered something into the officer's ear. He then reached inside his coat, pulled out a piece of paper and showed it to the officer. "Thank you for your cooperation, captain," he finally said, when the officer returned the document.

The man noticed us, as he started climbing back up the escarpment, but kept walking in silence. It was only when he was passing us by that he acknowledged us. "A dangerous night to travel," he said with a wry smile and walked off towards the back of the train, not waiting for our response.

After he was gone I checked for the bulge in the inner coat pocket on my chest. All the documents were there: Swedish, Turkish, Swiss papers, for delivery to Athens, to be handed over to a Jewish member of the underground. Thank God.

Shit. But I wouldn't be delivering them to Athens. It would take at least a day before the wreckage was cleared and new tracks laid down. At least a day. And dawn couldn't be that far away.

Away from the train, in the darkness, I handed over the packet to Von Schellendorff.

"I've got to go," I said.

"Where to?" he asked, not knowing whether I was serious. "Are you going to walk? The other train will be going back to Saloniki with all the wounded pretty soon. I'm sure we can get a ride. In the meantime –"

"I can't stay," I said and started walking off. Athens was still at least a hundred miles away, and I knew I wouldn't get there. I left Von Schellendorff behind, and the night swallowed me whole.

* * *

I kept wondering what it would be like to tell them the truth. Dear Baroness Molodyi, dear von Schellendorff; I'm not who you think I am. My name isn't Bittmann, which I guess you know, but you see, I'm not from around here, either. I am ... Who? I don't know myself. I come from a different world and different time. I come here because one night I started seeing things. Now I go to the train yards every night, close my eyes and catch a train. The trains take me here, to meet you, good people.

So as you can see, my dear Baroness and Herr von Schellendorff, I'm not really a local boy. Where I come from it's all over. Your world, your lives, your struggles are nothing but fading memories. The people like you, if they have survived, ponder the past on the verandas of retirement homes or their half-empty houses, cold feet wrapped in tartan blankets, eyes clouded by age, and cancers slowly finishing the job the war never did. Every year, there are less and less of you and when the last dies, the memory will turn into history, forever and ever.

On the positive side, though, in the world where I come from, my dear friends, there is a state of Israel, and the Germans are a peace-loving nation of dour hard-workers shackled with war guilt. Where I live, the drone of a plane doesn't send people running for cover, and the only real blood most of us have seen in our lives comes from accidental cuts in the kitchen.

So no, I'm not from around here.

What would you say, my dear Baroness Molodyi, my dear von Schellendorff? Would you think I have lost my mind? I wouldn't be the only one; madness grips the entire continent and so many simply cannot cope anymore. Or would you perhaps think that I'm joking? To stay human one has to try to find humor even in the midst of hell.

And yet ...

Do you ever wonder why you only see me around the trains? Doesn't it strike you as odd that you only meet me at night? Do you ever wonder where I come from and where I go to after I vanish so suddenly as if I were never there with you in the first place? Maybe you have learned not to ask too many questions, even in the sanctuary of your own mind. Maybe these are all trivial matters, compared to the fact of my assistance.

Maybe.

For now I'm a just a guest. I can't tell you, and I can't tell anyone else back where I come from. So for now just call me Bittmann, and I'll keep calling you Molodyi and von Schellendorff.

You see, I wonder about you too. I'm retracing my journeys on old maps, joining the dots, remembering alien names from painted signs. I leaf through books, hoping maybe, just maybe, to chance upon an old black and white photograph. Just one would be sufficient. And I move my fingertip up and down the columns of small print in indexes at the back of books, in search of familiar surnames. But I can't find von Schellendorff, Molodyi, much less Bartok. Much less Bittmann. Maybe somewhere out there, in some forgotten archive, covered in dust and smelling that old musky smell, is a volume or even a single document, the evidence that my past was everyone else's past. If there is, it's out of my reach.

X.

She was cradling a parcel, the size of a shoebox, wrapped in plain brown paper and tied around with packaging string. When she saw me walking over, she put it down on the bench beside her, next to her purse. I kissed her on the cheek and sat next to her. She smelled of wild flowers, a strong scent, an expensive scent.

"The Major sends his regards," she said.

Her voice had acquired a patina of sorrow, as if the gravity of the situation was finally starting to weigh her down. In the past, her position, the connections, her lovers, have always shielded her from the worst of it. And so she has managed to flutter like a butterfly, from day to day, from one experience to another, barely brushing everyone else's reality with the tips of her wings. But in the end not even she could escape the darkness.

I felt sad for her, and then I felt ashamed of my weakness, for even now she was so much better off than millions of others. Beauty truly has its own rules.

"And how is the Major doing?" I asked.

"On the edge, as always," she said. "The situation is ever so delicate, you know."

Yes, I knew. Himmler has finally achieved his dream: the Abwehr subsumed by the SS. Canaris was gone, and four hundred Abwehr officers warned by Himmler at the Mirabell Castle in Salzburg to demonstrate nothing but unconditional obedience to their new masters. Von Schellendorff was still an army officer, but his superiors now wore dark blue uniforms and looked at him with a mixture of suspicion and contempt.

"What's in the package?" I asked to break the silence.

"Things," she said.

"What things?" I persevered, more to keep her talking than out of any curiosity.

She sighed. "It doesn't matter. We do what we have to do," she made a vague gesture with her hand and pretended to look at the timetable on the opposite wall. A small gnomish-looking railway employee was updating it with meticulous care.

We do what we have to do, yes. There were things people wanted, but they usually came at a certain price. The economist inside me understood – demand was great, supply very small, prices were driven up. There could have been anything in that parcel; the war turned many things into priceless commodities. Its previous owner was likely well past caring for material possessions, and the new owner would unknowingly perform a good deed. A life saved perhaps. Like an organ transplant. All for a good cause. But we still wouldn't want to talk about it.

"Why are you doing it, Martin?"

She continued to call me Bittmann, and I continued to call her Miss Molodyi or Baroness, until too many nights travelled together made it seem silly. She was the first to finally relent.

"Doing what?"

"What we're doing."

"I have to."

She raised her eyebrows, questioning. There were many compulsions driving people to risk their lives these days; mine was too different to share with her.

I excused myself and made my way to the toilets. There was no one there. The lingering reek of urine and stale garbage hung heavily in the air.

The door of the first cubicle was marked with two black dots in the lower left hand corner. It signalled that the person I was trying to make contact with would be waiting for me outside, behind the left corner of the station building from the street side. I looked at my watch. If I failed to show up within the next fifteen minutes another time and place would have to be arranged.

I walked outside. There was no light by the main entrance to the station and the sky was overcast with a low, almost motionless blanket that made the night safe from bombing raids. I put my hand on the wall and started walking alongside the building, feeling the uneven plaster surface brush against my fingers. The paint had peeled away in several places, exposing a damp, gritty surface underneath.

A woman was standing behind the corner. She was young and pretty, maybe just out of school.

"Excuse me, are you waiting for the train to Nice?" I asked.

"Sorry, I'm catching the 12:05 to Bordeaux," she said and handed over the parcel she was holding in her hand. She didn't say anything more, only gave me a fleeting smile and turned around, walking back to town. Most likely she didn't know what the parcel contained. Neither did I. It might have been yesterday's newspaper torn into strips, yet we were both risking our lives to deliver it.

I walked back into the unreal bluish glow of station lights. It made people look pale and lifeless, like stuffed exhibits at a provincial museum. How I longed at that moment to see this world in the light of day instead of the washed-out monochrome of the man-made twilight. How pale would von Schellendorff look in the sun? What rich tone would Katrina's skin be? Would the steam escaping from the valves of engines finally look like smoke and not the phantasmal bodies invoked at a séance? Maybe day would finally reveal what night was hiding from me.

"I was talking to a nice man while you were gone," she said when I sat back on the bench next to her.

"Were you?" It was difficult to imagine anyone nice sharing the wait tonight.

"He said he was attracted by my perfume. Apologizing constantly in a sort of charming, shy manner, but wanted to know the brand so he could buy it for his fiancée," she explained. There was a hint of disappointment in her voice, I thought, that it took strangers to notice and appreciate.

"A German?" I asked.

"Yes, a German. A civilian. They haven't yet quite managed to put the whole country in uniform."

As she was speaking I glanced around trying to spot the German civilian with the good taste in perfumes. I could only see soldiers waiting for their train and an old man sitting by himself on the bench against the opposite wall. He didn't look like somebody about to get married, unless for the third time.

"He said that here it's still relatively safe to travel," she said. "Unlike Greece, where he just returned from."

Yes. Greece.

She turned towards me and whispered. "We could now be in Greece. So, lucky us."

"Yes, lucky us."

The man standing in the middle of a carriage. The gun aimed at me. The finger on the trigger.

"Lucky us," I repeated and closed my eyes.

"Is something wrong, Martin?" she put her hand on top of mine and squeezed.

"I'm tired," I said.

"We all are. One day we'll get some sleep, too," she smiled.

How true that was. If only she knew.

Later, when we stood on the platform, about to step onto our train, she gave me a nudge. "Over there," she nodded. She was looking at a man who was climbing up the steps of the last carriage, tipping his hat towards her.

It was him.

*　*　*

"When did you start smoking?" asked Julie.

"Yeah, yeah. A filthy habit," I said stubbing the cigarette into a saucer, which doubled as an ashtray. "Stress, you know," I tried to smile but I was so out of practice.

Julie only shook her head and marched off. I was spared a piece of her health-conscious mind.

I sighed to myself. I couldn't tell her that it was all a certain retired station master's fault. Or whoever was arranging the logistics of my night trips often left a packet of cigarettes in my coat pocket. Until recently, I had probably smoked no more than a dozen cigarettes in my entire life, mostly on occasions I had been too drunk to refuse. Now it just seemed appropriate. It didn't soothe and relax me, but it gave my hands something to do during those long stretches of useless time. They still shook, but less, I think.

Next morning I came close to self-immolation in my bed. I woke up unusually early, around nine o'clock, with cattle stampeding inside my head. Blindly I felt around, looking for the pack hidden under the tangle of my old clothes and garbage on the floor. Then I lit up and lay on my back with eyes closed, too tired to even watch the rings floating towards the ceiling.

Then I must have fallen asleep.

I woke up probably only a minute later, with the sheets in flames where the cigarette fell out of my hand.

It took me a frenzied fifteen seconds to choke the fire with a blanket. All that remained was a stench of smoke, a charred hole in the bedspread, and a blackened mattress. I sat on the bed for quite some time trying to calm down. Then I went onto the veranda and pulled out another one. I struck a match ...

* * *

... and brought it closer to my face, shielding it with the palm of my hand, even though the night was calm and there was no wind.

Jesus.

As if it had suddenly hit me that the dangers we were all facing didn't always have a simple accidental quality, like a cosmic lottery of misfortune. There could be something more behind it, a counterforce working in a methodical, intelligent way.

"You haven't seen him before, have you?" I asked her. Something was turning in my stomach. It wasn't the best idea to light up now but it had become instinctive. I inhaled so shallowly that the smoke mostly swirled inside my mouth.

"No, I don't think so," she said. "Why? Have you?"

"I think I might have. I'm not sure," I lied.

"So?" she shrugged, somewhat impatiently. The train was already in motion but we didn't enter any compartment yet. I didn't need anyone listening in.

"I think he might be following us – me, you, von Schellendorff," I said.

"They don't operate that way, Martin," she shook her head. "What's the point of watching someone if you let them know you're doing it? Believe me, when they fall upon you, it's like a bolt out of the blue sky."

I hesitated. "I don't know. I think this might be different." Yet, I didn't know quite how. Or why.

"Let's go," she took my arm. I hung on, briefly, to throw the cigarette butt out of the half-opened window, and then let myself be led down the passageway.

* * *

I told Bartok about the man following us.

"What do you want me to do about it?" he asked.

"I don't know, but I don't like it," I said. "I think the whole operation might now be in danger."

"You know," Bartok said. "Only a few weeks ago you would have threatened to walk off because it was all getting too much. Too dangerous. Too scary. Not now. I wonder what has changed?"

A very good question.

"Just pull your head down and try to survive," he added, very matter of fact, as if we were talking about something completely different, and completely unimportant.

"And what happens if I do survive to the end of the war?" I asked him. "Mission accomplished, here's your medal for bravery; you're going back to civilian life?"

Bartok smirked.

"I'm not joking," I said. "What the hell is going to happen? Because from what I can see, time is moving forward there too and the war isn't going to go on forever. And then what?"

"I do not know. What would you want to happen?"

"You know –" I started and then my voice trailed off.

What did I really want? All of it to finish? The nights to become nights again, the yards to became what they were before, the trains to disappear into the darkness forever? Taking Katrina with them? And Von Schellendorff? Leaving me here, safe and alone?

The only thing I was reasonably certain about was that the old me didn't exist anymore. Something has ended, just as inevitably and irreversibly as childhood does. My parents didn't know yet, some of my friends only started suspecting that something was badly wrong, but I – I knew. The secret I was carrying – a secret life – had eaten me from the inside, so that only a façade of me has remained. Does it sound too melodramatic to you, a tad self-pitying, perhaps? Yes, I know that a long time ago, millions of people, a whole generation, went through hell and yet came out of it and continued to lead normal lives. The greatest generation, and all that. The difference is, I'm alone. It's not the whole world that has gone crazy, only my world. After everything I've gone through I know I will always be a stranger in a strange land that once used to be my land, too. Not anymore.

That's what has changed. At least one of the things that did. And that's why, on a certain level, it didn't really matter if I lived to see the end of the war. Didn't really matter what would happen after that. Didn't want to think about it.

XI.

Sometimes I would wonder what it would be like just to jump off a train and run. Run ahead, run without a thought, run through the fields of wheat, like a ship plowing through the waves, run gathering dew, stumble, fall, get up, and run again, until I would lose my breath, tumble to the ground, onto the wet mattress of fragrant soil and twisted and crushed corn.

How far would I go? How long would it take until the sounds of the train receded further and further away, and silence rang in my ears?

And then what?

I didn't know. The trains seemed to be the magic bond between me and that world at night, the only tenuous link to reality, my only return ticket home. If I broke the bond would I be sentenced to walk that land forever, confused and distraught, unable to make it back, unable to catch that one right train that would get me out and get me home?

I was never tempted to find out. The train tracks covered Europe like a giant web, and I was its creature, part spider, part insect prey. But either way, there was no life outside it.

*   *   *

I am dressed in a Franciscan habit. There are ten people with me, clutching rosaries and mouthing silent prayers. They are all Jews. The priest seating opposite me is a rabbi. His eyes are closed as he caresses the beads like a blind man trying to absorb the essence of the world around him through his fingertips. I imagine him repeating in his mind "Lead my cause, O Yahweh, with them that strive with me: fight against them that fight against me."

The clothes are lent from a monastery, documents forged by a friendly printer and smuggled inside a bicycle frame. We are pilgrims now. That's what we are going to say if we are stopped and questioned by a patrol. We're returning from Assisi, strengthened in our faith after praying at the grave of St. Francis. What we're not going to say is that the Bishop of Genoa will arrange for my companions to be smuggled out of Italy on ships sailing under neutral flags. To safety, we pray.

I look from face to face and see a doctor from Trieste, a bookkeeper and his wife from a small town near Perugia, a young girl who for nine months was given sanctuary inside a convent in Rome. The silent words form on her lips, "Hail Mary, hallowed be thy name ..." She's had nothing but time to learn how to blend in.

My own thoughts wander away, to the man who follows wherever we go. Is he here tonight too?

"– excuse me, Father."

I jerk awake.

A woman is standing in the aisle, by the rabbi's side. Her fingers tug at her long, black skirt, self-conscious and embarrassed.

"Excuse me, Father," she says. "Sorry to disturb you, but I'm traveling with my mother and she's not feeling very well, and she's got it in her head that she might not make it to the end of the trip, and she would like a priest to hear her confession," she blurts out, her eyes cast down.

There's a moment of hesitation from the rabbi, and then he says as he rises, "Of course, my daughter, it's fine." He briefly touches the woman's elbow to reassure her and throws a glance in my direction. Our fellow travelers look much more discomfited than he is.

"That's fine, my daughter," he repeats. "It's all the Good Lord's work."

I hope that the Good Lord will recognize this absolution given in good faith by a rabbi. There are a lot of absolutions needed to go around these days.

* * *

"I know who he is," said von Schellendorff.

"How?" I asked. "How did you manage to find out?"

The corners of his mouth twisted with impatience. "We still have ways of making things happen. Or at least of learning things."

Congratulations, I felt like saying, it's good to be going down in high spirits. "So?" I said instead.

"His name is Kurt Behrnard. He works at the SD. Directly answerable to that son of a bitch Schellenberg."

He waited until the train moved on and the noise abated. "I don't know much about his past, which means there's not much to it. All the small timers want to rise to the top quickly, but the army's not like that. The SS, on the other hand, will accept and promote any dregs of society, all the malcontents and criminals. Twisted but faithful. Either way, it didn't take long for him to get noticed and transferred to Department VI at the SD. Foreign intelligence. When the war came he had the command of an Einsatzkommando unit. He spent a year in Russia, behind the frontlines. Cleansing the new territories, that's how they used to call it. God only knows how many thousands of Jews they've murdered. He's been back for two years, and now he's working on us."

I caught myself looking around, trying to see whether his face would stand out somewhere in the crowd. It didn't.

Von Schellendorff excused himself to go to the toilet. It was time, again, with a sick regularity. Every twelve hours, his own private clock chiming, his body sweating and shivering, demanding to be fed.

"Why do you do it?" I asked him when he returned, and before I finished I realized the stupidity of the question.

But he thought about it, nonetheless, and then said slowly, "You know, every time I do it, is like dying. And it feels good."

"Why don't you just take your Mauser, put it under your chin and pull the trigger?" Another stupid question.

He chuckled, "I don't like blood," and then he was serious again. "You see, I play a game with death, I tease her and entice her. Come, come, embrace me, I call out to her. But calling is all I'm doing. I'm not going to grip her by the hand and say: I'm not letting go unless you take me with you. So death comes, and stares me in the eyes, and I stare back, and we smile at each other, and then she leaves me. Until the next time."

He referred to death as her, as if she were a jealous, scorned admirer who couldn't bear to see him in the arms of another lover. So she killed her rival, and almost killed him, and yet she still cannot possess him. And I guess that's how he saw her that first time, when he was laying in the wreck of his car, falling in and out of consciousness, with Helena's body slumped in the seat beside him. She, death, had left him tantalized and yearning, and after that he had to keep on seeing her again, but on his own terms, of his own invitation.

"Our illustrious Minister of Propaganda does it," von Schellendorff added. "If it is good enough for Herr Goebbels, it is good enough for a lowly officer of Wehrmacht."

He pulled out his handkerchief and wiped his nose.

"You know, Bittmann, I'm not even a true hero. The true hero acts despite his fears. I don't care about my life, I don't care if I die tomorrow. I would like to be a hero before I die, even if for a brief moment. Do you know what I mean?"

I left him to go about my business, as he went about his. I thought about how I felt shit scared all the time. If that was what heroism was, von Schellendorff could have it.

XII.

The wailing started off in the distance, at the outskirts of the city, before rushing towards us. One by one, the sirens joined in a chorus of sorrowful cries like women mourning the coming death of a loved one.

The agitated murmur swept along the carriage, followed by a man in a dark blue railway uniform who flashed passed our door only to stop long enough to bang his fist on the window pane. "Get out! Get out as fast as you can and run!" he shouted.

I looked at Katrina questioningly. Her body froze in an unfinished gesture and she now sat stiff and alert, listening. Already the doors of other compartments were being slammed open and the human noise spilled into the corridor, filling up the narrow space with a mass of agitated bodies. The narrow exits of the carriage couldn't cope with the sudden evacuation of a few dozen people trying to get out all at once and as quickly as possible, pushing, screaming, cursing, shoving, desperately trying to hang onto their luggage and their children.

"They always go for the train stations and tracks," Katrina said. "To mess up communication." She stood up. "We have to get out, or we'll get it together with our train."

I glanced at the corridor. Our exit was blocked by an obese older woman in a tiny hat and a dead fox wrapped around her neck. She was struggling through, trying to force forward the man ahead of her, using her luggage as a battering ram. "Oh my God, these barbarians, they're going to kill us all," she was screaming as the hat kept sliding off her head.

"The window," I pointed. "I'll jump out first and catch you."

Katrina nodded and I lunged forward towards the handle. I gripped it tight and pushed down. The window screeched and moved maybe an inch. I swore under my breath and pushed harder. The frenzied mass had already started pouring out of the train, and into the relative safety of the darkness. Outside, abandoned luggage started snaring escaping passengers like treacherous rocks where sailors meet their doom. Somewhere out there a woman was screaming like she was possessed, looking for her children, and another woman was beating her husband with her fists trying to convince him to drop the heavy suitcase he was trying to drag along.

The window moved a further inch. I stood back and banged the metal frame on both sides of the window. For a second I thought the glass would break, but it only rattled. I gave it another whack and pulled down. It still resisted but it slid open. I threw a glance over my shoulder at Katrina. She gave me a weak smile, "My knight errant."

I stepped onto the seat and then onto the fold-out table. It shuddered and almost gave way, but before it could collapse I pushed my head and chest through the window and hung on the precarious pivot of the window frame. I wasn't alone. A few compartments down someone was throwing out their luggage and in the next carriage somebody else was passing down a little child to a man standing outside.

I swung my right leg trying to get it over the window. No use. The window was too narrow in length and I was gripping the frame in the wrong place. My fingers hurt and the frame dug into my stomach squeezing the breath out of me. Oh God ... I kicked my legs wildly trying to balance myself and not to fall back in. There was only one way out. "Shit," I whispered and launched myself forward. My fingers loosened their grip and I toppled down. My heels banged against the top of the frame and my shirt ripped open on the window handle. I only had time to put my hands in front of my face before I hit the ground.

The impact knocked the air out of me and then I rolled over a few times. The gravel managed to scrape my hands, the side of my face, my shoulder and my back, before my body stopped and rested. It wasn't as bad as it could have been.

I struggled to my feet. All over the city the light beams of the anti-aircraft batteries were pointing in accusation at the sky, dancing in circles, the prey desperately trying to locate its hunters. The heavy guns rattled, but the bombers must have been well out of range. When I caught my breath the first explosion sent shudders through the city and lit up the horizon with a fierce flash of brilliance.

Our train had almost emptied by now. Some vanished into the meadows stretching on one side of the tracks, others towards the city.

Katrina was now climbing through the window.

"Jump. I'll catch you," I shouted and extended my arms.

She hesitated and then tumbled forward just as I shifted my weight onto the wrong foot in a momentary miscalculation. I caught her under one arm and swung to grip her waist, but her falling body pushed me backwards and I felt my center of gravity displacing to somewhere outside of my body. I still tried to grab hold of her as I fell backwards. I crashed on the ground, and she crashed on top of me. A large stone dug in close to my left kidney and I yelled as the sharp pain shot through my body.

"Oh God," she whispered and tried to pick herself up. Her hand slipped and she fell on top of me again.

"God, it hurts. My ankle," she winced and rolled over. "I must have twisted it."

My lower back still felt as if it were on fire. "I'll carry you," I said through clenched teeth, only half believing I could do it.

The sky was now lit with the dancing hues of red and yellow. The bombers must have scored some big hits, for in a few places something more than mere tenements was burning furiously. The explosions kept on ripping through the city like a slow burning string of firecrackers. And yet, it still seemed somehow unreal, like watching a theater of lights and shadows from a far distance.

I stood up, at the same time trying to raise Katrina with me. "I'll carry you," I repeated. I gripped her arms, steadying her as I steadied myself.

"It's nothing, it's all right," she said and coughed. Her nostrils flared and her chest rose in a succession of quick sharp breaths. She had a small cut on her forehead. A single tear of blood oozed slowly from it. I eased my hold and let her drift back until she was leaning against the side of the carriage.

"I think I can walk," she said. The glare of fires lit up her face and gave her more color and life than I could ever recall her having. What the war taketh, the war giveth back.

I was going to say something when a huge explosion shook the ground under our feet. It must have been a munitions factory, for the first explosion set off a chain reaction of little earthquakes. My legs didn't steady me enough and I fell towards Katrina.

"I don't think they're going for the train lines," she said. "At least not in the first wave."

The sudden gust of wind enveloped us with the stench of burning rubber.

I reached, haltingly and uncertainly, to her forehead.

"You've got a ... small cut."

I touched her. Her skin was hot. I wiped the blood with my fingertips. "There ..."

My fingers didn't stop; they slowly slid into her hair, soft like velvet. I brushed the restless strands away from her cheek and tucked them behind her ear, tracing its contours like a sculptor admiring his work.

"There ..." I whispered.

Two explosions, one after the other, louder and more thunderous than before, sent tongues of light and fire high up into the sky. Closer. But it didn't matter. It was all happening somewhere else, not here, not now.

It seemed that my heart stopped beating and my lungs ceased taking in the vile air. The seconds stretched themselves into eternity, and eternity became seconds.

She drew her body up to me, and I felt myself falling into the bottomless wells of her eyes. There was nothing I could do and nothing I would rather do.

"Oh God, I love you, I love you." I whispered before her lips closed on mine and she silenced me.

*   *   *

We became one that night on the track, alone in the desolate field, shrouded by the mist of drifting smoke. The funeral pyre of a city, whose name I never learned, illuminated the night for us as we bathed in the glow of its immolation.

Soon – or so it seemed, for time had disappeared – after she collapsed into me and I held her in my arms until her body stopped trembling and her breathing became shallow again, the bombers came again, in the second wave, searching for virgin targets.

Then we ran.

One bomb hit our train. I didn't look back to see the carriages raised into the air by the blast and then sent crashing down, mangled and set alight. I felt the explosion on my back as the shock wave almost threw us to the ground. We stumbled but still we ran.

I didn't care if I died then and there because I could imagine nothing better and more beautiful than to die with the perfect memory of the moments before still fresh in my mind.

But I didn't die. We held hands and we ran, we ran, we ran.

I love you, I love you, I love you ...

*   *   *

I don't know when exactly I realized I was in love with her. Not the first time, I'm sure. It wasn't love at first sight, that mad wave of feeling that washes over you and drowns you with its sweet undertow. No, it was a slowly rising tide that crept up on me night after night. And when I finally knew, there was no doubt, no regret, not even a feeling that there was something else before, a different life, a different world without her.

I can't really put it into words.

It's such a cliché, isn't it, in all those films and books, the man and the woman who spend so much time together and share danger always end up falling in love with each other. Everyone wants a handsome star and a beautiful starlet finally brought together, and the money rolls in for the writers and producers.

So it's a cliché, until it happens to you. Then it's called life, and you then understand why it is a cliché.

"Will you leave ... your ambassador?" I asked. I wanted it to sound more like a statement, even an order, rather than a question.

"My my, you're jealous," she gave an exaggerated sigh. "Even in times such as these."

"What, as if times like these could make me any different," I protested.

She smiled and kissed me. "All the things I have to do, I do for no other reason than to make my – our – life possible."

I would have liked to be able to flatter myself that she fell in love with me because of the man I was, but I think, deep down, when you strip off all the pretenses, it happened because I was so much more like her than anyone else she knew, a fellow chameleon in a world that had stopped making any sense, or rather made too much terrible sense. We were both many things to many different people, but we could be truly ourselves only to each other. Or so she imagined. And in the end she simply could not go on living without being true to somebody else, even if for the briefest of moments.

XIII.

Remember, T.J., that time when you took a week off from work and came back to town to see me? You looked much better than I remembered when you left. You jumped out of your Italian black suit into a pair of jeans and a sports coat, but it all still looked pretty expensive. A new pair of frameless glasses, a new haircut, too. Working for the government has been good for you.

I asked how the capital was.

You said it was an acquired taste, but aside from that it was okay.

I asked how work was.

You said it was all right, a job is a job, pays your bills, all that. You laughed that I should have gone with you, we would have had fun together. As a matter of fact they were recruiting some people now, you said.

I laughed, too, and thought that if I were to believe Bartok, the trains would have still caught up with me, no matter where I was.

You asked how my work was going.

I said it was going. Slowly, but going, nonetheless. I lied, of course.

You asked how my love life was.

I said it was fine.

You asked whether it was anyone you knew.

I said no. Nobody you knew. That happened to be the truth.

You didn't press the point. That was good and I appreciated it. What would I tell you? I could not have told you anything then. Now, it's different.

That night we went on a pub crawl, trying to visit all our favorite hangouts from the university days. I don't think we quite managed it in the end; we've gone soft in our old age. My memory towards the end is pretty hazy, though, so it must have been a pretty decent effort nevertheless. I know that I woke up the next morning in pretty terrible shape, my wallet a lot lighter and my stomach trying to crawl to the nearest exit. You were sprawled on the couch. I think you might have spewed outside one of our pit stops and your clothes looked all the worse for it. How we got home was a mystery.

Fortunately the trains – Bartok – did not call me that night. It would have been somewhat embarrassing to try to split and leave you in some pub, just because ... No excuse would have been convincing enough. One night off is all I got. I don't think it was meant to be this way but it looked like a very cruel tease: have one last taste of the life that you've lost forever, boy.

Came the very late breakfast and we all talked around the kitchen table; you, me, Brad. Everything seemed so normal, we had a few laughs, we dragged out all the classic tales and urban legends of our past. Fortunately the conversation stayed away from me and my current life. But Brad couldn't help himself and kept glancing at me ever so often, as though not entirely believing that it was really me who was sitting there at the table, eating corn flakes, telling fart jokes, laughing like the good old times. He couldn't believe that I was back. It must have seemed a small mystery for him, that fine Saturday midday.

Then you had to go and spend a few days with your parents, up at the farm. I was grateful for those twenty-four hours without too many lies and too much pretending.

So I dropped you off at the bus terminal in the city. You said you'd stop by on your way back. I said I was looking forward to that. I saluted, you saluted back.

That was the last time I ever saw you.

XIV.

Krakow is now called Krakau. The old city of Polish kings now has a new, alien overlord at the Wawel castle that overlooks the city.

Poland, of course, doesn't exist anymore, except as a memory, hidden away for the future, if there will be a future. I look into people's faces, and they lower they eyes as they hurry on, but I know it's there inside, their last precious possession.

It's raining again. The rain turns roofs into percussion and coats the worn-down stone with reflected light. But people still come out, for the opportunity to travel is too precious nowadays to be given up on account of mere weather. They will dutifully if not gladly wait for hours, for days if necessary, rain, hail or storm, until a train can be put together, coal spared, or lines cleared.

I'm alone tonight. No fugitives to shadow, just a capsule with undeveloped microfilms. Isn't there anything more important for me than to carry some photographs around, I asked Bartok. Like save lives, for example. Everything can save lives, he replied.

I found the capsule, as he had told me, in the middle cubicle of the toilets at the station, securely taped to the water cistern. I had to step onto the rim of the bowl to reach up and feel around the porcelain top, my hand gathering the filth of uncleaned years. Now I'm waiting for the train to take the capsule up north, towards the port of Danzig where I'll have to leave it exactly the same way as I've found it. Another courier will take it with him onto a merchant ship sailing to Sweden.

I stand on the platform opposite the main station building, a long two-story brick structure built in the railway gothic style, in vogue when the Austro-Hungarian emperor was in charge around here a few decades back. That occupation now doesn't seem all too bad by comparison.

The train is late. I look at my watch, look at the clock hanging over the main entrance on the platform, and then look to where the tracks come together and merge into one point before vanishing into a black hole. Nothing happens on time any more. Time gets stretched in all directions like a rubber band. Stretched by fear, necessity, shortages, or accident. But even so, why do these nights seem so long?

I shift my weight from foot to foot. It's bitterly cold. How much longer?

Suddenly, there is noise, distant at first, and I start thinking that the train is about to roll into the station. But the noise is coming from both sides at the same time, closing in on me, and then finally I am able to untangle individual sounds. Boots crush on the stone, there is shouting, in German and in Polish. People around me try to peer into the distance, beyond the curtain of rain, where darkness and lamplight fight for weak supremacy. Instinctively we all tense, like animals in the wild. Life has conditioned us so well.

Somebody yells out on the top of his voice: "*Lapanka, lapanka.*" Somebody else starts wailing, "Oh my God, oh my God!"

Lapanka.

The area is selected, usually a street. The army closes both exits, and all those snared inside are rounded up, packed onto lorries, and driven off to concentration camps. A perfect terror tactic; every time you come out of your house it can be your last walk, for a return from the camps is unheard of. A nation's death by a thousand cuts.

Now people are running in all directions. We are trapped, squeezed between pincers. The whole station must be surrounded, yet when hope should be dead, pure instinct takes over.

A young couple is standing next to me. Fear roots them to the ground. He doesn't look over twenty, she's even younger. He is tall, with an open, clean-shaven face and broad forehead. She's a head shorter than him, seems lost in his embrace, cradling a baby not more than a few months old in her arms. In a moment they will be bundled off into oblivion, their life together over almost before it had a chance to begin.

I step forward and grab both of them by their arms. They shudder, startled, and she gives out a little cry. But of course, I'm wearing a uniform. A German uniform. Moments ago a fellow commuter, now I'm a tooth of the steel trap.

"Quiet," I whisper in Polish. "Everything's going to be all right."

I break up their embrace and swing them outwards. We're all standing shoulder to shoulder now, me in the middle, and I can't see the expression of bewilderment on their faces.

"Walk with me and pretend that you understand what I'm saying," I whisper as I put my hand on her back.

All around us is panic, but we walk calmly forward, as if this were an afternoon stroll in a park with old friends. I smile and turn to them as I speak about my wife and my little boy, having to grow up without his daddy in Vienna, and how I hope I'll be able to see them soon. I complain about the Polish weather, about Polish food, about trains always being late. And about tonight. What else can go wrong? They try to smile back. They nod, and say "Ja, ja," maybe one of the few German words they know.

The soldiers are now all around us. They herd travellers into small groups, hands over heads, heads cast down, faces flushed with despair, denial, resignation. The soldiers glance at me from under their helmets, surprised to see an officer caught up in the dragnet, but who will stop their superior strolling with his friends?

"Damned inconvenience," I say as we squeeze by one soldier. He turns around and salutes me. I shake my head but return his salute.

We continue on walking, up the stairs, over the pedestrian bridge, onto the other platform, and then through the station building. Outside, people are hurried on with rifle butts onto the waiting trucks. No one gives us a second glance.

It's still drizzling. Large pools of water ripple and shimmer under the shower, and our boots spray water around with every step. I keep on talking. Then I run out of things to say and I go back to where I'd started; my wife and my little boy, how he's growing up without me ... By now they have stopped smiling and nodding.

We're on the street now, walking away. We've left the commotion behind and we're all alone in the dark stone canyon, between uneasily sleeping four-story tenements. How far should I go before it's safe? How far can I go before the link is broken? Maybe the distance doesn't really matter as long as I'm able to catch the train – my train. As long as it doesn't take off without me. Either way, I have to get back. I hope my train will wait even though all its Krakow passengers are no more.

We stop on a street corner. All the windows are dark, curtains drawn to grant deceptive isolation and deceptive safety to tomorrow's condemned who toss and turn inside.

"Go," I say, and release the woman from my grip.

They both look at me speechless, still uncertain as to what exactly has happened, still caught up in this surreal dream.

I turn around and start walking back towards the station.

"Dziekuje," Thank you, I hear her say, quietly, but the night is so quiet that every whisper carries.

I'm thinking: why couldn't have I saved more? But I couldn't have put my arms around everyone at the station and led them out, like Moses, parting the olive sea of uniforms, returning salutes, and talking to myself about my non-existent family. I could only save whom I have saved. If they then live to see the end of the war, how many more children will they have, and how many children, in turn, will the children beget? So how many people have I really saved tonight?

When I get back to the station the trucks are driving away with their miserable cargoes. The officers stand around their staff cars and finish filing reports. The task accomplished; in less than ten minutes all the potential futures contained within the train station are erased forever.

I wait until the last truck drives off, escorted by the last motorcycle. The engines drone through the labyrinth of the old town, and I walk from behind the street corner, cross the cobbled plaza slashed across by shimmering tram tracks, and walk up the few steps to the station hall. There is no sound, no movement. Terrified railway workers still gaze through the gaps in curtains, thanking God for the sanctuary of their uniforms. Bags lay scattered everywhere, some ripped open and spilling their contents. I step over a teddy bear trampled face down on the stone floor. It looks like an overgrown dead rodent.

I come out onto the platform, the only passenger left now. Of my train there is still no sight. But I assure myself that if it had gone already I would have heard it, even from outside the station.

"That was very charitable what you've done, if very misguided," I hear a voice behind me.

No, I'm not the only passenger.

I swirl around. Kurt Behrnard is standing by the doorway, like a statue of the guardian spirit protecting the station. He's leaning against the wall, his left leg bent at the knee and his foot resting flat on the building's sandstone, cigarette in his hand, at his mouth. It's difficult to see where his uniform ends and the wall begins.

Behrnard exhales and the smoke obscures his features for a second. "I watched you from a distance," he says as he lowers his cigarette hand to his side. He moves as if he were underwater; unhurried, with a smooth, subconscious ease. "Quick thinking, good execution. Pity to waste such talent on actions like these."

Can my heart really gallop any faster than it did when I was leading the young couple away to safety? You bet it can. "I'm not sure what you're talking about," I say.

His head leans slightly to the side as if he were gazing at some curious phenomenon. "Let us not insult each other's intelligence. Please."

Why didn't you stop me, then? I want to ask him.

"I've been looking for you," he goes on. "What a night to catch up with you, finally."

"What a night," I echo.

He nods while taking another drag. "You see, lately you have become my very own private riddle. I'm quite confident I won't be able to rest until I solve you."

He pushes himself away from the wall and starts slowly circling around me.

"Now, normally my professional pride would suffer from admitting that I don't quite know who you are. But I don't think anyone else really knows either," he says. "You are a special case."

"That's not good, is it?" I jump in. "It shouldn't take too much time to check with the authorities and establish my identity."

He comes into my view from the left, the cigarette dying on his lips. "Oh, we do know you have papers from Abwehr. We also know that you – or rather whatever your official identity says you are – don't exist."

"Why don't you arrest me then, and find out?" I ask nonchalantly. Ah, how brave one sounds a blink of an eye away from home. But how frozen I feel underneath this veneer.

"Arrest you? Don't ever think we couldn't," Behrnard's features harden. There is a momentary gleam in his eyes and then he's his old self again. "But I enjoy playing games."

Bullshit, I think. There's something more to it than that. You're nothing but a pawn for the organization whose one and the only mission is to ensure that all the threats to the eternal Reich are extinguished with maximum efficiency. If it was all so simple and straightforward, I would be dead long time ago, and not before my mangled body had passed all my secrets into your inquisitive hands.

"What if I won't indulge you and play games with you? What if I just –" I wring my wrist in search of the right word, "– disappear, instead. If I weren't who I am and if I had anything to be concerned about, that is," I add.

"Somehow I don't think you will," he says. "You see, I've been watching you for quite some time. Well ... That's not quite accurate. I've been watching some of your friends for quite some time, and then you came into the picture. And from what I've seen so far I don't think you would do it."

Then you haven't seen enough, obviously. "Do your superiors know we're having this conversation?" I ask.

He raises his eyebrows.

"My superiors, as you know, are people who know everything," he says. A nice, evasive answer.

"Behrnard," I say. Two can play this game. If he is surprised that I, in turn, know something about him, he doesn't show it. "You are dealing with forces you don't know anything about, and can't even hope to comprehend. The people who stand behind me will be most displeased. And they will most certainly know by morning about this conversation," I wish I myself knew something about these forces. I understand so little – for all I know it could be true.

"Well, perhaps then, your superiors should talk to my superiors," he smiles humorlessly.

"Perhaps they will, once they decide that your superiors need to know." What I'm saying will sound utterly ridiculous to me when I'm back, and in the light of day, but at the moment nothing else comes to mind. "Now, if you'll excuse me. I have to go and catch a train."

"Why hurry?" he drops what remains of the cigarette onto the ground. He doesn't bother to step on it and extinguish it. "The train isn't here yet."

"I always like to have a few quiet moments to myself before I board," I say.

He rolls his lips. "Well, I won't intrude on your privacy then. Until the next time." He rises his hand in a stiff salute, "Heil Hitler."

I watch him walk away, through the hall, meandering among the abandoned luggage. Then I give the pedestrian bridge a miss and walk straight across the lines to my platform.

XV.

"Where the hell have you been?" Brad was standing in the middle of the corridor, blocking my way. He must have just gotten out of bed and his face was still swollen with sleep.

"Out," I said.

I have always managed to be exceptionally quiet when sneaking in and out of the house in the middle of the night. The few times I did run into one of my flatmates I offered the standard excuse of coming back from parties, or a late walk to clear up my mind before going to sleep. Sometimes they didn't even ask, accepting in silence yet another symptom of my ever progressing weirdness.

Now, after touching base with Kurt Behrnard, I certainly didn't need this.

"What do you mean 'out'? Could you please elaborate?" Brad growled at me.

"For God's sake," I looked at my watch. "It's two in the morning. I couldn't sleep, I took a walk. What's the big deal?"

"What's the big deal?" he exploded. "We've been worried sick. That must have been some bloody long walk, mate. Forty eight hours."

"What are you talking about?" I felt all the blood leaving my legs.

"We haven't called the cops, but we were going to do it in the morning if you still didn't show up by then. God," he shook his head, "next time you want to go walkabouts, at least have the decency to tell one of us, so we have some idea what's going on."

The commotion must have woken Julie up. She emerged out of her bedroom with a sheet draped around her body.

"Martin, you're alright?" she squeezed past Brad to take a closer look at me.

"The return of the prodigal son," Brad murmured to no one in particular.

"What happened to you, Martin?" she asked again. I've never seen her show such genuine concern for me as an individual, rather than in the abstract, as a member of the human race.

I didn't reply, just dashed towards my room, pushing them both aside. I slammed the door behind me and leaned with my back against it, as if expecting they would try to smash their way in. My mind was on fire and I couldn't think straight.

After what might have been a minute, there was a knock on my door. I didn't answer, and after a while, soft footsteps, Julie's, creaked on the floor away from my room.

I left for Krakow at 11 pm. I returned a few minutes before 2 am. Not three hours, but fifty-one hours later. That never happened before.

* * *

Please come, you old bastard, I was thinking to myself, please come, and explain to me what the hell is going on. Please explain why the rules of this game are changing in the middle of the round, and please explain what it all means for me.

Come, you old bastard.

He did. This time he wasn't concerned about anyone else being in the house. Around two in the afternoon there was a soft knocking on the door of my room, and I dragged myself out of bed. Julie was standing outside in the corridor, looking like she'd rather be anywhere else but here.

"There's some old guy to see you," she said. It sounded almost like a question and I could see in her eyes that she was looking for a reaction, any explanation, some hint to make her understand the last three days.

"Oh, yes," I slowly uttered the words.

She hesitated for a second. "I'll get him to come to your room," she said with disappointment in her voice and glided down the corridor towards the front door.

Bartok came in shortly after. He closed the door behind him and pulled out a chair from under the desk. I was sitting cross-legged in the middle of my bed, hunching over. The curtains were drawn across the window, leaving only a thin line of light that expanded and contracted with every breath of wind. Bartok put his hat on the desk and leaned towards me. I thought he would make the opening move, but he just sat there, waiting for me.

"I'm scared," I finally said.

He didn't respond.

"I'm scared. Do you understand? Not like normally when I'm scared all the time, because even if I can blink I might not blink fast enough or it might stop working. No, I'm really scared like you're scared because you know that's something's wrong, seriously wrong, but you can't exactly put your finger on it, and even if you could, you feel like there's absolutely nothing you can do about it. Do you understand?"

I waited for any reaction from him and this time he nodded, almost imperceptibly.

"What happened last night? Is it ... him?" I asked, and didn't really understand why I said it.

But he knew. I looked at him and I knew that he knew everything. Like a prayer – I didn't have to say anything aloud; he would understand almost before I thought about it.

"He is worrying you, is he not?" Bartok said.

"Of course he's worrying me," I flinched. "Suspecting something is one thing; knowing that somebody already knows is another. Particularly when that somebody is playing games with you. Screwing with your head. Why the hell is he doing it?"

"Because he is enjoying it? Because he can?" Bartok shrugged. It sounded again like his standard throw-away lines that don't really mean anything.

"Sometimes I think that you don't really have any clue what's going on," I shook my head. "You come here, give your little speeches like you're some goddamned sage, and in the end you tell me shit –"

"That is not the only reason why he is worrying you, is it not?" he interrupted me.

"What?"

"There is something about him, no?" Bartok said.

"It's everything about him, everything about the whole goddamned situation," I jumped out of bed and started pacing.

"Do you really want to know?" he asked.

"Know what?" I asked. I felt like I was going to burst out crying any second, totally lost, totally powerless, beating my – or his – head against a brick wall, yet still not achieving even a moment of relief. I leaned over him and grabbed him by his wrists, pinning him to the chair. "Oh, hell ..." I said. "Yes ... I really want to know."

He didn't wince even if he was surprised and uncomfortable. I didn't have any illusions that gripping his wrists or shaking him violently would make him open his heart to me and divulge his secrets. Not unless he wanted to.

But this time he did.

Four words.

Four words only.

"He is your grandfather."

The Dead of Night

I.

DEAR DIARY, I don't know what's happening to me. I'm no longer certain who I am, where I live or what I am doing. I'm standing astride two worlds, one of which shouldn't exist, yet is now more real to me than the one where I have lived in for the past twenty-plus years.

I lead my double life and I can't confide in anyone; not in my friends, not in my flatmates, not in my family. Mom, Dad, guess what? Every now and then – actually every night now, come to think of it – I take a ride on a ghost train and I rescue a few Jews here and there. What d'you think? Cool, eh? You see, I get up in the middle of the night, go to the railway yards and jump on one of those funny old trains and, lo, they take me away to Europe like it once was but, mercifully, is no more. And wherever I go there's bound to be trouble. Gestapo, Reich railway inspectors, black marketeers and criminals, the human refuse and human rodents you meet on public transport these days. But on the positive side I'm saving all those people from a certain death. If only I could be sure – absolutely and unequivocally certain – they existed. No matter. But now you understand why it's taking a lot of my time? I don't seem to get much sleep lately and when I return from my night missions sometimes I sleep a whole day, or I can't sleep at all. I can't interact with people either ...Talk ... But there's nothing to talk about. What's Paul up to? No idea, haven't seen him for weeks. How about the championships? Oh, the championships; missed the last few games. Other commitments, you understand. And I certainly can't concentrate on my work, can't analyze, forecast, advise. That killer instinct seems to be gone.

I've got unseemly dark rings under my eyes and I lost some weight, too. I don't look too good. Von Schellendorff, my dear imaginary friend, is into morphine, but in a way he's still looking much better than me. He seems to cope with the situation better. Then again, he knows where he stands.

What's the matter with you, everyone asks, you look like you could use some rest. Oh well, lots of work lately and I seem to have caught some nasty bug; it doesn't want to let go, you know. Hope it's not some chronic fatigue syndrome or some shit like that. That's alright, they say, yuppie flu, and you are a yuppie, aren't you? Ha ha, we all laugh. Try to take it easy, they say, more serious now, maybe take a week off, don't think about work or anything else and just relax. Thanks, I'll do that, I smile, and funny you should mention it; I'm going away tomorrow. There's a train ticket laying inside my desk drawer as we speak; a nice and comfortable ride from Paris all the way to the Spanish border. I'll be accompanying some family acquaintances who are really keen to go on a very long holiday under the hush-hush hospitality of Generalissimo Franco.

I don't say that, of course.

When I was seven I stopped believing in Santa Claus. Uncle Harry wasn't discreet enough when putting all those glistening silver-wrapped packages under the tree. He spoiled it for me, and when a year later my mother tried to gently disabuse the childish notions, I still pretended to be hurt and disappointed because I though that this was expected of me.

Then when I was seventeen I stopped believing in God. I got tired of sociology masquerading as religion, or politics masquerading as religion, and the Almighty as a school counsellor who normally would pat you on the head and give you a pep talk, but lately he's been on a long term stress leave anyway, and we don't really know where he is now. I pretended – yet again – for a year or so, went to church with my parents every Sunday until I moved out to go to college. They never asked and I never told them. We were all mature adults, rational, intelligent and perfectly capable of making these sorts of decisions for ourselves. And perfectly capable of respecting others' choices, or so the story went.

I had become rational all right. The university did the rest. Two plus two equals four, never less, never more, no point arguing needlessly about it. I have no time for empty words, imagined worlds, inquisitors and missionaries. I know who I am, I know what I know, I know what I'm doing and where I want to be in five years' time. I know a good deal when I see it, and I know how a woman's lips taste at three o'clock in the morning. I know.

And then I met Mr. Bartok and started riding the night trains. And now I know who's the deputy boss of Abwehr's Group I, Branch VII, I know whom he tries to backstab and which secretary he is banging before he comes home every night to his heavy-hipped bovine frau and blue-eyed cute kids in their freshly pressed *Hitler Jugent* uniforms. I know how to forge the best travel documents and turn a stolen passport into a kiss of life. I know how the rugged spine of the Carpathians dissolves into the muddy, sad plains of Poland, how the moon turns the waters of the Seine into a river of silver, how the vastness of Russia makes you feel so small as if you were in the presence of God himself. I also know how it feels to make love to a Hungarian Baroness, pressing her against the cold metal of a sleeping carriage as it rests briefly on some uneasily peaceful station in central Europe, gravel shifting under my shoes, her hot breath caressing my lips.

The only thing that I don't know is, what the hell is going on?

And now, this.

II.

"You're mad as fuck. I know who my grandfather is –"

"I do not know whether you would ever find out the truth otherwise, but I am not going to say that I am sorry that you had to find out this way," Bartok strained breathlessly as he spoke. Long sentences were not his forte.

"You're not listening to me," I said. I didn't know quite what to say. I didn't know what Bartok was up to now. "I know –"

"You think you know who your grandfather is," he said very calmly, putting all the stress on the second word.

It was like having a dialogue with a radio.

"My grandmother met my grandfather after he returned from the war, got demobilized and started his own business. My father was then born in 1951 –"

"You are both right and wrong," Bartok said. "The second part of the sentence is correct. As to the first one ... Your grandmother met Kurt Behrnard in 1950. Your father was born in 1951. In March to be correct. By July, Kurt Behrnard was dead. Your grandmother met the man you know as your grandfather towards the end of that year." He paused, "Do you want to hear the story?"

I only found the strength to shake my head.

"Do you want to hear the story?" he repeated, not giving up.

What was there to say?

He straightened up in the armchair like an experienced storyteller preparing to charm the children gathered in a circle around his feet. But there would be no 'Long, long time ago ...' and certainly no 'They lived happily ever after.' Not for me. Not in this lifetime.

"Kurt Behrnard survived the war," Bartok said. "Got rid off his SS tattoos, just enough to escape a superficial scrutiny. He put on civilian clothes and disappeared in all the chaos. Many of his kind got caught. He was luckier and managed to survive in displaced persons camps. He was eventually allowed to migrate towards the end of 1949."

Bartok shifted in the chair and continued.

"It was somewhat of a misalliance, your grandmother and Behrnard. She, as you know better than I, was from a good family. He was a migrant from Europe, no money, no past, only just learning the language and the new way of life. He did not know any profession other than killing when he came over here, you see, but he quickly learned carpentry. He was good at it. He came to your family house to rebuild the living room after your great-grandmother decided she wanted changes. Your grandmother was convalescing in bed after a tuberculosis scare. He was handsome in a way, and alluring, like a, what do you say? A forbidden fruit. Exotic. She was bored, lonely, impressionable ..."

My neighbor was playing techno music at full volume. Everything but the distinctive umph-umph-umph of the beat was lost on the way, but it still jarred with Bartok's monotone delivery.

"No, she did not know about his past; never did," he answered my unspoken question. "All that she knew about him was what he told her. For her, he was a refugee, like millions of others, a victim. Lost everything and everyone, nothing to come back to. Making a new life over here."

It's as if I were reading a story somewhere in a newspaper, or some women's magazine in a dentist's waiting room. I wanted it to be somebody else's story, some other family's private odyssey, some others' deep secret. Anything that would mean I wouldn't have to be concerned, try to believe or disbelieve, even think about it.

"Then your grandmother got pregnant. Her parents were shocked; they tried to solve the problem by removing Behrnard and covering everything up to spare the family the embarrassment. Those were different times, you understand."

He didn't have to be so patronizing. I did understand.

"They offered him money, there were even some threats made. They tried to send your grandmother away, to relatives down south. 'Going off to study' or 'Convalescing in a better climate, you know'; that is what they would say. But it did not work. In the end they proved too weak, they loved her too much to really hurt her."

The noise from outside died down now, just when it almost began to give the story an additional dimension, au ugly metronome to measure Bartok's every word.

"They had a secret wedding, and your father was born soon after. They were just starting to find out what sort of life they were going to have together when one evening Behrnard did not return from work. Next morning some people found his body in a ditch. The police said there was a car involved but they could not find what happened."

Secrets taken to the grave. Except that some things just can't die, can they? They come back to life years later, in the middle of night, and flicker at you from the depths of dead railway yards.

"I think it was an accident. Nothing more. Even those happen occasionally," he mused. "In any case, now was the time for your great-grandparents to finally cover everything up. They did not waste the opportunity. All the traces of Behrnard were erased from your grandmother's life.

Photographs, documents, you would not even find the entry in the church register. All the traces ... Except your father."

No, you can't erase blood flowing in living veins. You can't put out a child on a cold winter night to be devoured by wolves. Not in our age of tender sensibilities. Can't punish a child for the sin of having a parent like Behrnard. But you can destroy the grandson's life. That's so very easy.

"She cried, oh, she cried, she loved him, really loved him. But what was done was done. Your ... grandfather chanced by. An honest man, an honorable man. He fell in love with your grandmother, accepted some tragic, likely story her parents gave to explain the baby. Your grandparents got married soon after, this time in the open, and he accepted your father as his own son. I think he suspected something was not quite as it seemed, but why ask questions, why put happiness at risk? Some truths should just remain buried. The price is just too high. And your grandfather, I think, knew that in this case the price would indeed be too high."

His voice grew hoarser and fainter with every word. He would be finishing soon.

"And so it stayed a secret. Two years of family history were rewritten with scissors and an eraser. And at the end of it, who would think it was ever any different?"

And that was all he said.

We sat there, facing each other. Silence hung between us like an old but invisible curtain, heavy with the dust of many years.

"Yes," I said slowly. "But is it all true?"

I didn't feel like kicking and screaming anymore. All the will to shout and throw abuse, to smash my clenched fists against the walls and faces, all that drained out of me while he was speaking. I was left numb and empty inside. His words gutted my mind. There was nothing left.

"Oh, yes," he said. "It is all true."

III.

My mother was looking at me intently, a whole palette of emotions flashing across her face like a crowd of multiple personalities struggling for ascendancy. There was a question mark marring her forehead, a whiff of disappointment, a washing wave of concern, and a grimace of a crossword puzzle solver stuck on the last word.

"You don't look too good," she said.

"You, on the other hand, look fabulous," I tried to smile.

"Don't change the subject," she cut me off sharply, just like she used to when I was a teenager.

"I mean it." I didn't. I didn't expect this visit and I really didn't feel like talking to anyone. Having a conversation meant putting on a mask – the old Martin – and I knew that was going to take too much out of me.

"Is anything wrong?" she asked.

That was pretty much what I thought it was all about. Straight and to the point. It also meant she knew something; surprise visits were not her style.

"Everything's fine," I threw it back at her. "And what brings you here?"

"I was in town for business," she shrugged. "I thought I might drop by and see how you're doing. Can't a mother do that anymore?"

"You could have called."

"Why? So you could put on some make-up and make yourself look decent?" Normally, it would have been one of my mother's little jokes, but this time she sounded almost angry.

I sighed. "I wasn't expecting you, that's all."

"Well, here I am. And you still don't look too good."

"Oh, God," I stood up. The kettle boiling in the kitchen provided the excuse. If I could, I would have walked out of the house. "Do you want me to give you the same story I'm telling everyone? Tea or coffee?"

"No, I want you to give me the truth. Coffee."

"It is the truth. White?" I shouted from the kitchen.

"Yes, please," she shouted back.

I brought back the coffee and some sugar and put it on the table in front of her.

"It's just that it's a particularly tough time for me," I continued. "The work, this and that."

"Please, don't lie to me," she said very calmly, stirring the cup. "You haven't been to work for weeks." She took a sip and looked up to see my reaction.

Well, I was thinking, she's been checking on me. Somebody must have told her something. Who? Julie? Brad? Who else? Bastards. She must be really worried. What else does she know? Shit.

"I've lots of other work," I lied nonchalantly, in one of those flashes of inspirations that come to you at the time of greatest stress. "I do it from home now. It's called the new economy." It all rolled off my tongue so naturally and effortlessly.

"Oh?" It didn't sound like an expression of genuine surprise. I don't think she believed me. As if she knew more. She did. "And your new work takes you on long walks at night, doesn't it?"

And how quickly masks can slip.

"If you excuse my language, mother, but what the fuck is going on?" I barked at her.

"I was hoping you could tell me exactly that," she retained her composure and pierced me to my seat with her steel blue eyes, "just what the fuck is going on?"

It was one of the few times in my life I've heard her utter a curse. I was always repulsed – the hypocrite in me – by women who swore. Now, I was merely thrown off balance.

"What is going on, Martin?" she shook her head but her gaze had locked in and would not let go.

There was no point inventing stories on the run. There was also no possibility of telling the truth. And the skeleton in the family closet rattled its bones. Good God.

"I appreciate your concern, although I don't appreciate you spying on me, and I also don't appreciate my flatmates ratting on me," I said. She didn't try to deny the charge. "The last time I looked at the calendar I noticed that I'm no longer twelve years old and I have my own life now. Which means I can pretty much do whatever I want, without consulting you first. I'm not living at home anymore, I'm not living off your money –"

"That's all very wonderful," she finally interrupted me. "But you're still my son, and I think I'm not being unreasonable when I say that as your mother I have a right to know what's going on in your life, whether you're in trouble, whether you're sick ... whatever. Don't you understand?"

"I do."

"Will you tell me what's going on, then?" she came back with a persistence I hated – Bartok's persistence – except it was her who was asking all the questions now. So maybe it was my persistence. All in the genes. So much in the genes, indeed. But I hated it anyway.

"There's nothing to say."

She stood up. "You give up on your job, you look like a ghost of your old self, you start disappearing for days and nights ... That's not 'nothing'."

I threw my hands in the air but said nothing.

"What is it? Drugs? Do you have problems with the law? Gambling debts?"

"Mother!" I shouted.

"What?" she shouted back.

"Go," I said. It was almost a whisper.

There was a painful silence between us.

"I love you," she said.

"I know," I turned away. "Go."

She lingered for a moment and then she picked up her bag and walked out of the house.

God, it was all wrong, the whole conversation. I should have been prepared for something like this. I should have had a story – a good story – ready to go. Something. Anything. Now, if she didn't before, she definitely knew there was something wrong. So, hello trains, hello mother.

Something had to give.

* * *

My patience was first.

I thought that I'd calmed down over the next few hours, put my thoughts into order, started to make plans how to get out of the quagmire. I was doing reasonably well as the afternoon turned into evening. Then Julie and Brad came back home and all bets were off. I didn't care enough anymore not to lose it.

They both stared at me impassively when I asked which one of them had talked to my mother. They didn't exchange quick, guilty glances but somehow I knew that whichever one of them had ratted on me, the other one knew about it, too.

"What's your problem tonight?" Brad finally spoke.

"What's my problem?" I raised my voice. "Why the hell does everyone keep asking me what's my problem? What's your problem? Can't you just leave me alone? Did you have to drag my family into it?"

Brad exhaled loudly and shook his head. "Listen, it's not like we went out of our way to contact your mother. Actually, it was the other way around –"

"I don't give a –"

"– she called one day," Brad bellowed over me, "and one thing led to another –"

"As I said," I resumed. "I don't give a shit how it happened. Which one of you was the brain behind the operation?"

Brad hesitated.

"It doesn't matter," he then said.

"Well, I knew it would be you," I looked at Julie. I've never seen her so uncomfortable as she was this moment. Her fingers nervously rubbed a silver bracelet on her other wrist. She kept looking away, at anything but me, and I really hated her for her gutless humanitarianism. "I'm sick and tired –" I started.

"You're sick and tired?" Brad jumped towards me so that his face was only inches away from mine. "Not as much as we are sick and tired of the new and improved you, you turd. What the hell is wrong with you? Can't you really see what an asshole you've become lately?"

I turned around and started walking towards my room before one of us lost all control. Suddenly I felt really cold inside and nearly in tears, as if somebody close to me had just died. But that somebody was only me, and it was too late to do anything about it.

"I was only trying to help," I've heard Julie's voice, wavering on the verge of breaking.

"Well, fuck you, and fuck all your good intentions," I yelled without turning to face them and slammed the door behind me.

I could hear Julie bursting into tears and then running to her room.

Brad banged on my door for a while trying to shout through the wood about what a prick and asshole I was, but even he gave up after a while.

IV.

The meeting with Hitler was supposed to take place at 1 pm. On the agenda, the formation of new home guard units to throw at the advancing Red Army. The meeting had been rescheduled half an hour back to allow Hitler to see Mussolini, recently rescued by SS paratroopers from the internment by his treacherous compatriots.

At 12:42 pm, an explosion ripped through the conference room. It was an hour earlier in Paris.

Around 4 pm, the conspirators in Berlin began transmitting coded messages to all the army command centres in the German controlled parts of Europe. Operation Valkyrie has begun, three hours too late.

When I stepped out of a toilet at Gare Saint-Lazare station in Paris, 9:04 in the evening local time, the coup had already failed in Berlin and the chief conspirators had about two more hours to live. But Paris ... Paris was still free, even if for one night. In three hours' time it would be the 21st of July, 1944.

* * *

In a more peaceful time, what seemed an eternity ago, Gare Saint-Lazare serviced the most populous, western part of Paris. Tonight, the civilians were few, and none going north. The Allies have managed to break out from beachheads and their armored columns were now pushing through the plains of Normandy, east towards the Belgian border, and south to take the capital. German reserve units from southern France and from the Reich were now streaming through Paris to plug the holes. The station has become an anthill, full of warrior ants waiting to be shipped to the slaughter.

A few Frenchmen and Frenchwomen would try their luck tonight. As I looked around me, I couldn't distinguish the innocent from the guilty, those trying to escape the uncertainty, and those trying to escape justice. All I could see were tired, drawn faces, and sunken eyes casting nervous glances.

The soldiers were different; there was only the air of resignation about them. They sat on the platforms in small groups, some leaning on their backpacks, some standing against the pillars. Among privates, cigarettes were making rounds from hand to hand, while the officers huddled together discussing important matters and looking impatiently at their watches.

The arching construction of the steel and glass roofs made the Saint-Lazare look like a fin-de-siecle cathedral dedicated to the worship of Engineering and Progress. Tonight it seemed like all the believers have lost their faith, and the temple has been overrun by the barbarians.

The constant clamor made the public announcements barely audible. The male voice, alternating between German and French, was getting drowned out by marching footsteps, the buzz of conversations, and fits of coughing. Somebody was even trying to play a mouth organ, but no voices joined in to carry the song.

Von Schellendorff was waiting on platform number three, next to a stairway descending underground. Every time I now saw him he looked worse. Now he was paler still, and his irises looked at me through mere slits between puffed up eyelids. "Captain," he acknowledged me when I stopped at arm's length from him.

The uniform was the right size, but still somehow uncomfortable. It felt stiff, as if it had come straight from the factory and no one had worn it before me. The boots, on the other hand, were a size too large. No matter. It was the second time in my life that I was in a uniform, and it was like wearing an amulet that would keep the chaos and the danger around me at bay. Yet it also made me feel so cold.

Von Schellendorff offered me a cigarette and I took it with gratitude. I put the officers' flat hat under my arm and ran a hand through my hair. It was a hot night.

"It's good to see you, Major," I said.

"It's good to be still alive," he said. "Although some think the experience somewhat overrated."

It wouldn't be Jews tonight. With the Allies pushing from the north, the liberation seemed only a matter of time. A few weeks at most. After years of hiding successfully who would want to take any chances in such circumstances and move now? Wait it out, was the advice of the day.

Instead, it would be two people from the underground. There were no safe houses left and they could not afford to wait. Von Schellendorff was supposed to pass them onto me, together with two brand new sets of documents from the Ministry of Labor. The papers were very much a second best, but nothing better could be done anymore under Himmler's watchful eye. It was truly the endgame now.

The two of them stood behind von Schellendorff, leaning against the stone barrier of the stairway; a man and a woman in their mid-thirties, dressed their best, to make them look like those who have chosen to work for the victors and have feasted on the carcass of Vichy for three years. I was to take them on the train to Dijon, or however far I could travel, and intervene if there were any unexpected problems. The uniform would help, I suppose.

I looked at my watch. It was 9:15.

"You know what our prehistoric ancestors used to think?" Von Schellendorff asked suddenly. "They thought that spirits, the souls of the dead, travelled in straight lines from this world to the next."

"Fascinating," I said. "Why are you telling me this?"

"I must have read it somewhere years ago and now it's all coming back to me," he pursed his lips. "Maybe it's these train tracks cutting through the land like silver strings ... Poetic, no?"

"I was never much into poetry," I shrugged.

He ignored me, "If you were dead wouldn't you want to sail along those tracks to your afterlife, your Valhalla, the Elesian Fields?"

If only you knew, I thought. "If I were dead –" I went to say in response when a commotion on the opposite platform distracted me. Other heads around me started turning, too.

Two SS officers in their dark navy blue uniforms were surrounded by a group of soldiers pointing their rifles at them. A Wehrmacht officer was waving his pistol in front of the SS men's faces, trying to shout them down.

I gave von Schellendorff a quick glance.

He shrugged and shook his head, also confused.

The SS officers slowly raised their hands to the back of their heads and the soldiers were removing the guns out of their holsters.

"Let us inquire," said von Schellendorff and motioned with his head towards the spectacle. He walked over to the edge of the platform and jumped onto the tracks.

"Don't move. Wait here," I whispered to the two French people and followed after von Schellendorff.

By the time we crossed the tracks and climbed onto the other platform the agitated murmur was rippling through the crowd. Everyone stopped to watch the spectacle, curiosity banishing tedium.

"What's happening here, Sergeant?" von Schellendorff approached the officer.

"Major," the officer turned around and saluted von Schellendorff. He was in his twenties, with a badly healed scar running down his cheek and an eye patch over his left eye. "We were given the order to arrest on sight all members of the SS, SD and Gestapo."

"What the hell, Sergeant –" von Schellendorff started a question, but the officer took out a piece of paper out of his top pocket and started reading: "The Fuhrer, Adolf Hitler, is dead –"

Von Schellendorff tore the paper out of the Sergeant's hand.

"The Fuhrer, Adolf Hitler, is dead," he read aloud. "An unscrupulous clique of non-combat party leaders has tried to exploit the situation to stab the deeply committed front in the back, and to seize power for selfish purposes." Martial law has been declared, the order went on to say, the secret service dissolved, party members placed under military authority. It was signed by Field Marshal Ervin von Witzleben.

"Impossible," von Schellendorff murmured. "How can this be?"

"Who gave you orders, Sergeant?" I asked.

"General von Stulpnagel, Captain" the officer answered. He was getting impatient, casting glances over his shoulder as if to see whether the SS men he had just arrested were still there.

"I know von Stulpnagel," von Schellendorff said. "He's the commander-in-chief of our forces in France."

There was no point prevaricating. "Do your duty, Sergeant," I saluted him and he saluted back relieved to be dismissed.

Those standing closest to us have heard von Schellendorff read the message. Now they started throwing questions at us and talking to each other, passing the unbelievable news to those further behind. The Sergeant had to shout and wave his gun again to part the crowd and get through with the SS men in his custody.

"Calm down, men. Your officers will be issued with new orders in appropriate time," I shouted over the noise, turning around to face those around us. "Martial law has been declared. You'll be told more later."

Then Von Schellendorff was tugging my sleeve and dragging me away, back to our platform. "Calm down," I said once more. It was just as successful as trying to calm the sea.

Von Schellendorff stopped in the middle of the tracks and turned towards me.

"He's dead ... It's all over," he said, looking at me, expecting a confirmation, as if I would be able to give him one.

"Hans," I started, "let's wait and see what's going on, before we do anything rash."

"We know what's going on," he protested. It was the first time I've seen him truly agitated, truly alive.

But he was wrong. We didn't know. I did. At some point I had remembered the day's date, and then everything became obvious. But could I really tell him? Could I tell him that the windows and the massive oak tabletop, four inches thick, took the force of the blast, which killed a colonel, two generals and a stenographer, but had left Hitler with only slightly charred hair, damaged eardrums, and shredded trousers? That by the time the two of us were having our conversation, countermanding orders issued from the Fuhrer's Wolf's Lair headquarters were slowly reaching all the military outposts across occupied Europe? That in two hours time, von Stauffenberg, the man who had placed the bomb under the table, will be put up against the wall in the courtyard of the War Office in Berlin and shot, *"Es lebe unser geheimes Dutschland!"* – long live our secret Germany – the last words on his lips? That in the morning, General von

Stulpnagel will be forced to release all the SS personnel arrested during the night, and will then attempt to commit suicide in his office? I truly couldn't tell him all that.

"Hans, I have to go and take care of our charges," I said. Soldiers were now running all around us, jumping off platforms and crossing the tracks in a frantic mill. I was afraid that our French might get lost in the chaos.

"Don't you see it doesn't matter?" he tried to argue with me. "There's going to be a settlement with the Americans and the British. These two are now safe."

"Hans," I shook my head. "Of all people you should have the least illusions that whatever might or might not have happened today, the Allies will never agree to any separate peace. It's too late for that."

He shook his head, impatient with my obstinacy, and looked away. His foot started a nervous tap on the gravel.

"I have clear instructions to make sure those two get as far away from Paris as possible," I still tried to argue with him. "As far as I am concerned, nothing has changed. I could never forgive myself if something happened to them because I got overenthusiastic in the middle of an operation."

"What the hell are you talking about?" he turned at me. "It's not getting through to you –"

But I was already heading towards our platform. "Take care of yourself, Hans, and don't do anything stupid," I said. "I'll see you shortly."

My two fugitives were still standing by the stairway, looking anxious. Maybe they haven't heard what happened, maybe they didn't know German well enough to understand.

"Don't worry," I said, switching to French. "Martial law has been declared."

The woman went pale. "Oh my God," she whispered.

"It's not going to affect our schedule," I reassured them.

They both looked at me with questions in their eyes. I chose not to elaborate.

The train arrived half an hour later. I didn't see von Schellendorff during the wait. He melted somewhere into a sea of olive uniforms. When we left, the station still looked like an anthill after a little boy had stuck in a stick and stirred.

* * *

The next time he asked me how I knew.

"I didn't," I lied. "Hasn't your work taught you to be wary of stories, particularly the good ones?"

I don't think he believed me. I don't think I would have if the tables were turned. But he had to come to terms with me and accepted my explanation. What was the alternative? To think of me as a part of a conspiracy that was much greater than the one that had just failed? Sheer madness. But I think a splinter of doubt remained with him from that night onwards, a feeling that there was something not quite right about me. Or, should I say, even more so than he thought before. Of all the people he had to work with I must have seemed the most peculiar.

And I, in turn, remembered the fire, which for that brief moment had lit up his eyes; not the sickly glow of addiction that nowadays never went away, but the pure fire of hope. Maybe he really did go through life not caring whether his next morning would be his last, but maybe somewhere deeper, underneath all the layers of self-delusions and self-justifications, he held a secret wish to live to see the moment of freedom, to finally wake up from the nightmare. How cruelly, then, his hope must have been dashed after only a few hours into the holy night.

I also kept thinking what would have happened if in my travels I had met Claus von Stauffenberg, the steely-eyed colonel who had lost his left eye, right hand and three fingers of the left one in the desert of North Africa. What if I had whispered in his ear: for God's sake, try to put the briefcase with the bomb somewhere closer to Hitler, on the other side of the wooden slab that supports the table, somewhere out of Colonel Brandt's reach, so that he will not accidentally push it further under the table with his foot. For God's sake ...

All the lives I've helped to save so far, even multiplied thousandfold, would still not equal the number of lives I could have saved in such an indirect way. Even if von Stauffenberg had listened to me, however dumbfounded by the conversation with an angel, even if he had manage to place the bomb exactly how I suggested, what would have really happened? Would I wake up in a world where the different future was my new present? Or maybe whatever happened was meant to be and I could never change it, however hard I would try? Or maybe there was no link between my two worlds at all.

I don't know.

In the end nothing was any different.

* * *

I'm sure you must be sick of all the questions to which I have no answers.

Not as sick as I am.

V.

It's a town square, small, almost claustrophobic, surrounded on all sides by low buildings, their wooden surfaces weathered almost black. There's a well in the middle of the square, rising like an ancient pagan monument out of the hard-bitten earth.

I stand on the front steps of the largest house, looking at the crowd milling in front of me. All the Jewish men from the town and nearby are herded into the square, dazed and fearful. My men are among them, with their easy laughter and swinging rifle butts. Their dark blue uniforms make them blend in with the crowd where everyone is wearing dark, but you can always distinguish them by the way they move, so confident, purposeful, at ease with themselves.

Somebody – Kurt? – is cutting off an old man's beard with his hunting knife. He's laughing as he triumphantly shows his trophy around before throwing it on the ground. Others are making the Jews leapfrog around the well. The men, most of them old, strain and stumble. One of them loses his balance and collapses to the ground. Werner jumps out of the crowd and kicks the man in the gut, screaming obscenities at him until the old man slowly picks himself up and rejoins the exercise.

My boys are chuckling. Somebody's now taking a photograph.

The locals, Latvian farmers in their black trousers and white shirts with sleeves rolled up, are hanging around on the edges of the crowd, trotting about in a hesitant yet expectant manner. Their faces glisten with sweat, eyes dart around, and only a few words pass through the corners of their lips.

Old Hauptmann has dragged a rabbi and one other elder from among the crowd. They are now kneeling before him, heads draped with shawls, their hands outstretched in an ignored plea. They look like downed cherubim. Old Hauptmann holds the Torah scroll in his hand. He orders the rabbi to spit on it. The rabbi is impassive, his head raised to heavens, eyes closed, his lips mouthing a silent prayer. Old Hauptmann gets impatient; he whips out his Mauser and shoots the rabbi in the head. The whole town square falls quiet for a brief moment.

The other old man is trembling, hands in prayer in front of his pale face. Old Hauptmann kicks him in the thighs and yells at him. It must have been something funny because a few of my men watching the scene burst out laughing. The old man closes his eyes and tries to spit but the saliva only drips down his chin. Old Hauptmann kills him anyway.

The second in command shouts the order for the Jews to kneel down. They slowly sink to their knees, prodded with riffles and boots. The sun beats down mercilessly. I wipe my forehead with a handkerchief. It's midday.

My men start to move out to the edges of the square. The Latvians suddenly have long pieces of wood in their hands. They are moving in, uncertain at first, looking over their shoulders for instructions or reassurance. My people cheer them on. The Latvians stand among the kneeling Jews like harvesters in the sea of black wheat. There, bent on his knees before you, is the baker who you think overcharged you last winter. There's the publican who got rich while bad harvests drove you into debt. Look at him, the wily Christ-killer. They can almost feel that scent in the air. The nostrils flare, the heartbeats quicken.

Then one of the Latvians swings his piece of wood ...

Oh, God.

God.

God.

God.

*　*　*

I look at myself in the mirror. Very carefully, as if my very life depended on memorizing every square inch of my skin, every shade, every contour, every texture. It's me, all right, on the surface at least, so how much of me is him?

Are we all merely parts of our ancestors or are we something else, something more? And if so? Surely you cannot pass evil in your genes onto your unsuspecting descendants? Not like a genetic disease, surely. The sinner's child can be a saint and the saint's progeny a scoundrel. Otherwise, what's the point? Where's the free will, where is some elementary justice that would allow each one of us a fresh start, a new chance with a clean slate? That whole stuff about sins of the fathers visiting their descendants for ten generations was supposed to have ended quite some time ago, in ancient Israel, wasn't it?

I sit on the edge of the bed and run my hands through my hair and then all over my face as if I was trying to rub off the last remains of a dream. Or to tear off a mask, a mischievous voice whispers in my head.

No! What the hell am I thinking? I'm normal, damn it, I'm all right. Even if what Bartok says is true and I am Behrnard's grandson, then so what? I must just as well be the grandson I always thought I was. My father's real father was a man that should have hung from the gallows at the end of the war. He did despicable things, but what does it have to do with me? I wasn't there, I wasn't even born.

I have never done anything evil. I haven't even torn the wings off flies, for God's sake. I have never fantasized about abducting a little girl, raping her, then strangling her and burying her body somewhere in the forest, much less made fantasies a reality. Of course not. Then why do I think that it matters at all who my grandfather was?

And yet ...

* * *

I got the message on the train from Berlin to Hamburg. Katrina was supposed to wait for me somewhere in the last carriage. She couldn't tell me which compartment exactly, she would have been lucky enough to get on the train in the first place. It was getting more and more difficult to arrange an exact rendezvous. Trips that once took hours now took days, and the trains were always packed with weary, easily irritable people on the move. The bombed-out families in search of a roof over their heads, scavengers and black marketeers scouring the countryside in search of food, we would all cram together without privacy and without high hopes.

Katrina wasn't in any of the compartments. I went back again, past the obstacle course of luggage mushrooming in the corridor. I was thinking of going to the next carriage, just on the off chance there was some misunderstanding or some unexpected problem, when the doors of the last compartment slid open and a man come out onto the corridor.

He was young, about my age, but short and stocky, with thin blond hair and a face of a professional boxer, or at least a pub brawler. He made sure the doors were closed behind him before he spoke to me. "On the train to Vienna one can still read a book in peace," he said as he leaned against the window.

I turned towards him, caught off-guard by his remark. He stood there, not looking at me, absent-mindedly scratching his chin. The boxer reading anything other than the sports pages, what a thought.

Then it clicked.

"I found Victor Hugo to be particularly rewarding on long trips," I said.

One train ride with Katrina, some time ago, when we became for a few hours a small link in a chain passing a microfilm from Berlin to Bern, Katrina whiling away the long hours reading *Les Misérables* aloud to me.

"Bittmann, I presume?" His German was good, but not native.

"Yes," I nodded. He looked me up and down, trying to compare the description with the reality.

"I've got a letter for you," he said and reached inside his coat.

It was a small, unmarked envelope. I ripped open the seal and pulled out a single piece of paper. The corridor was dark; the light slipping through the doors of compartments did little to dispel the internal twilight.

I took the lighter out of my pocket and flicked it open. The flame threw a dancing glare on the paper.

"Martin, my love," the note read. "Forgive my absence. There has been an emergency. My grandparents are in grave danger. I had to go back to Budapest as fast as I could. Francis, my trusted friend, who will deliver you this letter, will tell you more than I have time to write now. He is aware of my family situation. Please, be careful. I shall remain in touch with Mr B. Wait on any news through him. Love, K."

Francis, if that was his real name, gave me time to finish the letter. I slowly folded it and put it in my pocket. Sheer helplessness. Katrina, somewhere in Hungary ...

"Let's catch some fresh air," Francis motioned with his head towards the rear door of the carriage. The train was slowly coming to a halt, for God knows which time that night. Soon, inevitably, the heads would start popping out of the compartments, hoping to find answers for this particular delay.

What used to be the glass pane on the door had been replaced with a wooden board crudely nailed to the frame. I pressed on the knob. It turned but the door only moved an inch. I put my shoulder against it and pushed. Still nothing. Impatiently, Francis leaned against the door alongside me. We pressed on and it gave way so suddenly we had to steady ourselves against the frame not to fall outside.

There wasn't much room on the rear platform, but enough for the two of us standing. Francis closed the door behind him, leaving only a paper thin gap.

The train had stopped by now. There were no stars and no moon either over the vast, featureless plain. It felt like standing at the bottom of a tar pit.

"As you know, things in Hungary got a lot worse recently –" Francis started.

"Actually I don't," I interrupted him. "I've had no chance to follow what's been happening."

He sighed. "Well, it's all gone to hell ... for some, at least. The circus's finally over. A wonder it lasted as long as it did."

He pulled out a small flat box of cigars and offered me one, taking another for himself. I didn't inquire how he got his hands on such a rarity. In times like these one learned to appreciate without asking.

"When our own were running the country, the Jews could still manage. After the Germans finally took over in March all bets were off."

We both took slow drags. They were good, these cigars, with the insidious salty taste they left in one's mouth.

"Eichmann divided the country into five zones, and started making Hungary *Judenfrei*, free of Jews. They were all rounded up, loaded on trains and taken away ... wherever they take them away to. Budapest ... some called it Judapest before the war, did you know? ... Budapest, that was zone five for Eichmann, the dessert."

The train started moving again, slowly at first, as if uncertain how long the new spur would last.

"The people, the Horns, that the Baroness has ... a sentimental attachment to, they could have laid low in their town. The documents they had were beautiful, believe me, top quality, very expensive. No one knew who they really were, no one suspected anything. But old people sometimes get strange ideas, don't they?"

His cigar went out and he started fumbling about his pockets looking for matches. I offered him my light.

He lit up and pulled back. The tip of his cigar was glowing faint red again, the only color on the dark tapestry. "Maybe they got scared seeing all the other Jews being taken away around them. I don't know. They packed their bags and a few days later they were back in Budapest. Meanwhile the Russians crossed the border and Admiral Horthy broke away from the Germans. The same day the Germans and the Arrow Cross overthrew the government and started rounding up Jews in Budapest."

I nodded, trying to make sense of the Byzantine goings on in Katrina's homeland.

"I wasn't in town at the time, thank God, but I've heard it was bad," Francis went on. "They would tie three people together, shoot the middle one and then throw all of them into Danube so that the dead would drag the living to the bottom. Anyway, the Baroness' people still had their good papers and would have gotten through all this but someone from the past recognized them and informed the police. They were taken away a few days ago. That's the whole story, as far as I know."

"You don't know where they are now?" I asked.

"No, I don't," he said.

But there was really only one question on my mind, "Where's the Baroness?"

Francis extinguished the stump of his cigar on the iron railing and shrugged, "No. As I said, I was only asked to carry a message to you. I don't know anything more."

"Will you mind if I ask you what's your role in it?"

"Yes, I will mind," there was impatience in his voice now. "Let's just say I owe the Baroness a favor. Other than that I've got nothing more to say."

He opened the door and peeked inside the carriage. "It has been nice meeting you. Maybe next time we have a chat, the times will be better," he said. The corridor must have been empty for he took a step in, but before he disappeared he turned and said to me, "From now on I don't know you and never've met you, Mr Bittmann."

Then he was gone, for the rest of the trip. I saw him come out of his compartment a few stations later with a small carry-bag in his hand.

I was going to nod towards him in acknowledgment but then I remembered what he said. He didn't look my way.

*   *   *

Everything was starting to fall apart. I now thought almost fondly of all the trips of the past months. For all their discomfort and casual, unplanned danger they seemed somehow reassuring in their predictability and routine.

Next morning I went to the letterbox to check the mail. The only envelope inside had Bartok's handwriting on it. I expected an instruction for the coming night. Instead it was a short message.

"The crackdown after the assassination attempt is in full swing," it read. "V.S. is on the run. Will keep you posted if contact is re-established."

I went into the kitchen and put the match to the corner of the paper. It trembled in the sink as if it were alive, suffering terribly while consumed by fire. I washed the ashes with cold water and then I put my face under the tap.

VII.

I put the gun to the back of the woman's head. The muzzle almost brushes against her bronze hair, once glorious, now matted and lifeless after all the sleepless nights and the long journey on the back of a lorry. Her body quivers and she whimpers something in the incomprehensible gibberish of Yiddish.

It's a beautiful day. The summer is so intense, so warm, so determined to stamp her full glory on the world before she'll wither away in a few weeks' time.

The crisp, fragrant air fills my lungs, and I feel they could burst through my chest and float to the sky like two balloons. Above me, pine treetops spear the deep blue sky. There's hardly any breeze to sway them. I have never felt so alive.

I pull the trigger.

A clap of thunder rings through the forest. And yet there are no storm clouds in the sky.

Blood, brain, and bone splinters rain on me, spray my face, coat the front of my uniform. Again. I'll have to get it washed tomorrow. I wipe my cheeks with a handkerchief. The cloth is no longer white.

The women collapses as if the ground had suddenly disappeared from under her feet. A few short spasms convulse her body and then everything around me is still again. Only other thunders explode among the trees. No other sound intrudes. The birds are long gone, and the flies haven't arrived yet.

The woman is lying a few feet away from a girl, seven, maybe eight years old, and a younger boy. I gave the mother a choice: which one of her children did she want to save? She took too much time deciding, so I shot the boy first, then the girl, and then, finally, her. By that stage, I suppose, her mind was already gone. Next to these three lay an old man, half his face missing, his long white beard matted with blood that has already started drying out in the warm sun. And further away, another woman. She screamed, tried to run, took two bullets.

I weigh the gun in my hand. The magazine is empty. I eject it and slip in a new one. Time for a break. I walk back towards the edge of the clearing. Werner's there, leaning against a tree, smoking a cigarette. He offers me one from a pack and I take it.

"How's the pest control going?" he asks.

"Good," I say. "Hopefully not many more today. I want to go swimming."

"Yes, a nice day for a little dip, isn't it?" Werner says, looking up to the sky.

Somebody, somewhere out there cries out. The shots keep on ringing.

* * *

Now I'm afraid to sleep at all. At night I go out, get on the trains and ride to save the few who would otherwise perish. Isn't that enough? I don't want to go back in my dreams, too. I don't want to come back as him, even in this strange way, even for a brief moment.

In my sleep I look through his eyes, speak through his mouth, think his thoughts, do his deeds. I have no power over it; we merge into each other; he becomes me, or maybe I become him. And I can't stop it.

I'm afraid to sleep, but how can I not sleep at all?

* * *

I am back in Hungary again and I don't know whether it is merely an accident of timing. I don't dare question my luck. It is as I wanted it, yet somewhere else still, on a different mission.

Some time ago, the authorities had stopped recognizing the Portuguese and Swedish documents that gave protection to the lucky few. Then a Swedish diplomat, Roaul Wallenberg, spoke to Baroness Elizabeth Kemeny, the wife of the Foreign Minister. Baroness Kemeny, six months pregnant, threatened to leave her husband if the documents were not officially respected again. There was rage, there was love, and in the end love won. Now I'm back with more good, freshly printed papers from neutral countries.

I walk toward the train. Along its whole length, men and women –

mostly men – stand around, looking harangued and exhausted, their gray and washed out clothes often no more than torn rags. Only the yellow stars of David shine from their chests. They wait, suitcases at their feet, rolled up blankets and bales of clothing hanging precariously around their necks. Strong lights, suspended from tall poles, beat down upon them. The mist of breath dances in the beams of light, slowly drifting skywards. It's early November. The winter is still a few weeks away but people shiver all the same and pray to God to hurry the morning sun.

The doors to the wagons are already slid open, waiting to take them onboard. The SS men and local gendarmes shuffle impatiently, passing around cigarettes and talking quietly to each other. The bureaucrats of death consult their documents, trying to tally up the final figures.

Heads turn when three cars pull up. I'm still some distance away when Wallenberg and his people jump out of their Mercedes limousines and hurry towards the crowd.

Wallenberg.

His open, boyish face disguises the ruthlessness of purpose. At just over thirty, he is prematurely balding. His long nose, full lips and prominent chin give him a look of a soft and spoiled adolescent. He could be that – back home, enjoying the carefree lifestyle his family can offer him. Instead, he chose to turn the Swedish mission in Budapest into a rescue agency for the Hungarian Jews.

I intercept him half-way to the tracks. He shakes my hand on the run, fleetingly, but with a surprising strength. "Mr Cabriz, of the Portuguese legation, I presume?" he asks, but doesn't wait for my reply. "Thank you for coming. We've received a communication about you." Precise, very matter of fact. He despises having to waste even one word, one unnecessary movement. There is so much to do and so little time. I nod, pretending to know what he's talking about. I'm only a busy actor, whose appearance has been efficaciously arranged well beforehand by his trusted agent. No need to worry about the precise mechanics.

"I'm also looking for two specific people," I say. This wasn't in my brief, but right now I don't care.

"By all means," he nods.

I reach inside my coat for a thick envelope. This is, after all, what I'm here for. Before I can pull it out, Wallenberg catches my movement and his hand shoots out to grip my shoulder. Almost imperceptibly he shakes his head and motions towards one of his associates behind. I understand.

One of the junior officers steps into our path, hands on his hips, ready to put a stop to this distracting spectacle. Wallenberg side-steps him and bellows out, for the benefit of all gathered, the captors and the captives: "My name is Wallenberg, and I'm from the Swedish mission. There are people here who hold Swedish passports."

The officer turns toward his superiors, uncertain how to proceed against this intruder. Those in charge have by now raised their eyes away from the paperwork as Wallenberg's entourage descends on the crowd. The jaws of the master race warriors tighten. It's an uncomfortable situation, but he is a diplomat from a neutral country.

By now Wallenberg is taking people by their hands out of the crowd. "You," he blurts out to those he's dragging away. "You've got a Swedish passport. I remember issuing it to you."

I know he hasn't seen any of these people in his life. They don't have any passports in their pockets –

"All those who have Swedish papers, please hand them in to me," his voice rings with authority and confidence. It's so quiet now that everyone would be able hear him even if he was whispering.

– maybe only some pieces of paper.

There are puzzled looks on people's faces. Hardly anybody moves. Then one elderly man fumbles around in his pocket and pulls out a folded piece of paper. He hesitates, and then hands it over to me. It isn't a passport; it is a page torn out from a scrapbook, with some illegible scribbling on it. I half-turn to Wallenberg, but before I can say anything he snatches the paper from my hand. "Thank you. Please step out and move over there," he gestures towards his cars. Now lorries with the red cross painted on their sides are pulling up just behind the Mercedes cars.

It's a dangerous bluff. As long as the Germans don't look too closely it doesn't matter whether there are any Swedish papers at all. I'm sure the new ones will be issued later, on the way back to Budapest, but for now any scrap of paper will do the trick.

People start catching on, desperately searching through their pockets for any sort of identification, any piece of paper, however small, however insignificant. There are hands extending towards me from everywhere, holding out their fake passes back to life. I gather them as fast I as I can, praying the make-believe will not wear off too soon. Thank God it's not daylight.

But neither the SS nor the Hungarian gendarmes seem keen to step in. Wallenberg keeps ploughing into the crowd, pulling out people like a mad god, all the while repeating his mantra about the Swedish documents.

I pass on the pile of papers to his assistant. And my envelope. The saved ones are moving towards the parked lorries. One, two, a dozen, two dozen, then more. The drivers have switched off their engines but keep the lights on, glaring at the train. The silent figures drift like moths to a lamp.

I walk along the edge of the crowd, scanning faces, looking for a flash of familiarity, though I have no reason to expect it. "Mr. and Mrs. Horn?" I raise my voice to be heard over the fray, "The Horns?" There is no reaction. People give me quick glances, but no one says anything.

Wallenberg now gets into a heated exchange with a group of SS officers. A hundred Jews are climbing onto the trucks. This is too much for the Germans. Not even diplomatic privilege can be allowed to interfere that much with the transport schedule. But Wallenberg is determined to make his point. He whips out a thick folder with his list of names and drags the SS men into a time-wasting, bureaucratic haggle. The papers collected from the Jews have by now conveniently disappeared out of sight.

"Mr. and Mrs. Horn!" I call out. It becomes clear that Katrina's grandparents are not among this group and that no one here knows them. Or, if they do, time is too precious to spare to enlighten me. I know that I'm merely a nuisance, a distraction from the main game of miracles in the middle of a November night. "Does anyone here know Mr. and Mrs. Horn?" Yet I persist, hopelessly.

Wallenberg finishes his negotiation with the SS officers. The bluff works, there's not much they can do tonight. They will report the matter directly to Eichmann in the morning, complaints will be lodged with the Swedes, and precautions worked out by the SS for any future eventualities. Meanwhile they can only watch impassively, seething and waiting to unleash their rage afterwards on those not fortunate enough to have found their way onto the Red Cross trucks.

Wallenberg comes over to me, his face sweaty and flush with excitement, but not betraying the satisfaction of the task accomplished. It's but one small step; the work never ends.

"I have to go," he says. "There's nothing more I can do tonight. The trucks are full. I will come back tomorrow."

I suspect that tomorrow there will be no one to come back for. I suspect he know that too. But one must go on.

We shake hands.

"Did you find the people you were looking for?" he asks.

I shake my head.

"They could be anywhere," he says. "Give me their names, and I'll see whether there is anything I can do. If I find them somewhere back in Budapest I'll try to help them and I'll pass the information onto you."

I scribble the names on a piece of paper and pass it onto him. He folds the paper in half and puts it the inside pocket of his coat.

"I'll do my best," he says and brushes the rim of the hat with his fingers. "We're working under difficult conditions, you understand."

I do understand.

"Thank you for your help tonight," he says. Then he turns around and hurriedly walks off towards his limousine, where the embassy workers are waiting for him. The engines rev up, the final crescendo of defiance.

"I haven't really done anything," I say to myself. I can only think about Katrina's grandparents, not the unnamed ones I helped to get off the train to perdition. Tonight was a one-off chance. Too good to be true if I had found them. Yet I cannot but think that I've failed.

The air is fresh and biting cold, but suddenly I feel out of breath. I have to get out of here, walk it off, past the trains – past this train – past the guards, past the lights. Nausea slowly rises from the pit of my belly.

So I walk. Down the labyrinth of other trains, through the dark corridor of wood and metal. Absentmindedly I stretch out my hands and reach out towards wagons on both sides of me. My fingertips brush against the paint. It feels greasy under my touch, and sharp where it's peeling off.

This time he makes no attempt to hide himself and startle me. He is there, between the tracks, silhouetted in a dim light that shines somewhere behind him. I can't see his face, yet I recognize him immediately, even before he opens his mouth to speak to me.

He's straddling my path, his feet apart, his hands clasped behind his back. The easy pose of learned superiority. Only his officer's hat is slightly skewed, breaking the symmetry. It makes him look as if his whole head was mockingly inclined towards his shoulder.

"We keep running into each other, don't we, Herr Bittmann?"

It's so damned hard to stop one's heart from racing.

"You didn't expect to see me here?" he asks rhetorically. "I, on the other hand, kind of expected to see you. Soon, I might start thinking there is some invisible bond between us."

I stiffen, but he only sniggers and there doesn't seem to be anything more behind his remark.

"Maybe we're twins. Astral twins. Reichsfuhrer Himmler believes such phenomena exist," he adds.

Not quite astral twins, I think. Oh God, how would he look at me if I now told him: you are my grandfather. I think he would laugh, a statement as absurd as the situation we're in.

"So you're looking for Mr. and Mrs. Horn?" he starts slowly walking towards me. "A passing acquaintance, or a family connection, perhaps?" he asks.

"I'm sure you can find the answer to that yourself," I swallow hard. A few lines away, somewhere to our left, wheels are woken up from slumber. They screech like tormented souls as the engine starts pulling them on their way. The death train goes forth.

"Maybe I do already," he stops a few paces away from me.

"Then why are we playing this game?"

"Games," he says. "We've talked about games once already, haven't we?"

"What do you want?" I ask. There's no way I can back out before this conversation runs its course. Well, there is a way, but I have to stay longer.

"What do you want?" he echoes with his own question. There is a moment of uncomfortable silence between us before he snaps out of it. "Meet me here three nights from now. Then we'll talk."

I don't know what to say to his invitation.

"I might give you something you want," he adds. "Like the Horns, for example. For now, farewell."

He turns around and starts walking away down the train alley. He gets down the length of two wagons before he turns around abruptly as if he suddenly remembered something very important. "The Baroness is such a beautiful woman. It would be terrible if anything were to happen to her," he says.

"You're not going to do anything to her," I say quickly. Too quickly.

"Oh?" I can't see but I can picture him raising his eyebrows.

"You don't care about her," I regain composure. "You don't want her, you want me."

"Perhaps yes. Perhaps not. But you don't really know," he says and turns around, again walking away, this time for good.

And I'm left standing, thinking how in the world I am going to arrange to be back here three nights from now.

VIII.

Oh God, how I needed to go back to Hungary.

I was going insane not knowing what was happening to her, where she was, not knowing whether she was safe. If the net hadn't closed around her quite yet, it seemed only a matter of time. Maybe Katrina's diplomatic connections were still protecting her, or maybe, now that all bets were off in the collapsing house of cards that was the Third Reich, maybe nothing really counted any more except what you held in your hand. Or whom you held in your hand. Maybe.

"I want to – I have to – get back to Hungary," I told Bartok.

He looked at me without surprise. He understood but didn't respond.

"It's not just her grandparents," I continued. "She too is in danger now. I have to go back."

He frowned, "My dear Martin, please remember this is not your own private adventure."

This time I was silent. I knew what he was going to say.

"The whole world does not revolve around you. You were sent over there to save lives, not to fall in love and engage in escapades of your own."

Yes, I was right.

"Can't stop life from taking its course," I said. This was not a convincing riposte to somebody who has always put the mission above its participants.

"As you are risking your life every night, so are they," he replied. "Von Schellendorff, the Baroness, all the people who work with them. That is the price of being human these days."

"Listen to me," I said through clenched teeth. "I don't care whether there is a war out there or not. I don't care what you think. I don't care about anything much at the moment except about this."

"Martin," I could see his upper lip twitching slightly. "You can shout at me all you want but it is not going to change anything. I do not put together the timetable."

"Then who does?"

He thought about his answer for a few seconds. "What does it matter if it cannot be changed?"

What, indeed? But tell that to a drowning man.

"I am not saying that you will not be allowed to go back to Hungary," he suddenly added. "What I am saying is that it does not depend on how much either you or I might want it."

"On what does it depend then?"

"On whether it is meant to be," he said.

Whether it is meant to be. I fell back into my chair and hid my face in my hands. Had they ever existed, that's how the Greek heroes must have felt, at the mercy of their stupid and vengeful gods. How much worse for me, all flesh and blood.

"Listen, Martin," Bartok said. "You do have to understand. You have to continue doing your work. Think of all the people who will die because you are too weak, too absorbed by other things ..."

He put his hand on my shoulder and squeezed it lightly.

I didn't say anything.

*　*　*

And so I went to the train yards that night, yet again, and closed my eyes on a freight platform that was almost empty, except for two rats feasting on garbage and a middle-aged priest in a long dark coat buttoned half-way up his chest. The priest noticed my presence but did not acknowledge me. I disappeared before his train arrived to take him away on his own journey.

When I opened my eyes I was in the toilet cubicle on a train speeding through what remained of Hitler's Reich. And I prayed that the next time it's meant to be.

*　*　*

Two days later I picked up the phone and heard Bartok's monotone voice.

"Tonight, 1 am," he said. "This is a favor. The biggest one you get in your whole life. The only one."

So the powers that be did let me go, I thought when I put down the handset.

I didn't kid myself that it was the strength of my prayers, or the sincerity of my contrition. No, it happened, as Bartok would say, because they wanted it to happen. Yes, it was meant to be.

I think I now know why.

IX.

In three nights' time, the train did not stop. I should have guessed that much; it was always a freight depot and not a station, even if the Germans had used it for their human cargo.

The SS weren't here tonight, their job accomplished, which is why I almost missed the rendezvous. Only after the train had made its way past a group of buildings did it occur to me they looked familiar. If the lights were on, like the other night, the recognition would have come earlier. Now I only had the silver platter of the moon to illuminate my blind man's kaleidoscope.

I was travelling inside an empty freight wagon. The floor around me was covered with moist straw, which stuck to my palms when I felt my way around. The air inside still smelled of urine and animal sweat, even though the door was not closed properly and night air was sneaking in. I crouched down by the gap and allowed myself to be washed by the wind.

The train was slowing down. I pushed the door open and grasped the edges of the door. There was a moment of hesitation, as if a quick rethink was going to change anything, and then I launched myself into the air.

I don't think I closed my eyes even for a fraction of a second but I don't think I saw anything either until I hit the ground. Hard earth knocked the breath out of me, and as I rolled down the escarpment I thought I would suffocate.

My body stopped some fifty meters down from the tracks, finally rolling to a still in tall grass at the bottom of a marshy gully. I lied on my back for some time, oblivious to the wetness slowly seeping in through my clothes and caressing my skin. Afraid to open my eyes and move, I was trying to somehow feel whether all parts of my body were still intact. Every bit of me ached, but there was no sharp pain.

Finally I stood up slowly, stretched and ran my hands along my legs, chest, and over my head. All normal. Time to go, boy. My boots kept sinking into the turf with an unpleasant squishing sound as I climbed up from the ravine. My left ankle was hurting a bit, but not as bad as if I had twisted it.

Back on top of the escarpment I thought I could still hear my train. Instinctively I looked at my wrist but there was no watch there. I took a few deep breaths and started following the tracks back to the station.

Five, maybe ten minutes later, the shapes of buildings detached themselves from the black background and came towards me.

He was there, somewhere. I was trying to feel with all my senses for any sign of life. To feel him. Blood calling blood, isn't that what they say? But I felt nothing.

Then I saw it.

Like a star that fell down from heavens and rested on the earth, a storm lamp was hanging on the wall of a shed. There was no other sign, only this beacon to guide me to him. This was it.

I walked towards the shed. No sound was coming from inside. The lamp was swinging in the light breeze, casting strange, dancing shadows on the wall. I put my hand on the door and hesitated. Here we are, I thought.

I pushed the door open and walked in.

It once used to be a tool shed. Now all that remained was a phantom smell of oil and lubricants, mysteriously lingering within the wooden walls that looked too porous and fragile to hold anything inside.

There was a table of sorts in the middle of the room, a piece of board placed on an empty box. On top of it, candles, five or six flickers multiplied in the shards of glass that still remained on the inside of boarded-up windows.

He was sitting on a chair just on the edge of the pale circle of light, like a magician reluctant to step into the protective pentagram of power. The other chair stood empty opposite, waiting for me. He motioned with his hand inviting me to sit down. I descended down carefully, not quite trusting the old wood to support me.

It was only when I rested that I saw three other figures in the room, hiding in the twilight against the wall.

Katrina.

My heart stopped for a moment.

She was sitting behind Behrnard, silent and composed, only her eyes betraying that she saw me too.

Oh, God.

Her posture was so stiff and unnatural that it could only mean she was bound to her chair. I couldn't see the ropes, only the gag in her mouth. So, her diplomatic immunity only extended thus far and no further. This was the end game, after all.

I wanted to jump out of my seat, climb over the table, over Behrnard, to catch her and hold her, to put my arms around her like a magic cloak that would make us invisible. But even if I had somehow managed to knock Behrnard to the ground and trample him, I would still run into the two guards who flanked her. The black, metal helmets of Waffen SS overshadowed their stony faces. Like ice sculptures, I thought. Black ice. Two dragons guarding the gate to heaven. The light of candles played gently on the barrels of their submachine guns.

"Thanks for coming, Herr Bittmann," Behrnard said. "I knew you would."

"Let's not waste time on niceties," I said. The burning ember in the pit of my stomach was the realization that he was the first person in my life I wanted to kill. And that I had never been in a worse position to do so.

"In that case, I'll tell you what," he said and opened up his hand. He was holding a pack of cards. "Let's have a little game of, say, poker."

"Mind you, it's not as good with only two people playing," he continued. "We'll have to make up for the lack of excitement in some other way. What do you say?"

"I don't know what you're getting at," I said. That wasn't quite true; the sick feeling rising up in my throat was telling me otherwise.

"Well, such an intelligent man like you, Herr Bittmann," Behrnard shook his head in a theatrical gesture of disappointment. "It will be very simple. If you win, I'll give you the Horns back."

I was dimly aware that my breathing became so shallow my chest was hardly moving. Katrina was staring at me, her eyes wide open, terrified.

"And what if you win?" I asked.

"Nothing," he said. "So what do you have to lose?"

What indeed? There must have been a catch.

"Where are they?" I said. "I want to see them first, before I do anything."

"Don't you trust me?" he asked, breaking the pack. The silence around us only magnified the crack of cards.

"Trust you? Of course not."

"That's not good," he put the pack in the middle of the table. "That's no way to start a good relationship. Cut it," he motioned with his head.

I didn't move. "I haven't decided yet if I'm going to play."

"What other choice do you have?" he looked at me for a few seconds, waiting whether I'll oblige him. Then, disappointed, he reached out and took the cards in his hand. "It's not as much good luck as if you'd cut it," he murmured under his breath.

"I want to see them," I repeated.

Behrnard split the pack into three lots and then quickly gathered them up again. "I'm afraid you can't," he said. "They're not here."

I looked at Katrina. She turned her head away and shut her eyes.

"I thought it would be unconscionable to drag people of their age and failing health around with me in the middle of the night," he said. "But one word from me will suffice, and they will be free. If you win."

There wasn't really anything I could say or do. We were already playing the game and he had all the best cards. And at the same time he was also the dealer.

Behrnard took my silence as acquiescence. "Let's say we'll have three rounds. The winner of the series takes all."

He dealt us five cards each and put the rest of the pile in the middle of the table. "It's not going to be normal poker," he added. "For the sake of simplicity we'll have to dispense with a few of the rules. Let's call it the Behrnard poker."

If a mother asked her child: what were you doing tonight? And the child answered: I was playing cards with my grandpa – how innocent it would sound. Yes, I was playing with my grandfather, and the stakes were the lives of two people who meant so much to the woman I loved.

I picked up my cards. A pair of threes, a seven, a nine, and a Queen of Hearts. Not good enough. Not with these stakes.

Slowly I threw the seven and the nine face down on the table.

I tried to concentrate on the cards but I couldn't help stealing glances at his face, now that for the first time I was seeing him in a better light. I was cursing myself for trying to calculate the odds of getting two pairs, three of a kind, or a full house, while at the same time mapping his features, in my mind analyzing every line, shadow, and contour. I was looking at him and not finding a resemblance, not even a fleeting one. But it didn't calm me down.

Behrnard put down three of his cards on the table.

Our eyes met and the corners of his mouth twitched in a ghostly smile.

He dealt me two cards and three for himself.

I picked up the first one.

A two of spades.

Shit.

And a second one.

Another three.

Yes.

I strained not to allow my expression to give the game away.

"As you can guess, there won't be any bets or raisings," he said. "There's only one pot."

I nodded.

"You first," he said.

I swallowed and put my first three on the table.

He smiled and put down a king.

I put down the remaining two threes.

He hesitated for a fraction of a second, shook his head and threw his cards on the table.

"Very good, Herr Bittmann, very good," he said, suddenly expression-less.

He gathered up all the cards again and started shuffling them.

"They say he who has luck in cards has no luck in love," he said as he dealt the second round.

I didn't rise to this. Outside, another train passed by, rattling on the tracks. I picked up the cards.

A two, a four, a seven, an eight, and a king.

Not good.

I left the eight and the king. Behrnard threw away two cards and without a word dealt out for both of us.

A two, a queen and an ace.

Nothing.

"Your turn," I said.

He put a pair of tens on the table.

I threw my cards down.

"That only makes it more exciting now," he chuckled.

I'm sure Katrina couldn't see the table, but she must have been hearing everything that was said. God, what she must have been thinking.

Behrnard was taking his time, first shuffling then dealing as if it were some holy ritual to be solemnized by strict observance.

This was it. I closed my eyes, slid my cards to the edge of the table and picked them up.

A four, a five, a six.

And a pair of aces. Hearts and diamonds.

Again I threw away three cards, and he threw two.

How long could these black statues remain motionless, I thought. Maybe Behrnard was trying to deceive me. Maybe he had robbed Madame Toussard's museum and dressed two wax models in vile uniforms peeled off the corpses of his dead comrades in arms.

I picked up my three cards.

A ten.

And a pair of eights.

A pair of aces and a pair of eights. A dead man's hand. The hand that Wild Bill Hickok held when some small-time shit had sneaked up behind him and shot him in the back of his head.

"Please," Behrnard motioned with his head.

I put down the pair of eights.

He smiled and put down a pair of nines.

I added the aces on the table in front of me.

The face behind the mask collapsed into itself. The remaining three cards stayed in his hand.

"I've won," I said, not quite believing it.

The hearts and diamonds were staring back at me, alive in the candle-light.

"You've won," Behrnard echoed.

He turned his head to the side and his brow furrowed as if he was pondering on some difficult philosophical proposition.

I could see a single tear rolling down Katrina's cheek.

Then Behrnard turned back to face me. Now his eyes looked like they, too, were burning candles.

"Take the girl away," he barked at the two SS-men behind him.

"No!" I jumped to my feet.

He was as quick as I was – quicker than I was – as if all that time he had been sitting down he was winding up the spring to release it in a fraction of a second. He was on his feet before I could make any other move, and his gun was now no more than two inches from my face, pointing squarely at the ridge of my nose. He was leaning forward over the improvised table, pushing it forward. The edge of the board dug into my calves.

"Sit down," he told me, and then repeated to his underlings, "Take her away."

I didn't move.

One of the guards untied Katrina and lifted her off the chair. They held her under her arms and dragged her with them around the table, towards the door.

I extended my hand out to touch her as she passed by and her body instinctively drew towards it.

Behrnard leaned across the table and hit me across the face with his gun-clenching fist. My head twisted sideways as fire erupted on my cheek. I sank into the chair. The room swirled in my eyes. My tongue was cut and I tasted blood.

Katrina cried out, muffled by the gag, and paused in mid-step, but the SS men pulled her through the door.

"Now we're comfortable," said Behrnard. He, too, had now sat down.

"What are you doing?" I asked. The words came out with difficulty. I felt like somebody had stuffed my mouth full of hot pebbles.

"We didn't play for the girl, did we?" Behrnard said. His elbow was resting on the table and the gun was still pointing at me.

"I've won. I want the Horns."

He leaned back in his chair. "I'm afraid that's impossible. They're dead."

The room suddenly felt darker, as if the candlelight had dimmed.

"I don't believe you," I swallowed blood and bile. My throat almost refused to pass it through. Oh, God, I thought, oh, God. Other than that my mind was empty.

He was still aiming at my chest while with his other hand he started playing with the cards strewn across the table.

"It would be good if you'd finally learn to believe me. To trust me," he said.

"Trust you? You must be completely insane," I said. How could I know? Maybe he was lying, still playing his game. That was his sort of amusement, wasn't it? My last slim hope.

Behrnard took one card and started spinning it around on the table. "Do you want to see the bodies?" he asked a matter of fact.

"Why?" I almost shouted. "Why did you do it?"

"Did you really think I would just let them walk away?" he picked up the card and put it the face up. It was the king of spades.

"Why?" I said again.

"You ask too many questions, Herr Bittmann," he said. He stood up but his gun remained aimed at me. "We'll be in touch."

He put two fingers in his mouth and when he took them out, with a connoisseur's smack of the lips, they glistened with saliva.

"Where are you taking her?" I asked.

He started extinguishing candles with his fingers. The flames resisted bravely and died with a soft hiss, their souls drifting upwards on thin threads of smoke. Then, there was only one left.

"We'll be in touch," he repeated.

And then there was darkness.

I heard his footsteps as he left. The door swung on its rusty hinges a few times before it was quite again and I was alone.

I did not find it in myself to try to follow him – them. I swept all the cards off the table and rested my forehead on the edge of the board.

X.

Germany always gave me the creeps. Feeling like Jonah in the belly of Leviathan. Ironic, since in many ways it was safer than all the other places I had to travel through; no partisans blowing up trains, not so many trigger-happy soldiers, not all passer-bys presumed hostile by watchful eyes of secret police. We were all Germans after all. Still *ein Fuhrer, ein Reich, ein Volk*, maybe not Hitler-lovers all anymore, but all in this together, bombed out just the same by the British and Americans.

There were about two dozen people inside the station hall. All civilians. People who couldn't blink. A few spoke in hushed voices, but most remained silent, avoiding eye contact, too preoccupied with their own private predicaments to care about others. Children slept on the seats, huddled against their parents who were denying themselves the luxury of rest. Every few minutes, public announcements would come out through the megaphones, but even the station master's voice was no more than a barely amplified whisper. There wasn't any good news tonight, only more delayed trains. No apologies anymore from the railways, no anger and frustration from the passengers. Resignation hung in the air like a heavy mist.

I had only just caught up with von Schellendorff before it was time to say goodbye again.

"How are you keeping?" I asked him.

"Still surviving," he shrugged. What he must have thought was: just.

"How close are they?"

"Close," he said.

The contact had been re-established. Now the helper needed help.

"You know the biggest problem about being on the run?" he asked. "It's so damned difficult getting your hands on some morphine."

I didn't have any either. Bartok didn't turn me into a night pusher. Keeping von Schellendorff alive took priority over other concerns. I had carried a new set of fake documents and a box of bullets for his Mauser. After a quick exchange behind the building the contraband was now safely packed away in his coat pocket. God, it was strange seeing him not in uniform. He looked almost naked, a different person. He hadn't shaved either for a few days, something that was starting to make him stand out from the crowd. Bartok should have given me a razor instead of bullets.

"Will you manage?" I asked.

Von Schellendorff shrugged again. "I don't feel quite ready yet to shake hands with Miss Death." He winked at me, with a lot of effort, and then cast a slow glance around him, careful not to be too obvious. "Have to go," he said.

I nodded. We didn't shake hands.

Von Schellendorff turned on his heel and started walking towards the exit.

He was passing an elderly men who sat on top of his two suitcases in the middle of the floor when they moved in.

They appeared as if from nowhere, but they must have been hanging around all that time. Somehow, for all his careful glances, he had missed them. I had missed them too.

They didn't look like they normally did. That was part of the problem. No ankle-length leather coats and fedoras, much less uniforms, just normal woollen suits, bare heads, open faces. But the same air of purposeful, professional menace – once they sprung into action. Once they did, you knew. Once you knew, it was too late. Almost too late.

Von Schellendorff now saw them too. There were two men coming briskly towards him trying to catch him in a pincer. He couldn't see the third one, approaching him from behind.

Von Schellendorff froze in mid-movement, as his brain must have made a lightning calculation and instinct took over. He spun around and started running back. The third man lunged straight at him but the momentum was with von Schellendorff and he pushed him aside. The man tried to stay on his feet, and he took a short step back to maintain balance. He didn't see the elderly man and the two suitcases blocking his way.

Out of the corner of my eye I saw them both topple to the ground. The other two men leapt forward after von Schellendorff. "*Halt*," one of them shouted. They both reached inside their coats to pull out their guns. A woman somewhere behind me screamed and a child started wailing.

One of the men extended his arm and fired a shot at von Schellendorff. I heard the explosion, magnified by the vastness of the hall, and a ricochet spinning off the masonry like an angry bee.

More screams. Crazy movement on the periphery of my vision, people ducking to the floor, bodies crashing heavily. Somebody crying for help. "Stop," the man yelling again.

I should have started running too, but my feet froze to the marble floor. I half turned and saw von Schellendorff disappear among the colonnades along the far side of the hall.

The two Gestapo men – that's who I assume they were – were sprinting past me and the second one was also aiming in mid-run. I heard another shot. The man closer to me spun and stumbled. His gun crashed onto the floor and skidded away while he fell to his knees clutching his right arm.

The other Gestapo man stopped, crouched and fired. His shot hit a column and sprayed shattered flakes of sandstone.

From somewhere behind the colonnade von Schellendorff fired again. Before I heard the discharge, I felt the blast of wind passing too close to my left ear.

Fuck.

I crouched down instinctively.

Another shot went over my head, this time from behind. The third Gestapo man must have picked himself up from the ground.

I dived head first towards the nearest wall, away from the action. Bartok sent me with a box of spare bullets but not a gun of my own. Just as well; I don't think I would have been able to use it.

I landed on the floor and skidded forward just as another two shots sounded in quick succession. My elbow connected with the marble and pain shot along my hand, all the way through my shoulder and to my head. I grunted and swore and rolled onto my back. There was screaming all around me but it couldn't drown out the echoing ricochets.

I was turning my body to the side, when I felt something grasping at my right hand, now twisted behind my back.

"Daddy, daddy."

I turned my head and looked over my shoulder.

A boy, maybe four or maybe five years old, his face red and puffed up with tears, was sitting on the ground clutching my forearm. "Daddy," he kept repeating between loud sobs.

I'm not your daddy, I thought. I've got no idea where your daddy is. Daddy must have chosen the worst possible time to go answer the call of nature, or wherever the hell else he disappeared to.

Shit.

I rolled my body and was reaching with my left hand towards the boy. If not for that I wouldn't have noticed another man. The fourth one. Sprinting low to the ground.

Towards me.

Shit.

I closed my eyes.

* * *

No bullets whizzing above me, no woman shrieking madly, calling for God. No marble floor underneath me; more like concrete.

I opened my eyes and saw no lit-up arched roof, only the blackness of moonless sky. And the familiar humid summer air pressing down on me, with a fragrance of rot and industrial lubricant.

Welcome home.

Thank Christ, I exhaled under my breath.

I started moving my hand when I felt a tug of resistance.

"Daddy."

* * *

Oh Christ, oh God.

I kicked back and shot up standing, as if I just got touched by a plague victim.

The weight slipped off my hand and a body – a little body – hit the platform. The boy gave a cry of pain and erupted into sobs.

"Where is daddy?" he wailed, choking on his snot.

Oh Christ, oh God.

How did this happen? How the fuck did this happen?

How?

Bartok, you-

I dropped to my knees. My eyes had adjusted enough to the darkness and I could see the boy, sitting on the ground, his upper body rocking back and forth, his voice piercing the night like a little fire engine.

The boy I rescued from the shoot-out and brought back with me onto a filthy concrete platform of train yards in a kingdom far, far away.

"Where is daddy?" Another snort.

I grasped his shaking body in my hands and this only made him howl even louder.

"Shhhhhh," I stupidly implored him. As if that was going to make any difference.

Bartok, I'll kill you.

"Shhhhhh, everything will be all right," I said, knowing full well that whatever happened next, there was no chance of it being all right. None.

"I'll take you back to your daddy," I said.

How, you fool? I thought. Just how will you do it?

I don't know but I can't leave him here, can I?

Shit.

So I held him in my grasp and did the only thing that came to mind, the only thing that I could have done.

I closed my eyes again.

* * *

God help me, now I was hoping for the screams and the gunshots. Positively looking forward to it.

Strange how things turn out, isn't it?

To find myself again on the marble floor, caught between flying bullets, with a Gestapo man coming straight at me. Just for a second though, one second; long enough to shake off the little hand gripping my arm. And then bye bye again.

Just for a second.

Before I opened my eyes, there was sobbing. The familiar sound.

And nothing else.

I loosened my grip on the boy and pulled back.

Do you really want to look?

Yes. I have to.

"Daddy."

Much weaker, exhausted exclamation, drowned in hiccups.

I opened my eyes.

Same place.

The same arched ceiling supported by steel beams, illuminated by hanging lights; seats against the walls, colonnade along the length of the hall, obscuring the exits onto the platform.

And not a soul in sight.

I stood up and left the boy on the floor. There was no point even trying to console him.

The ticket window was boarded up. The clock hanging above it showed the time as being 4:35. I wish I could remember what time it was when I was here with von Schellendorff.

I walked around the hall. In the middle of the floor a rusty, dried-up stain. It didn't look good. On one of the columns a small crater chipped by a bullet. Did it happen only hours before? Or maybe days? One thing for sure; certainly not five minutes ago.

"Anyone in here?" I said. My voice came back to me as an echo, the only response. Somewhere behind me, the boy was still sobbing, but his spasms were quieter and further apart, as if he had finally cried himself out.

"Anyone?" I repeated, my stomach again curling itself up inside me. You just can't win; you feel sick when the guns are blazing, you feel sick when they're not.

I walked through the colonnade and through an open door onto the platform. The wind was swinging the lights, which creaked softly as they cast strange shadows on the walls of the building. A page of a newspaper shuffled slowly along the platform opposite, on the other side of the tracks. Somebody built a damned good station and forgot to put in the people. What a waste. Like some bloody ghost caravel.

I went back inside the building. The boy saw me again and that was enough to bring fresh tears to his eyes. I hurried across the hall and came out the other side, onto the street. The lights weren't working here and it was dark. The light coming in from the inside cast an uncertain circle that illuminated the pavement and the asphalt of the road within a radius of maybe seven or eight meters, beyond which the world stopped. There was no sound; no dogs barking in the distance, no car engine, no human voice.

I took the Lord's name in my thoughts. Again, in vain.

I could go out into the darkness, try to find the nearest house and ask for help. Dear lady, would you like to take care of this little boy? I slipped and fell in time and we lost his daddy. That would be the humanitarian thing to do, the only decent way out of the whole shambles. If only I knew it would work. If only I knew what would happen to me should I choose to stay here for another – what? – few minutes? Few hours?

You silly little brat. Why did you have to come to the station tonight? Why did your father have to leave you alone? Why did you have to grasp my hand? All good questions, but the answers didn't matter any more.

I could try to do the right thing. Or I could get the hell out of here. Now.

Suddenly a wave of fear hit me in the gut, and I saw myself stranded forever on a deserted train station, with an orphaned five year old in tow. And no way out, for him or for me. I gripped the doorframe to steady myself and took a deep, deep breath of fresh air.

Why don't you take him back with you, again?

But the thought wilted very quickly, a little flower under the scorching desert sun.

Take him back and then what? Hello sonny, welcome to the new world. If we have some time tomorrow, we'll look up on the internet the German White Pages and try to get you in touch with your grandchildren. If they exist anywhere in this world, that is.

Better to leave you. At least you belong here. Surely, somebody, sometime soon, will find you.

It's just bad luck that everything had to turn out the way it did. Real bad luck.

This was the hardest decision I ever had to make.

In the end, I leaned against the door and the last thing I heard as I closed my eyes was soft sobbing, echoing inside the station hall behind me.

* * *

And there was sobbing again.

I opened my eyes and sat up, so fast that my head spun.

I was in my bed, the sheets crumpled around me, the window in front of me open to the brilliance outside. I blinked my eyes a few times before they adjusted to the sunlight.

The sobbing.

Ah, the sobbing.

Again.

Somewhere inside the house, muffled by the closed door of my bedroom, a woman was weeping uncontrollably. There were other voices there too, but all I could hear was an indistinct murmur.

I stood up and stretched.

Not good, said the little voice inside me. Not good.

I opened the door and the sound of misery hit me with all its splendid force. The sobbing was coming from the kitchen, and as I walked down the corridor towards it I realized that I recognize the voice.

It was Julie.

My legs felt like they were made of lead, and I put all my strength to force each step. My heart pounded inside my chest, and the little voice fell silent, too scared to discover what lay ahead.

An hour, or more likely ten seconds later, I entered the kitchen.

Julie was sitting at the kitchen table, her head in her hands, her body shaking with hysteric tremors. Sitting next to Julie, with her arm around her was a girl whose face I vaguely remembered from somewhere but the name was escaping me. She turned her head towards me as I entered the kitchen and I could see that her eyes too were ringed in red. Another girl, Julie's friend Jackie, stood a few steps away, leaning back against the kitchen cabinets, her hands clasped together under her chin.

I opened my mouth, but the nameless girl beat me to it.

"Brad," she said.

Julie cried out and her body collapsed into her friend's arms.

"He's dead," the girl said. Her eyes bore into mine for a moment, before they clouded with tears, and they both sobbed, clutching each other desperately, like shipwrecks.

I took a step back and discovered the wall behind saved me from falling. Inside my head the little boy kept crying for his daddy.

*   *   *

"They were walking back from a party, early this morning," Jackie told me some half an hour later. "It was him and a few friends, just walking down the street, a bit drunk, but not that much. Then a car came, like out of nowhere. Brad was the one walking furthest away from the curb, and –"

She bit her lip and turned away to blow her nose.

"The car didn't stop afterwards. Just sped away. Brad was still alive, but when he got to hospital –"

It was too much for her now. She screwed her eyes shut but that couldn't stop the tears. I leaned across the table and put my hand over hers. I closed my eyes too, wishing – for so many reasons now – that I could turn back the clock by a few hours.

XI.

"You know, a few hours ago, I could have killed you, but now –" I merely shook my head.

"I am sorry," he said softly as he sat on the couch next to me. "About your friend."

He knew. Of course he knew. He knew everything, didn't he? Everything except how to unmake the whole mess.

It was afternoon, now. The first afternoon without Brad. The last few hours of all the tears, all the phone calls, all the meaningless words of sorrow, stirred into one horrible, never ending, unreal out of body experience. The police have taken care of notifying his parents. They lived in another city and wouldn't be here for some time yet. The funeral, the goodbyes and loose ends never to be quite tied up, Brad's possessions haunting the bedroom we locked up hours ago; all that we would have to face at some point in the future. Soon. But I couldn't think about it anymore.

"Why didn't you tell me?" I asked him.

This time he didn't try to twist and skulk around. "Knowing too much would not have helped you at all," he said.

"But you lied to me, you bastard," I raised my voice. I was angry about so many things, about almost getting shot by my friend, about the little boy ... about not having had the chance to say goodbye to Brad. And Bartok was here, and he'd better be ready to take it, because there was soooo much to take. "You lied to me. You told me that von Schellendorff and Katrina can't blink. Remember?"

"I –" he opened his mouth.

"Don't even try to bullshit your way out of it," I cut him off. My body rose and tensed as if I was preparing to pounce on Bartok. "I know what you're going to say –"

"What –"

"You're going to tell me that you weren't lying. You said that they couldn't blink, and that's technically true. But you didn't tell me that they – shit, everyone – could just hold onto me as I blink."

"Martin –"

"So don't even think of giving me that crap," I shouted at him. "It's bullshit."

I collapsed back into the couch and caught my breath. My fists were still clenched and fingernails dug into my flesh.

I wasn't finished. "Instead of riding the night trains with these people and crossing my fingers that they'll get through the border, I could have just grabbed them and closed my eyes, and hey presto, they would be safe."

But more than anyone else I thought about Katrina. Because if I knew before what I knew then, I would have folded her into my arms and then taken her away. We knew that every one of our meetings could be our last; there were plenty of opportunities. Goodbye war, hello new life. Would the shock of it all kill her or make her insane? Somehow I didn't think so. I have managed, going in the opposite direction. She wasn't any weaker a person than I was. Stronger, in many ways.

"Martin," he took advantage of my silence, "do you really think that you could just bring all those people back with you? Do you imagine you could really save them like that?"

"Hell, why not?" I said.

"And then what, Martin? What would you do with hundreds – no, thousands of people here? How would you deal with that?"

I didn't say anything. My head was gripped in a vice of a pounding ache, and every thought – particularly every logical thought – made the vice tighten just that little bit more.

"But never mind that," Bartok droned on. "That is not the most important reason why you could not have done it." He leaned towards me, as if he doubted that I could hear him well enough. I could. "Yes, you can bring people over. But how many people over here, people close to you, are you willing to sacrifice?"

A second later my head exploded.

* * *

Yin and yang. The eternal balance.

For every action, an equal and opposite reaction. Nothing's free, buddy; for everything you do, you pay the price. Or rather, somebody else does.

I had a choice not to believe him. But why wouldn't I? Why wouldn't I, at this point in time, after everything that has happened before? Wouldn't you?

A little boy grabs hold on to me and hitches a ride back. Even if for a brief moment, he crosses the line, wherever the hell that line is, and makes it over. Shouldn't be here; one extra body, one extra soul that doesn't belong around here. The balance is thrown off kilter. And so, for every plus you need a minus to cancel it out and get back to zero, the status quo. Not just any minus, not some poor sucker in Africa, maybe somebody terminally ill, beyond hope, already on the way out. No. Because there is savage equilibrium in it all; you break it, you own it.

So, Martin, how does it feel to kill a friend?

Yes, be my guest, reunite with your love. But who will you sacrifice in exchange this time? Your mother? Your father? Your –

"Why didn't you tell me?" the little boy sobbing inside my head was now me.

"Because it would not have changed anything. And can you really tell me that now that you know, you are better and happier for the knowledge?'

And the boy wailed away.

XII.

The heavens opened that night and came down upon the sleeping world. The thunder rolled in from above, taking over where the guns had left off at dusk. I watched the lightning on the horizon. For a brief moment it looked like the sky was supported by brilliant crooked columns. Then they would vanish and darkness would collapse onto the earth again.

I did not make any attempt to shield myself from the rain. There was nothing to pull over my head, and nowhere to hide, except under the train itself. I threw my head backwards and opened my mouth to taste the water falling from heaven.

I closed my eyes and remembered the handwritten words of Bartok's last message: "V.S. will be transported on a special train. It is the last chance to rescue him before he disappears in Dachau. The engine driver knows."

Short and to the point, that's how it has always been. In my head I tried to fill in all the blanks. What was I supposed to do, exactly? I now knew there was one less option left open. Not after Brad. Not after all that. I knew that now, but at what price.

So whatever would happen, von Schellendorff had to remain here. Yet I had no sanctuary for him. Even if I somehow managed to rescue him from the train, there was nowhere I could take him. Would that matter at all, or was I merely supposed to make a futile and symbolic gesture in defense of friendship and honor, the last, suicidal cavalry charge? Still thinking about you, my friend, take heart – that sort of thing.

It was too easy to lose all sense of time and stand there, by the train, bathing in the deluge.

C'mon, knight in shining armor.

But all I had on me were some dirty, worn-out work clothes of a laborer. I checked the pockets. No documents. Only a box of matches, a matted handkerchief and a pocket knife. All I needed to rescue von Schellendorff. And still no idea where exactly on the train he was being held, how many others were there, and whether Behrnard was here with him, too. I didn't even know where I was.

The train itself was put together from passenger carriages, but each one of them different, a jumble of eras and nationalities. It looked like the last few spoils of conquests thrown hastily together in the service of a lost cause. Somewhere onboard this rolling museum was a precious artifact I came here tonight to fetch from the thieves who stole it. Very precious.

The thunder was now rolling away and it took the heavy rain with it. All that was left was a drizzle and sudden gusts of icy wind. The magic had vanished and my body was shaken by a violent shiver. It was time to go.

I started trotting, bent to the ground, almost on all fours, trying to hide from the wind and inquisitive eyes. The engine was just a few wagons away. The engine driver knows, I remembered.

When I was half-way there, the giant stirred. It came to life with a reluctant grunt and then a jerk. Couplings crashed together and the train began slowly inching forward, unhappy to be awakened from its slumber. I made the distance past the last few wagons and the tender in a few seconds. Then there was nothing ahead of me but the engine.

I grabbed the handrail and sprang up. Virtually the same moment as my feet left the ground my hand slipped off the iron rod. The rainwater. I tumbled down, my arms waving chaotically in front of me, trying to protect my face from impact. I hit the escarpment and desperately clutched the ground to prevent myself from rolling down the into the gully.

There was no time to worry about the pain. I scrambled up and lunged forward. I was out of breath when I finally caught up with the engine. Now there wouldn't be any margin for error. I threw my hands at both the handrails and grasped them very hard, as if I wanted to squeeze the life out of them.

I yanked myself upwards. Half-way through the movement a thought crossed my mind: what if the engine driver is not alone? What if there is a guard with him? But it was too late to stop.

He was alone.

I saw a man of uncertain age, a man whom years have not treated fairly. Deep lines ran through his face giving him a look of perpetual worry. He didn't betray surprise. He had obviously seen too much and expected very little.

I pulled myself up onto the floor of the cabin. By now the train was moving at some speed and I had caught him in mid-movement as he prepared to load another shovelful of coal into the firebox.

"Hello," I said. It sounded silly but I couldn't think of anything else to say.

He nodded in response.

I stood up and leaned against the wall of the cabin. It was warm here but I was still shivering.

"C'mon, what you're looking at?" he extended his hand towards me holding the shovel. "It's not gonna go on magic."

The wooden handle was blackened by soot, yet at the same time smooth, polished by a thousand hands. My palms were still burning fiercely after the fall but I gripped the shovel and got down to work. The driver didn't look like a man who would take any excuses about unfortunate tumbles.

There was still some coal left on the floor of the cabin. I shovelled it against the wall and dumped it inside the firebox. The heat was intense and my rain-soaked clothes started drying up on me.

After we were finished my companion closed the fire door and stood with his arms folded, watching with pride his engine at work.

"There's no other machine like it, my friend," he spoke out. "There hasn't been one and there never will be. Beautiful," he stretched the word.

"Yes," I said. He obviously didn't expect me to be a part of his fraternity.

"You see, there is a tank full of water with a furnace inside it," he spoke to me. His voice was strong and clear, easily audible above the noise of the engine. With his hand he was absent-mindedly caressing the blower valve, as if the machinery were his lover. "The coal burns and water turns to steam, steam moves through the cylinder and pushes a piston. The piston is linked with the wheels. The secret – one of them, in any case – is the water. It can't fall below the top of the furnace, otherwise everything's gonna blow up."

A very simple lesson, Locomotives 101. I nodded attentively. The coal burns on the grate, the water travels down the pipes to the boiler. Heated, it expands 1,700 times and in the form of steam animates the cylinder and the piston. Fire and water and steel, that's all you need. If everything was as simple in life, I thought.

In my travels I rediscovered an old love, the one from my childhood. There was something gorgeous about steam engines, and sad at the same time, like watching an aged starlet. They were a relic of the vanished world when progress was celebrated and not feared, and technology awed and enthused. It was our last altar where we could still worship fire and not appear barbaric.

And so my companion and I worshipped in silence as we ran through the night, safe and warm, encrusted in the armor of steel. For a while it seemed there was nothing else, just us and the engine herself. No war, no ravaged land around us, no von Schellendorff somewhere behind us on the train, in fact no train at all.

"Where is he?" I finally asked the engine driver.

"The sixth carriage down the train," he sighed and rubbed his nose.

"How well is he guarded?"

"Well enough, I think," he shrugged, pretending to pay attention to the gauges.

"Will you stop the train?" I asked.

"I can't," he said. "I can only slow it down a bit." He looked at me, and his face seemed even more furrowed with deep lines. "I guess you don't have much experience going over the roofs while the train's going?"

I shook my head. That, and rescuing heavily guarded prisoners, with no real means of getaway. When I really needed help, I was completely on my own. I didn't even have spare clothes or documents for von Schellendorff.

"Thank you," I said. "It will have to do."

He murmured something in response and turned back to his instruments. I think he was relieved to see me go. Who, after all, would want to take more risks so close to the end? I left him alone to ponder on the mystery and the beauty of steam engines and to dream of a new world – better world – where he would not have to tow their trains.

Getting on top of the tender was not difficult but even that left me out of breath and with my heart trembling uncontrollably somewhere close to my throat. I lay on the mound of coal for some time trying to calm down and to plan the next move. The sharp, jagged edges of coal blocks digging into my body finally drove me onward. When I crouched down on top of the pile the wind started rushing at me, urging me onwards to the sixth carriage down from the engine.

The train was steaming ahead fast. How fast, I couldn't exactly guess, nor did I want to. I braced myself, swung my arms and launched myself towards the roof of the first wagon, one meter away and half a meter up. My life didn't flash in front of my eyes. Only the old question: why me? Before

I had time to think of an answer I was lying flat on top of the carriage, my limbs outstretched in a physically futile attempt to grab hold of the edges of the roof.

If the rain didn't make the surfaces slippery, and I felt a bit braver, I would now sprint in movie-style action. Instead, the journey towards the sixth carriage was a slow, nerve-racking crawl. Down the length of each wagon, crouch, jump onto the next one, steady yourself and crawl again. When I finished my clothes were wet again. I stunk of fear, too.

The fifth carriage, finally. I lay myself sideways near the edge of the roof, gripped it with left hand and then threw my legs over the side.

In the fraction of a second after the bulk of my body left the roof I caught its edge with my other hand. My body swung like a wild pendulum and my arms almost gave way. I gasped as my muscles threatened to tear themselves off the bones, but I held my grip and after a moment steadied myself.

Slowly, I lowered onto the wagon's bumpers. I didn't want, but I had to look down at my feet. It was too dark to see anything more than the blurry movement itself. It was enough, though, to set my stomach churning. Only when my feet were firmly planted on the metal protrusions and my hands hugged the back of the wagon did I allow myself to close my eyes and breathe out.

Somehow I managed to turn around and move onto the bumpers of the next carriage, and then over the barrier onto the small platform. I gripped the door handle and squeezed my face against the window trying to peer through the dirty glass.

The only impression breaking out of the dark was emptiness. It looked like all the seats inside the carriage have been removed, leaving only empty space. A chapel without pews. No movement, no sign of life. Would they keep a prisoner like von Schellendorff here? Surely the engine driver must have been mistaken.

I had no choice, really.

There would have been a lot of noise had the train been standing still. Now, the screech was barely audible, a lonely false note lost in the middle of a wild symphony.

I squeezed in through the narrow opening and closed the door behind me. My body was still trembling and my ears buzzed with the wind.

I could see no more than from the outside.

My hand fished around for a while before I managed to pull out the matches. There weren't many left in the box. I took one out, struck it against the wall, and started walking down the carriage.

A naked shape was lying on the floor, only a few meters from the door. It was a man but the sight was barely human. His body was curled up in a fetal position and his limbs twitched continuously as if a low current was passing through him. A skeleton with a sheet of skin decently draped over the bones. His body was covered in the filth he was laying in, seemingly oblivious, unhearing, unseeing, unfeeling. Mucus, vomit, shit, all mixed together. I didn't want to see it, but it was too late. The wave of nausea hit me and I turned my head away, gasping for air.

Then my mind clicked, and the second wave punched me in the gut.

Von Schellendorff.

At the very moment that light lit up my mind, the match scorched my fingers and went out.

Oh, Christ.

With trembling hands I again took the matches out of my pocket. When I tried to open the box it slipped out of my fingers.

Shit ... Shit, shit, shit, shit.

I ran towards von Schellendorff. The absence of light was a blessing anyway.

"Hans," I whispered, kneeling by his side.

He didn't react.

My outstretched hand hovered in mid-air, hesitant to touch him. But I eventually did.

He was slippery like an eel, covered in his body fluids. I nearly threw up from the stench and the feel of filth under my touch. I twisted my head and buried the nose in my arm. I waited for the sick feeling to recede and then I shook him gently.

"Hans. Can you hear me?"

He grunted, but I don't know whether that was recognition of my voice or a plea to whoever was touching him to leave him in peace.

"Hans. We have to get out of here," I whispered, louder this time. "Quickly."

I had no idea what to do. Alone, I could countenance the crazy notion of jumping out of the train, even at this speed, and take the risk of broken bones and concussion. Jumping with him was impossible. I couldn't see whether there was an emergency brake anywhere in the carriage, but even if there was one, I couldn't use it.

There was nothing I could do, but I could not do nothing. I skirted around him and put my hands under his arms. His body glowed with an unhealthy warmth.

At that moment the door at the other end of the carriage opened and a beam of light shone directly at me.

* * *

"*Hände hoch!*"

The light is a blinding sphere that obscures everything behind it.

"*Hande hoch!*" the man shouts at me. "Hands up! On your head!"

I try to lay von Schellendorff gently back on the floor but he slips out of my grip and his back connects with the wooden boards with a thud. A gasp escapes his mouth.

"Hands up!"

I raise my hands and straighten up.

"Well, well, well," I hear another voice, one that I know so well.

The man with the torch comes towards me along the side windows. He stops a few paces away from me. The end of the barrel of his submachine gun and his knee-high leather boots materialize out of the glare. I turn my head away from the light. Behrnard is coming towards me. There is another man walking behind him.

"Voigt, you naughty boy," he wags his finger at his torch-bearing minion. "I told you not to leave our guest alone. You were supposed to protect him from ... intruders."

Voigt remains silent, letting his superior take center stage.

"Remember, if you see him closing his eyes, shoot," Behrnard tells his men.

My heart skips a beat.

He knows. Of course. You can't just disappear all the time without questions being asked. Particularly in the middle of a station hall, right in front of a Gestapo man's eyes. It's pretty clear, but the realization still grips my throat in a vice.

Hell, maybe I could try to blink, but can I blink fast enough?

"Herr Bittmann," Behrnard takes a mocking bow. "How rude of me not to introduce you. This is Herr von Schellendorff. Of the good von Schellendorffs." He steps towards Hans-Bernd and nudges him with the tip of his boot. "Old nobility," he winks at me.

"You fuck," I whisper through my clenched teeth. There's a rage in me, but it's a rage of helplessness. Complete and utter helplessness.

"Oh? Did I step on somebody's toes?" Behrnard sneers. "Or do you two know each other already?"

"You are a comedian, Behrnard," I say. The second SS man positions himself against the opposite side wall of the carriage, to my right. His hand gun is also aimed at me and I have no doubt that it can come alive in an instant.

"How noble of you to try to rescue your dear old friend," the mask of mockery slips form Behrnard's face. His voice is now steady, serious, a matter of fact. "And how stupid." He stands behind von Schellendorff's body, feet slightly apart, hands clasped behind his back. "Did you think that we were just going to wave him a tearful goodbye at the station and send him all alone on his journey?"

Von Schellendorff moans. The SS man on my left tightens the grip on his gun.

"Not after I've spent so much time on this chase," Behrnard says. "Him, and all his filthy friends." He pauses. "He and his kind always made me sick," he cringes, "a long time before he was covered in his own shit and stank to high heaven like some gutter vermin."

If I try to launch myself at Behrnard I will be dead before my fingers claw at his face. If I try to go at the man on my left and grab at his gun I'll be dead even quicker. And death solves nothing.

Even if I could blink I can't leave Hans behind.

"A bit worse for wear, isn't he?" Behrnard says. "Of course, I always knew that our friend had a little problem." He chuckles and starts circling around von Schellendorff like a museum guide explaining an exhibit to visitors; clinical and confident. I hate him so much that I forget for a moment who he is to me.

"Do you know what happens to a person who is denied his daily dose of morphine?" Behrnard stops and looks up at me. But he doesn't wait for any reply, "No? I'm going to tell you."

Von Schellendorff gives a barely audible whimper. I am going crazy, not knowing whether all my attention should now be concentrated on him or on his tormentor.

"Some twelve hours after the last dose of morphine the patient starts weakening," Behrnard continues. He is standing just outside the arc of light, and I can't see his face now. There's only voiceover to his documentary.

"He sweats, and is raked by shivers. A discharge starts running from his eyes and from his nose. In quite fantastic amounts. I would have never thought that a human body can expel so much water. And that's just the beginning."

He pauses to take out a cigarette and lights it. He tosses out the still burning match towards von Schellendorff. It flies off in an arc but falls short of its target.

"The patient is lucky if he can get any sleep. If it comes to him, it's short and restless. But usually it avoids the man altogether. The patient keeps yawning. Yawning so hard that his jaw dislocates. And the water just keeps pouring all this time. But that's not the worst of it. Around 24 hours after the last dose of morphine, his insides are like a sack full of fighting rodents. They convulse, contract, and twist, expelling everything there is inside and then some more. The patient vomits profusely, until there isn't anything more than blood left. But still he vomits. And he shits himself. Thirty, forty, maybe fifty times a day."

Behrnard takes another drag. "You see, I wouldn't have known all this if I didn't have a chance to observe it first hand." He exhales and a cloud of smoke drifts into the light. "They say you learn something new every day. How true that is. How true."

My jaw is clenched so tight it hurts.

"Thirty six hours after the last dose the patient starts having convulsions," he pushes on relentlessly. "Like epileptic fits but more violent. He keeps on sweating, keeps on vomiting, keeps on shitting, and water still comes out of his eyes and his nose. What he excretes he doesn't make up for. Since he doesn't eat, he loses weight. By that stage he becomes so weak that he cannot move."

He pauses for a moment, "You see, I don't know yet what happens after 48 hours because we haven't arrived at that stage."

"You motherfucker," I whisper. I want to shout but my voice gets lost somewhere inside my throat.

Behrnard appears not to have heard me. "And through all this I did not even have to touch him. Not at all. They didn't teach us this method." He flicks the butt of his cigarette away. " Fancy that. I didn't have to touch him at all. Yet he told me everything."

That could be all or nothing, or maybe a bluff, but in the end it doesn't matter. Von Schellendorff must be among the last to get caught. By now they must know as much as he does anyway. Behrnard might not have learned a lot about me but he knows the most important piece of information. He hasn't learned it from von Schellendorff either. And –

Before I know it, I feel a hand gripping my wrist.

I focused so much on Behrnard that I didn't notice the SS man on my right moved quickly towards me. Now my hand is caught in a human handcuff and I can't move.

"You see, Bittmann," my grandfather says, "We've been watching you too, and for quite some time we were mystified how you always managed to evade us. But then we finally had a breakthrough. One of our people saw you do your magic trick."

I feel the SS man's grip tighten even more and I wince.

"I, of course, was skeptical at first," Behrnard continues, "but then I was watching over a certain action, and I saw you make your unexpected exit. What's more, you even managed to take someone with you."

So he was there, that night, somewhere, observing us.

"The world's full of wonders," he says. "I have to confess that I didn't use to think much about all that stuff Reichsfuhrer Himmler cares about; astrology, occult, and the rest. But now," he chuckles, "well, now I'm a believer."

His laughter rings in my ears and I want to cover them with my hands to make it stop, but I can't. Or choke it out of his throat. I can't do that either.

"So, Bittmann, we decided that Ingo here," Behrnard nods at the SS man gripping my hand, "will keep you company. Just in case you get an idea to leave us he will go with you. He's also instructed to use his gun if necessary."

The other SS man, Voight, comes over to me and takes out a roll of bandages out of his pocket. He cradles his flashlight between his raised shoulder and his inclined head and proceeds to wrap the dressing around where Ingo's and my hand meet.

"That's just in case Ingo's grip gets tired," Behrnard explains. "He wouldn't want to lose you."

Voight finishes his work, and ties the bandage tight. Ingo is my wound. What an ugly cancer. Then Voight goes through my pockets and fishes out the knife. He shows it briefly to Behrnard before pocketing it away. Matches first, then the knife. Now all I have left is the handkerchief.

Behrnard looks happy. One problem taken care of.

"It's time to end the charade, isn't it?" he asks his SS men. They understand it's a rhetorical question. He comes towards von Schellendorff and slowly takes his Mauser out of the holster.

"No!" I scream out.

I feel a tug pulling me back and I cannot forget even for a moment that now I have my very own Siamese twin.

"No," I say again and this time it comes out so dull, as if something was sitting on my chest.

Behrnard extends his arm.

"Goodbye, von Schellendorff," he says and then he pulls the trigger. Once. Twice. Three times.

I look away but I still hear everything, amplified a thousand times. The thud of explosions, the groans, the echo that goes on forever inside my head.

"Shot while trying to escape," Behrnard says.

The darkness swirls around me.

"Take him away," he orders. He's talking about me.

Ingo takes a step forward.

"Where is she?" I ask.

Behrnard is not thrown off by my question. "She's safe," he says. He puts his gun back into the holster. "Such a wonderful woman. I wouldn't let anything happen to her," he forces his lips into a smile. The executioner posing for a snapshot with a gallows in the background bares his teeth and his eyes become mere slits. He extends his hand and taps me on the cheek.

Ingo pulls me along towards the back of the carriage.

"We'll talk in the morning," Behrnard calls after me.

So, I've failed. The first time there was no routine, the first time I had to show some imagination and initiative, I've failed. And someone ended up dead. Again.

All I have now is the memory of him as he was and as I want to remember him. I choose not to think of him onboard his last train. He was too far gone by the time I got there, barely a human being anymore, lost in his own private hell. I hope, at least, that by this stage he didn't realize what was happening around him.

* * *

I'm sharing a compartment with Ingo. We're in a different carriage now, one that still resembles the old luxury self. We sit on a plush seat that now feels grimy and damp to the touch. Our bodies are turned towards each other because of the way we're bound together. I know he's looking at me most of the time, so I turn my ahead away from him.

Behrnard doesn't know it, but even if I wanted to, I can't blink. And it's not because I'm afraid of Ingo's gun, although the fact that he can shoot me in an instant does play on my mind. But no, I simply cannot afford to bring that creature over and lose yet another person close to me.

So you see, we're stuck together. At least for the time being.

How do you separate Siamese twins, doctor?

Well, surgery is necessary.

But what if one of the twins dies during the operation?

Well, that happens sometimes. I still think surgery is the only viable option.

Doctor, one of the twins has got a gun. He's also a trained killer. Surely, that increases the chances of his survival?

Oh, yes.

Is the situation truly hopeless then, doctor?

Not necessarily. I recommend you wait.

Wait for what?

The right moment, my dear. The right moment.

So I wait, and the train inevitably ploughs its way through the night, all the way to Dachau, the end.

I know that Behrnard doesn't want me dead. At least not yet. If he did, there were plenty of opportunities; I could have taken the fourth bullet after von Schellendorff. But Behrnard needs me for now. I am Himmler's magic in action; I shouldn't exist but I do. What great many possibilities I might hold. Yes, I'm still more valuable alive.

That's why Ingo's gun is not aimed at me; it is the last resort. He does not put it away on the foldout table by the window, or on the seat next to him. After all, should I blink and take him with me to wherever I go to, he needs to have his weapon with him. It's in his holster now, but if I start causing any trouble there will be plenty of time to pull it out on me. In the meantime, he won't oblige me and fall asleep; there will be no chance for me to lean over and remove it from him. No, I have to wait for some other opportunity. What it is, I don't know, but I pray that it will come, and that when it does, my wits will be quick enough for me to realize what's happening and grab the chance.

And so I wait.

Later, our train starts slowing down. I feel him stir. His grip on my wrist feels warm and sticky, like some parasitic growth on my skin.

He looks towards the window. Are we coming to our destination? I hope not. Not yet.

He doesn't say anything but he drags himself to stand up and drags me with him. He's curious. This makes me think it's not Dachau yet. I think he wants to know why the train is now coming to a halt after such a long smooth run. So he lowers his head and tries to peer through the window, naively hoping that out of the darkness will come an answer.

Ingo is bigger, heavier and stronger than me. He's far deadlier too, trained to kill without hesitation or remorse, kill quickly and effectively. He's also attached to me. On the other hand, the only thing I've got going for me is desperation. I know that if the gods will smile upon me, it will only be a fleeting smile, and only once.

Doctor, is the time right now?

I think so, my dear, but you have to be fast.

I know, doctor. I know. Faster than I've ever been in my life. Move as if my life depends on it. Because my life does depend on it.

It is just one movement. With the corner of his eye he catches the glimpse of my left hand exploding towards the back of his neck. When his body reacts, my hand is already gripping the collar of his uniform. By the time he starts to half-turn towards me, I put the whole of my weight and strength behind the push.

It all lasts maybe a second, but I still see it as if in slow motion.

He tips forward, directed by my hand and propelled by the momentum of my body. His head connects with the window and for a briefest of moments it seems that he will merely bounce back.

But he doesn't. I hear the window crack and the glass explodes outwards as his head exits the carriage.

I lift my legs off the floor and let gravity take me down. He can't refuse me – his hand is still joined to my wrist and my other hand holds tight to his collar. Before he can do anything, my weight drags him down.

I can't see it, but I imagine how the shards of glass in the window frame slash his skin and dig into his neck. One long piece cuts his windpipe and slashes his aorta, before the weight of our two bodies pries it out of the window, still embedded in him.

We fall onto the floor of the compartment, and his blood, guzzling out of his neck like from a broken hose, showers upon me.

I hear his wrist bone give way as his hand twists in an unnatural angle. I roll on top of him and put all my strength, what remains of it, into holding him down. He doesn't scream, he can't, only gargles while his body thrashes around in violent convulsion. But he won't shake me off.

So we dance together. Until it's all quiet again.

How did it go doctor?

Operation successful, the patient's dead.

I lie on top of the dead body and think: I've just killed a man. But at this very moment, the thought seems no more shocking to me than if I had just swatted a cockroach. My heart races, my lungs are trying to keep up and stay in the race, my ears pound like a stadium full of fanatical fans cheering their team on. And the adrenaline floods my body like the surge of a broken dam. I've just killed a man, slashed his throat on a window, and all I want to do is sit on top of him and keep stubbing him with a shard of glass, a dozen times, a hundred times, a thousand times. He's not a person anymore, he's all of them, a symbol, and I want to wipe out all traces of him – them – all the memory, the last spark of life that might lay buried somewhere deep inside.

Excuse me, my dear, but the operation is not quite finished yet. Your twin might be dead, but you're still attached to each other, the good Siamese twins that you are.

You're right doctor. Absolutely right.

I sit up on top of him and with my left hand I feel around the bandage. Only now I notice that my hand is bleeding. I had cut myself too as I propelled him through the window. Broken glass must have slashed my skin when my hand went outside clutching his collar. No matter, a small price to pay.

Shit. I can't seem to untie the bandage. Voight has been very skilful. I don't know how he did it but I can't find the end of the dressing, or the knot, to start untangling it.

I hope that no one heard the sound of breaking glass. The train was still in motion at that time. I just hope that there aren't any other people in the neighboring compartments. I think not, or they would be here by now. Still, my dear, you don't have too much time.

Yes doctor, I understand. Unless I can separate myself from my twin, the operation will experience complications and both patients will end up dead.

I just can't get that bandage off. Just can't.

My mind still races ahead in leaps and bounds, but it's not aimless. It races in good directions. In a flash I know there's only one thing I can do, only one way out.

I plant my feet firmly on both sides of his body and bend over to put my left hand, still bleeding, under his body. I strain, hoping that my back won't decide to give up on me at this crucial moment. Slowly, very slowly, I manage to lift his body, first to the sitting position, and then get his ass off the ground. His blood doesn't gush anymore but it still spills his spent life force all over my chest. I pretend I can't see his face, hideously deformed by pain, bobbing from side to side only inches away from my own.

I don't know how I'm able to do it. Must be that pure adrenaline rushing through my veins now.

I lean Ingo against the window and with my free hand and elbow I smash out of the frame any remaining fragments of glass. Then I push both of us once again, praying that the fall will be gentle.

We pivot on the frame and then tumble outside into the night.

He breaks my fall, good boy. His wrist is gone, so it bends comfortably to accommodate my hand. The impact still pumps all the air out of my lungs and I choke as we roll down the gentle incline away from the train. Not too far away though. When we stop I finally manage to catch my breath.

I lay in the grass, still attached to my guardian, and after a few moments I realize that the train has stopped too.

This is the worst possible moment. What if somebody checks up on us and raises the alarm? Or maybe simply sees us lying on the escarpment. I can hardly run anywhere. Maybe now I can close my eyes. What would happen if I brought back a dead man? Would it work backwards, and require a plus to compensate for the minus that crossed over? Maybe one of my friends would get pregnant as a result.

I listen in, but there is no sound coming from the train.

My mind still doesn't stop. Before I quite know it, I'm crawling back towards the train, dragging the dead weight with me. By the time I reach the track I feel like any second I'm going to collapse from exhaustion. I would crumple if I already wasn't sprawled on the ground.

One last strain, one last effort and I roll Ingo's body over the track, under the carriage. Only his arm is sticks out, resting across the iron rail.

And I wait.

Eventually the train awakens again, and moves forward. Then I turn my head away and wait for the sound of separation.

Only after the train is gone I get up. My legs almost refuse to support me and I sway gently in the breeze. The cooling hand is still gripping my wrist but it's no longer attached to anything heavy and dead.

I hope that the whole thing with crossing over works on one complete human body as the basic unit of accounting. I hope that none of my friends or loved ones is going to lose their left hand after I get back.

Just before my legs are about to finally give up on me, I close my eyes.

XIII.

The question was so simple and straightforward, yet it eluded me until now. You see, it wasn't a matter of 'where' – it was a matter of 'when.' As in: when were the others?

By the time I asked the question, the answer was almost irrelevant, academic. But I wanted to hear it nevertheless.

A paradox: I was just another one of Bartok's recruits, a replacement for others who have come before me but didn't make it till the end. Yet, my missions started right at the beginning of the war and continued right until its end, which I was now approaching.

So when were they, these others before me? When did they have time to die?

I never asked Katrina and von Schellendorff. It simply did not occur to me before. They never mentioned anyone else, any others like me.

And even if they did not die, I never met them in my travels.

Or have I? How could I be sure? Would I have recognized a fellow traveller in a French peasant passing a small parcel to me, or in a Polish courier disappearing back into the darkness after I'd arrived to take over escorting some fugitives? Even if I had thought about it before, I couldn't have asked everyone I'd ever come across there under the cover of night: "Are you from my world?" Of course not.

"The others that you said died," I asked Bartok. "How could they have died before me if I started riding the night trains right from the start of the war?"

He opened his mouth to speak but I wasn't finished yet, "Or if they did not die before my time, but sometime while I was already involved, how could you have known that they would ... they would die, and therefore that you would need me? Can you see the future? And if so –"

"Slow down, slow down," this time he interrupted me.

"– tell me what's going to happen next? And tell me why we still do it if you already know the outcome?"

I caught my breath and waited on him to respond.

"Maybe," he said, "because it is all happening now, as we speak ... Many people, many places?"

He looked up at me and his eyes tried to fathom whether I understood his cryptic confession.

No ... Yes ...

Any answer was likely to disturb me. Wasn't ignorance bliss?

"But if there are dozens, thousands of ... whatever ... wars with their own night trains, then what does it matter if I get involved, if I succeed?" I asked him.

"Oh yes, it does matter," he said. "If you spent your whole life painting pictures, would you not like just one of them to come out perfect?"

"Good God. So that's what were doing here, painting pictures. What the hell am I, then? The picture itself, canvas, paint, the brush, or the hand that moves it?"

He only shrugged, as if my inquiry did not deserve an answer.

I persisted. "So it doesn't really matter whether I win or lose or draw if there are thousands of those ... paintings being painted. There's always going to be somebody who will succeed, get ten out of ten. So what does it matter in the big bloody scheme of things what I do?"

"You think it does not matter. And even if it did not matter ... in the great big bloody scheme of things, would it not matter to you?" Bartok leaned back in the seat and looked at me. "Would it not matter to you?" he repeated quietly.

How does it feel to be inside a game, toy soldier? Somebody out there must really love it, playing it a hundred, a thousand times. With me, with countless others before I came in, while I'm here, and after I'm gone. And if there really are hundreds, or thousands, or God knows how many, different Europes, all shrouded by night and by the war, then what is happening in all of them? Does Hitler win in some of them, or is history immutable? Is the purpose of it all to save as many lives as possible or to save oneself?

But most of all my thoughts keep coming back to her. Are there places where she dies, or does she survive everywhere? Will she always fall into Behrnard's hands or did it all happen this way just this once, just for me? And, in all those different worlds, with their own compulsory heroes dragged from our night to their's, whose lover is she then?

XIV.

The boy is looking at me intently as if trying to find something in my eyes – hope, reassurance perhaps. He must be fourteen or fifteen, I think. He still belongs to the warmth of home, among model airplanes made of balsa wood, and adventure books that take you to the wild savannas of Africa or the mysterious islands of the South Seas. But he's also quite big for his age, amply filling the dirtied Hitler Youth winter uniform. He looks so out of place in it now, like a boy who's lost his way home from a neighborhood parade and is still desperately trying to get back.

I must look strange and out of place to him, too, in my freshly pressed clean uniform. The boy is used to seeing trains and lorries full of soldiers with hollow faces and unseeing eyes. No one cares anymore to button up correctly, no one has time to polish their boots. It's the beggars' army. He must see me as a ghost from the old glorious times that now seem like they never really existed.

I am a ghost, I think to myself.

"How old are you?" I ask.

"Fourteen and a half, Major," the boy answers with a hushed voice.

"What are you doing here?"

"We are manning an anti-aircraft battery, Major," the boy says vaguely nodding his head to his left. "We were called a up few weeks ago."

Hitler has run out of warriors. It's time now for the Fatherland to devour its children. The boys and their grandfathers will make the final sacrifice. Duty calls. We're all so proud.

"What's your name, son?" I ask and then realize the absurdity of calling someone his age 'son.' It doesn't matter anymore, though. I'm the officer here and that makes me everybody's father.

"Helmut, Major," the boy answers. "Helmut Kohl."

Tanks roar along, somewhere off in the distance, crawling along the night roads on the last few drops of fuel. I slowly extend my hand and ruffle the boy's hair, somehow strangely embarrassed by this attempt to comfort him.

"You're doing fine, Helmut," I murmur, barely audibly.

It's time to go.

"Major," the boy calls after me.

I stop and turn around.

He is still standing in his spot, the palms of his hands self-consciously pressed against the sides of his legs. There is a question in his eyes.

I wait.

"Major, will it end soon?"

I think of other boys, elsewhere, unwisely asking some other officer the very same question. Boys then taken away, into some ditch or a grove or an empty yard, shot and hanged for exhibiting defeatist sentiments and lack of faith in the Thousand Year Reich. The last spasm of the Fatherland, the last sacrifice, no more and no less senseless than all the others.

"Yes," I say slowly. I'm glad it's me here to answer him.

The boy's not looking at me anymore. His gaze is turned away, and he tries to peer through the darkness.

"Yes." I turn around and walk away.

Not far to go. Only to meet him again. For the second last time, I hope.

*　*　*

How much a man can change in a short time, I'm thinking as I look at him. He still glows in his dark uniform, but it is a feverish glow. He's burning up the last of the fuel left in him and there is nothing more to replenish it. What animates him now is momentum; only to make it through one more day, then another, and then, maybe, make it through. He's got a restless look about him, a man who understands that the end may come at any moment, but won't invite it, and when it does come, he will fight against it until he's got no strength left in him.

How could I possibly pity him? His masters are dying, and with them, the dark spark that has fired him up and gave his life some semblance of meaning. He's built his life around hounding his masters' enemies only to discover now that it has all been in vain. For as the enemies were rooted out from within they're now pouring in from without, a hundred new ones for every one expunged before.

Surely this man cannot really be my grandfather. I must be mad to believe Bartok. I am not like him, I keep telling myself. There is nothing of him in me. I know that. And yet –

To find seclusion one has to break out of the crazy mill of disoriented refugees and shell-shocked soldiers, climb over mountains of luggage and discarded containers of provisions, leave the noise behind. Walk past the burned out carriages and charred, twisted skeletons of vehicles, abandoned in the ditches, walk past the last wagon of the last train, and follow the tracks to where the station's jurisdiction ends, where its lights no longer reach. There, one will find him, by the semaphore, sitting on an empty wooden box. The storm lamp rests on the ground next to him, casting an uncertain circle of luminosity around his feet.

"Let's make a deal," he says. The burning end of his cigarette looks like a distant railway signal.

Even now, this will be a standing audience only. A master race to the end, even on their knees.

"The war's nearly over. It will end in a few days' time, a few weeks' at most. Everyone can see that, so what are you hoping for?" I ask.

"Don't think me a fool," tension reverberates in his voice, like a metal string about to snap. Don't think me a fool. Is that what it all comes down to in the end – a peasant boy's inferiority complex? "I know that. I want an escape." He pauses to shake off the ash. "You can give that to me."

I'm tempted to shout at him: you will escape anyway ... But maybe you won't. Maybe in one story you will hang from a lamp post after somebody someday eventually recognizes you. Maybe in another one you will live to be eighty and will die in your bed, in sleepy suburbia, the matter of an embarrassing SS tattoo under your armpit only coming to light at the funeral home, when undertakers wash your body in preparation for burial. Or maybe somewhere else you're not my grandfather at all. But in this one? I don't know. This one is not finished yet.

"You've killed in cold blood three people I wanted to save. And now you want me to make deal with you?" I ask him.

"I still have the one you want to save the most," he answers.

That's right, I can never forget. It's the only thing I now think about. "Why should I trust you anymore?"

"Because this time I mean it," he says. "It's not a game anymore. Besides, the third time lucky, isn't that so?" in the past he would chuckle at his joke. Tonight his voice is halting and flat like a wine that has been left out in a glass for too long.

So this time he means it. But I can never trust him, even if I wanted to. And I don't want to. He would never honor his side of the bargain, not after everything he's done before. I look at him and I have little doubt that once he has what he wants he would kill Katrina and then kill me. It would be closure for him.

"The net has been cast and many will be caught by the Allies. Or the Russians," I say. "And you're thinking that – what? You will be able to evade the net and disappear with me? Disappear to where?"

"You tell me."

He, who had joyfully murdered women and children only because they carried in them the wrong blood, is gone. For the first time I'm talking to a little blond-haired boy from my dream, standing alone in the middle of his village green, innocent and vulnerable. But I know there is already a germ of decay somewhere within him, and with it, all the promises of evil. Even if I could hope to go back and run my hand through his hair, put my arm around him and wish him a better future, I know that it's too late, far too late. Maybe there is redemption, but I'm not the redeemer. And I know that salvation can't be attained through escaping forever. Not that he wants to be saved, not in that sense of the word.

So, grandfather, I can't make you disappear. I wouldn't want to have you in my world. There are enough bastards there already without dragging over another one from the past. Besides, you've already tried to enter my world – that's why I exist in the first place – and, let's say, the devil took his own.

But there is another voice that speaks up now. Ah, all these sensibilities, but you seem to forget about one small detail. It's actually not that small at all. Katrina. Wouldn't you do anything, absolutely anything, just to have her back? You do love her more than anyone, more than life itself. So maybe a free pass for your grandpa and killing another loved one are not too high a price to pay to make sure she doesn't die?

I only notice the train when it's rushing by, behind me. The air lashes at us, and I struggle to keep the balance. When the train is gone, Behrnard stands up and smoothes out his uniform.

"I have to go now," he says. "We will meet at 2300 hours on May the 7th. The Liense station, west of Chemnitz. Then I'll give you back your girl and you give me a way out." He starts walking back towards the station.

"Behrnard," I shout after him.

He stops and turns around. The storm lamp dangles by his side and he looks like a mariner from an old print.

"Who do you think I am?" I ask him.

He shrugs, "I don't care. All I know is that you're somebody who's got something I need."

"And if I do have that something you want, has it ever occurred to you that it is also in my power to get what I want without giving you anything in exchange?" I try to be clever but even before I finish I understand I have overplayed my hand.

He stares at me for a long while, as if he's trying to weigh his response very carefully. But it's simple, really, and must have been on the tip of his tongue right from the start: "Then why don't you?"

The slap in the face reaches me across the distance. So it remains a stalemate.

I watch his light get smaller and smaller until it disappears altogether, swallowed by darkness.

XV.

I scale the stairs to the house, a plastic bag with groceries in my hand. The midday sun is particularly harsh, the sweat runs off my body in streams and the sunglasses couldn't be dark enough.

With the junk mail under the other arm I fumble around my pocket, looking for the keys. They jingle against loose change but prove difficult to extract, intertwined as they are with the wallet, handkerchief and some old shop dockets.

When I finally get them out I'm just a little more irritated than I have been throughout the day. Having to provide for oneself, trying to maintain a semblance of living, is such a distraction from what I am supposed to be doing right now.

I turn the key and then the knob, but the doors resist. I must have just now locked the door instead. Either I forgot to lock it when I left, or Julie is back.

I fling the door open and step inside.

Hands grab me by my neck and my arms. I'm pushed forward. The bag, junk mail and the keys all tumble down to the floor.

"What –" I open my mouth to scream before my head connects with the wall and the pain explodes from the middle of my forehead, blinding me and washing over the rest of my body like a tsunami wave. Blinded, I roar and try to dislodge myself from the grasp. But the hands still hold onto me. We spin and with the corner of my eye I see a face of a retired wrestler, dumb and emotionless, set on its task. And another face, another pair of hands.

"Calm down, boy," the wrestler grunts, and it comes out as "buoy." His blinking beads of eyes are sunken deep in a red, sweaty mass of face. He's dressed in washed out white; short sleeves that expose his bulging bicepses. A huge watch circles his wrist.

I want to lash out madly with my legs, in any direction, to find somebody's shin, kneecap, better still, the balls, but even before my legs start to move I lose balance and we all tumble to the ground. I smash into the wooden floorboards and they smash on top of me. The air escapes from my lungs and it feels like I've been hit by a speeding car. I want to scream: get off me, get off me, you're crushing me, but sound doesn't come out of my mouth. It feels like it's the last few second of life.

"Goooood," grunts the wrestler, in a drawn-out way, as if he was pacifying a sheep at a farm.

I feel a sharp pain in my right arm as the needle carelessly breaks through the skin. "Good boy," I hear him say before everything, the sounds, the vision, all the sensations swirl into an incomprehensible kaleidoscope and I fall, and fall, and fall, and then there's nothing.

* * *

– and it all blurs into one, everything superimposing itself onto everything else. A collage of ghosts, ghost sounds, ghost visions, somebody's playing with a dial on the television set, going through all the frequencies ... then there are the periods of darkness, forgetting, nothingness, interwoven somewhere in between ... there is no sense of time. I'm an ant drowning in honey. I want to laugh. Maybe I am laughing. Sometimes I think can hear laughter, but I don't know whether it's mine or somebody else's ... The ocean – honey – closes over me ... who are all those people? ... it's so hot, please, somebody open the window, I want to stand up and take a few deep breaths ... My mother, and someone I don't recognize, a man dressed in a white coat ... a doctor ... 'The tests did not show any drugs in his system' ... I hear him say, a small, bespectacled man with wisps of white hair behind his large ears ... I want to scream: that's right, you bastards, the only drugs in me are the ones you keep on pumping into me to keep me up like a zombie in suspended animation. You ... No use ... 'We'll keep him like that a bit longer and run some more tests. It's too early to say, of course, but it could be –' I don't know when it's day, and when it's night ... I think the lights inside my head are burning brightly regardless of time ... My mother is leaning over me and whispering: 'It's all for your own good.' No, no, no. Hell. Don't you all realize I have to go? I have to run, before it's too late, I have to meet Behrnard, I have to ... I have to do something ... do something for Katrina. Please, let me go. You fucking ... Please. 'It's all for your own good. You'll be fine, dear, just rest.' Rest, rest, rest, rest, rest ... She kisses me on the forehead ... her lips aren't cold at all; it's like being touched with a fish taken straight out of water ... I can't lift my hand to wipe it off, I can't ... Mum, mum, mum, what have you done, what have you all done to me ... it's not just my life ... and I don't care about my life so much now anyway ... but ... God ... can you open the bloody window, please? ... It's like I can see Bartok, but is it him? Hello, thanks for coming to see me ... He is saying something; his mouth is moving but all that comes out is a bubbling sound, as if he was underwater ... or maybe I am underwater ... And Katrina ... As if she couldn't see me. I reach out for her but the closer I seem to get the more out of reach she becomes ... what day is it? ... I see von Schellendorff, too ... beautiful, shining, freshly-pressed uniform, with blood seeping through it ... why, why, why? ...

* * *

"Martin."
God, it's so cold.
"Martin."
And dark.
"Where am I?"
"Martin."
It's his voice.
I crouch down and throw my arms around me, as if trying to hug myself. It doesn't help at all; I keep on shivering uncontrollably. It feels like all the heat had rushed out of the air, soaked by a giant invisible sponge all around me.
"Where are you?" I cry out. "Where am I?"
The darkness is breathing.
"Martin," his voice reverberates like that of a priest in a Gothic cathedral. "You have to go."
"I know," I whisper. "I know."
"You don't have much time left."
His voice is everywhere, like the air. I look around but I don't know the directions; I don't know which way is up and which way is down. I guess I'm squatting onto something, but awareness of this fact does not help me at all.
"I have to go," I say.
Oh God, how cold it is.
"Is your mind clear now?"
I hesitate, but answer. "Yes ... I think so." I don't really know. Is my mind clear? That would be an unusual experience lately. I just don't know. It feels good, though. Cool. Sharp. Even though there are hardly any sensations to absorb. Hardly any. But those that are, feel fine to me. "Yes."

"Good. That is good."

That is good, indeed.

"Listen to me carefully," he says. Now I have the impression he's hovering somewhere above my head, with his clean, well tailored suit and felt hat, speaking slowly and annunciating clearly, as only he does. This time it doesn't even begin to irritate me. "It is about twelve o'clock at night – midnight. Everyone is asleep. You have to get out of there. I cannot actually help you do it. That part is up to you."

I nod my head and rock on the balls of my feat. I'm all ears.

"You are restrained and you will not be able to untie yourself. But you have one advantage now. You are awake, yes?"

I nod again. Yes, I am. At least I seem awake now.

"Good. You see, the staff, they do not know that. They expect you will be asleep for a long time because of all the drugs they gave you. But you are awake. That is the only thing I could do for you. So you have to use it."

Oh yes, I will use it all right.

"There is a camera in the upper right-hand corner of your room, but the man in the monitoring room will be watching sports. Make sure that before you go you roll up the blankets on your bed and cover them with the sheets, so it looks like there is still somebody in the bed. When you are out of the room, go to your right, down the corridor. At the end, turn left and go about ten meters. You will see a door on your right. This is an access to the stairway. Go up. Remember: go up. It will take you to the roof. There will a small metal ladder and a hatch. Do you remember?"

Yes, I remember. Blanket, right, left, ten meters, the stairs, up, the hatch.

"You will find yourself on the roof. Straight ahead of you will be ventilation fans. Make a hundred and thirty five degree turn to your left. Do you understand? That is ninety degrees and then half of it. Then go straight. It will take you to the corner of the roof. There is another metal ladder that leads all the way down to the ground. On your way down there is another security camera. You will have to trust your luck with this one. Once you are on the ground run towards the trees on your right. The fence is two and a half meters high. You will have to scale it somehow. It is not electrified and it does not have razor wire on top of it. It is just a private clinic; it is secure but not that secure."

That's comforting. I think I can see my breath rising from my mouth. But it could be my eyes playing tricks on me.

"You should be able to do it. The clinic is in Oxley. No public transport and I do not advise you to catch a cab. I am afraid you will have to walk home. You are weak but you will have to do it. Two, maybe three hours. Do you think you can do it?"

"Do I have any choice?"

"Go to your house. In the top drawer of your desk you will find a letter from me. That is all I have to say."

I wait in silence.

"Bartok?"

There is no answer.

"Bartok?"

That is all he has to say.

* * *

"Bartok?"

I open my eyes.

It's my own voice.

It is still dark, but it's a different kind of darkness. Not as dense, not as pervasive. There is some faint echo of light that travels from the far reaches of the corridor through a small window at the top of the door. There's just enough illumination to see the contours of the room.

Thank you, mother, I'm thinking. Thank you for your concern and thank you for a wonderful gift. A clinic for addicts and other embarrassing family secrets? Really, you shouldn't have. It's Christmas come early. I should have seen it coming.

But I do feel clear, as if somebody has washed me in pure light and wrung the last drops of all the chemicals out of my body. I have only cloudy fragments of memories of the past – hours? days? I have no idea how long I've been tied to this bed, drugged up to my eyeballs.

I move my left hand. An inch or so and I feel the tape restraining me. Yes, the limits of Bartok's magic.

So I wait, once again. I'm getting good at it.

Sometime later I hear the footsteps. They stop outside the door and I close my eyes. I hear the door open and the footsteps continue to my bed.

"How are we doing?" A woman's voice. Middle aged, slight accent, a forced familiarity.

I feel the blankets pulled away.

"Behaving ourselves, are we? Not causing too much trouble?"

Bet you say that to all the guys.

"Let's straighten you out, darling."

Hands playing around my ankles, untying the straps.

"We wouldn't want to get bed sores, would we?"

Oh no, definitely not. Keep talking dirty to me.

My legs are free and she moves to my hands.

"Oh, let's turn you over, darling," she sighs.

The straps fall off my writs and she now puts her hands under my back and my thigh and gives a soft grunt, straining to roll my body on its side.

I'm quick. Before she quite knows what's happening, before she has a chance to open her mouth in a scream, I'm onto her. Her hands are still imprisoned under my body, and my own hands reach her throat and close around it, squeezing the breath out of her. I use the grip to pull myself up and out of the bed. Her eyes bulge but still no sound comes and she grabs on to my wrists. Too late. I spin her in an arc and it almost looks like a waltz movement, if not for the fact that at the end of it the back of her head connects with the wall. I hear a thump and her body now slackens in my hands. I'm sorry, I'm so sorry, I didn't want to do it, I'm so sorry. She is no longer a marionette guided by my skilled hands, but a rag doll, her limp limbs overflowing my embrace. God, I hope it was hard enough but not too hard.

Too late to be sorry now.

I rest her body on the bed. This will be slightly more original than rolled up blankets. Bet that Bartok couldn't have imagined all this. Straps first, firm, then I tear off a piece of my pyjamas and tie it around her mouth. Then tuck her in under the sheet and the blanket.

I hope that the security guy is enjoying his football game. It might be the last one he will ever watch on the job.

And I hope that those closed circuit cameras will not instantly give away a middle aged nurse impersonating a young rehab patient.

I stretch. I'm sore as hell. I don't know how long I've been lying in that bed but all my bones, muscles and tendons tell me it's been too long.

No time to think about it now. I stand up and my head spins. Better hurry.

I pull the door ajar and sneak out of the room.

Turn right.

The corridor is empty. A perpetual dusk from a few weak light bulbs sparsely spaced throughout its length. I move with my back turned to the wall. My feet don't make any noise on the tiled floor.

The corridor ends. Turn left.

The door is only a few meters ahead. I sprint to it.

Thank God my mother did not put me into a really good, expensive clinic with top security.

I run up the stairs. One flight. Another flight. There's even less light in here than in the corridor. I wind myself along the handrail and fly up, hoping for the best.

The metal ladder. The strain of lifting the hatch with one hand, while the other clings to a step. Then the cool air enveloping me with all the unexpected passion and freshness, but it's not as icy as in my vision of Bartok.

There can be no pause now. I spin around just like he'd told me to and head for the corner of the roof.

The ladder goes all the way down to the ground. Three floors only; it's not a large building. I try to see where the security camera is, but it's too dark. As he said, I have to take a chance. The metal steps feel cold under my feet and the pyjamas don't offer much protection against the cold either.

Closer to the ground I jump off the ladder and sprint to my right, towards the trees. I haven't run barefoot on the grass since I was a child. Even now it feels just as exhilarating as I remember it.

The only thing standing between me and freedom is the fence. Bartok was right, it's two and a half meters high. No chain-link either, just straight metal bars every ten or so centimeters apart. I can't climb over it. There's only the tree. I scale the one closest to the fence. The bark scrapes my feet and my hands but nothing will stop me now. I yank, pull, and then push myself up until I'm on the branch that overhangs the fence. It takes me a minute of careful balancing before I can let my body down. It's a long drop from there. Landing with bare feet on concrete is not a good experience. But I don't feel pain now. I run.

* * *

I don't know how much time it took me to get from the clinic back to my place. Unlike sailors, I could never navigate by the stars and I wasted some quarter of an hour getting lost on the back streets of Oxley. I finally got to the main road I recognized from occasional drives and I ran north until I couldn't run anymore. Then I walked. A few cars passed me by, but only one, filled to capacity with drunken teenagers, sounded a horn at me. I think one of the passengers yelled "Nice pyjamas" but I wouldn't swear on it.

I had no choice but to break into my own house. I couldn't afford to wait until the morning to go in and grab whatever I wanted. The ruse with the nurse couldn't go on for too long. Until the morning rounds if I was lucky. If I wasn't, for all I knew, my absence might have been already discovered. And my house would be the first logical place to come looking for me.

But the street looked peaceful enough, and there were no suspicious looking cars parked along the sidewalk.

The fence around the house was a symbolic meter high hurdle I jumped over without any problem. I run around the back of the house and dragged the aluminium stepladder from the side of the shed. My window overlooked the back garden. I left it half open before going shopping, which was just as well since I didn't have any contingency plans if it was locked. Except a brick.

The bedroom was a dark landscape I had to steer using my memory as a map. Walking on my toes, praying that the floor would not squeak under my weight, I made it to the desk and pulled out the top drawer. The envelope was there, as Bartok had promised, on top of other papers.

I grabbed a pair of jeans, a shirt and sneakers; whatever I could pull out from under the bed. I dressed, put the envelope in my pocket, together with some loose change from the desk. I was on the way back to the window when suddenly I stopped and thought of you, T. J.

I came back to the desk, opened another drawer and took out a tape recorder and a few tapes. I dumped them all into a bag, and hurried out before I could push my luck any further.

* * *

There would be a whole day of hiding, somewhere not far away from the yards but far enough from my house.

I opened Bartok's letter and read by the light of a street lamp:

"Dear Martin,
As you remember, you will meet Behrnard on a small station in Liense, a few kilometers south of Chemnitz. It will be one hour to midnight on May the 7th, 1945. The Americans surround it from the West and the Red Army from the East but it will still be in German hands when the surrender is signed.
I wish you all the luck in your endeavour,

B.

P.S. By the way; your meeting is taking place an hour before the war comes officially to an end and before the Victory in Europe Day starts. At a quarter to midnight a train will leave the Liense station, bound for the American lines, with refugees from eastern Germany who want to escape the Russians. It will be the last train of the war. I thought you would want to know that."

* * *

No offer of help, no advice as to what I should do.

Tonight I will have to deal with Behrnard. I've got the way out, which I can't give to him. He's got Katrina, who I can't leave in his hands.

I'm sitting in the park, in a shadow of a giant tree. The bench is out of the way for all the joggers and mothers with little kids, so the sight of a young man talking to his tape recorder for hours on end doesn't turn any heads. When I went over to a nearby shopping center to get something to eat I had to buy one more tape to fit all I wanted to say to you. There's a prepaid postal package sitting on the bench next to me. It's got your address on it. I'll be putting it in the mail soon.

* * *

The pub is not a good place to write. The music's too loud, the light's too meager, and I feel as lonely as that forty-something woman sitting all by herself at the next table, onto her fourth gin and tonic.

I'm hiding in a corner, as far away from the bar as possible, trying to postpone the moment when the waitress will notice that all this time here and I haven't ordered anything. To be honest I wouldn't mind having something to drink but all I have left in my pocket is a few cents.

There's a sheet of paper in front of me, getting stuck to dried-out beer rings on the table. I'm trying to write something to my family. I'm not sure whether it's a farewell letter or perhaps a plea for understanding. Whatever it is meant to be, I'm finding it impossible to put into words how I'm feeling right now.

"I'm sorry for everything I've done, but I couldn't do anything else, I don't think ...

"... can't explain...

"Still love you ...

"Don't think ill of me."

The TV set hanging from the ceiling is showing a boxing match, but the regulars seem to ignore it. Maybe they know it's fixed.

To hell with it. Whatever I say will be wrong, or insufficient, or meaningless. I screw the page into a small ball and make my way out of the pub. There's no one outside, and only one lonely pickup truck is making its way on the street. I throw the ball of paper into the gutter and walk away.

* * *

So this is the story so far.

... the story so far ...

I am recording it and sending it to you because I don't know what will happen to me tonight. I'm sorry that you won't know the end. But it's probably better that at least you know most of the story rather than nothing at all. I want you to know. Not necessarily believe but know.

I remember Depeche Mode playing on my stereo, not that long ago. I know, I know, you hate all the '80s music. It's from "Violator." Dave Gahan is singing "I'm waiting for the night to fall, I know that it will save us all."

I hope it will.

Over and out, my friend.

To the Dawn

I.

T.J.? IS THAT YOUR NAME? I hope I am not mistaken.

We have a mutual friend, you and I. He was telling you a story. A curious story, an interesting story. I think he wanted you to know how it ends. He would think that he owes you that, and I think I owe him something, too.

So listen ...

* * *

The Liense train station does not exist anymore except inside the heart of its station master, as fleeting recollections of those who might have once passed through it, and an as yet unknown potentiality in the mind of the architect who will raise it from the ashes once the fighting is over.

The station, cradled in a valley and braced between a stream and a road, is still smoldering. A wing of the 5th Bomber Group has made Liense its last target of the war, reducing much of the station and the nearby town to rubble. Intelligence reports indicated that remnants of several Waffen SS battalions have taken over Liense, preparing for the last desperate stand on the road to Chemnitz. The intelligence was wrong. Only a flotsam of the regular Wehrmacht units, without orders, communication and hope, were still roaming the countryside around the town. Most of the casualties of the air raid were civilians from Chemnitz and beyond, escaping the advance of what they saw as Asiatic locusts which rape all the women and loot everything in their path.

And so the city burns, a few hundred meters down the road from the station, and the red glow hovers over the valley. There is no one to extinguish the flames anymore. Along the road the wrecks of cars and carts hit by bombs get pushed into the ditches together with the bodies of their occupants, so that the tide of terrified humanity can continue on its frantic exodus.

By some small miracle one of the railway lines remains undamaged and soon it will carry the last trainload of refugees towards the west. The engine and the remnants of the stock got stranded here about a week ago when the advancing armies cut off the lines further from the town. Now the train driver is being forced at gunpoint by one desperate man to make himself available for his last mission of mercy towards the American lines.

Martin stands alone and watches the apocalypse before him. He's thinking: as if a theater had been hit by an artillery barrage, the decorations are burning and the spectators are scrambling for a way out of Hell painted by a time-travelling Hieronymus Bosch on acid. Where, among it all, is Katrina? And Behrnard?

Three Tiger tanks stand abandoned behind the station after their fuel had finally run out. Their crews are not here anymore, ordered by their superior to march against the current of refugees towards Chemnitz. The officer's last communication with his field headquarters had taken place over 24 hours ago. He does not know where to go and doesn't yet realize that some time ago it ceased to matter at all. When the time to lay down their arms comes tomorrow morning, they will hardly have any arms left to lay. And the tanks only serve to remind those who swarm around them that they are all on their own now. Their country and its army do not exist anymore; there is only the last train.

The train waits on the siding. This is probably what had saved it a few hours earlier. Had it been shunted onto the main line it would have taken the brunt of the blast which levelled the station building and ripped apart the rails, pushing them grotesquely twisted towards the sky like the radix of an uprooted iron tree.

No one really knows who first noticed the train but the news spread fast. Those with carts or bicycles abandoned them, joining those escaping on foot in an unexpected detour taking them from the main road, through the desolation of the Liense station, towards the miracle train.

Martin wades into the human mill. People crash against him like waves, push him, tug him along, as he makes his way through the station's skeleton. He strains his eyes, looking around, trying to take advantage of the ever-fleeting moments when the fire's glare lights up the features of those around him. They are all strangers, a crying child dragged along by a panicking parent; a woman with empty eyes carried forward by the current, her mind left buried together with the loved ones under the rubble of her home; a well-dressed man straining to save his bulging suitcase. But no her, no him. God, he is praying silently, let her be somewhere here. I still don't know what I will do when I find her, but let her be here …

I see him notice me, as he zooms in on me among the sea of faces. His pace quickens, his shoulders open the way, and soon he is standing in front of me.

"The station master?" he shouts through the clamor. "Are you the station master here?"

"Yes, sir," I say and spread my arms in resignation. "A station master without a station."

Somebody running behind me shoves me aside and I stumble forward, but his hands reach out to steady me.

"Have you seen a man and a woman ..." he starts.

I throw my head back in laughter. "So many, sir –"

"No, no," he shudders. "A man in an SS uniform –"

"No," I say. "Nobody here in an SS uniform. No SS people for a very long time."

"God," he turns his head, trembling with impatience. "A man, blond man, about ..." he cuts the air with his hand in a horizontal slash, "about this height. And a woman. Shorter, dark hair. Beautiful." He pauses looking for words. "He's holding her against her will."

A scuffle erupts behind us and a maelstrom of human bodies starts spinning amid screams and cursing, gathering momentum with every body it accidentally attracts.

"They were here," he says. "They were here waiting, before it – the train – the whole thing started."

Through the conversation he never lets go of me. He's holding onto my arms like a shipwreck clinging to the last raft. I think he would start shaking me, shaking me really hard, if I do not say anything.

"Yes."

His eyes widen.

"Yes," I say. "They ... were here."

He drags me towards him so that our bodies are only inches apart and I can feel his breath on my face. "Where are they know?"

"They went off in that direction," I cannot point so I motion with my head towards the town.

"How long ago?"

"About an half an hour," I say. He loosens his grip and I almost topple forward.

"Thank you," he shouts towards me and disappears in the crowd.

Where have they gone? How far have they gone? he's thinking. We were supposed to meet at the station. Surely they couldn't have left. It's not the time yet ...

... what time is it?

Martin looks down to his wrist but there is no watch. He slows down to feel around all the pockets. It is unlikely that he will find a watch there or anything else for that matter. It is a brand-new suit. What a rarity, if only anyone would still pay any attention. The only object that Martin's hand encounters is a smooth metal shape tucked behind his belt against the small of his back, something he had been too busy to notice before. As his fingers close around the handle and the coldness of steel tingles his skin, he recognizes what he is holding, and a tremor of apprehension passes through his body. And of vulnerability. A gun. The only help.

The further away from the ruins he walks the smaller the crowd. The tumult recedes behind him and he no longer chooses to hear their noise.

By the side of the track rests the dead carcass of another tank, leaning on the gentle slope that rolls towards the unseen stream. The turret is turned backwards and the gun slumps down impotently. Through the open hatch, clouds of thick, oily smoke rise up in the still, motionless air, chased up by the tongues of red flame. The tank is a giant oil lamp made of metal, lighting the night around it. It's a beacon.

"And so we see each other, the last time."

The voice does not really come as a surprise but it still makes Martin shudder.

Behrnard walks out from behind the tank, moving warily in a half-circle, a predator by instinct. He once used to look like a black panther, now he is merely a hyena, scared and harangued, looking for scraps of someone else's kill. His uniform is gone now, abandoned like the rest of his unwanted past, and he's wearing civilian clothes. It's a strange metamorphosis that sees not a butterfly leaving its chrysalis but an even uglier grub.

"Where is she?" Martin asks. His calm veneer is hair-width thin and he prays that he does not lose his mind when he finally sees her.

Behrnard motions with his left hand and takes a step back. It's an invitation. Martin steps forward, but maintains some distance.

There she is, on the other side of the tank, kneeling down, her hands tied in front of her with rope, in turn tied to a handle on the side of the tank. Martin's heart skips a beat. He wants to run to her but Behrnard is standing between them, watching his every move, a gun somewhere close by his hand. But would Behrnard risk shooting a person who possesses the only thing he now wants? It's all endless possibilities and uncertainties, and Martin has come too far to risk everything now.

"I ... want to touch her," he says quietly, not wanting to betray the fact that an invisible hand is closing around his throat and squeezing the air out him.

"Later," says Behrnard. But there is so little time.

"What have you done to her?" Martin asks. He meets her gaze and does not let go. Will not let go. Thousands of words are being said now, silently, but he fears he does not understand them all. God, it has been, what? a week, two weeks for him? and it has been months for her ... But it seems like years. She is but a shadow of herself, or rather, the shadow of what he remembers of her; a shadow of a shadow: thin and pale, her hair matted and dull. Her body lost under the big army coat thrown over her shoulders. It is only her eyes that are still as he remembers them. She is there, inside her eyes. But barely.

"Nothing," says Behrnard. "I've done nothing to her. Just protecting my most valuable asset."

Finally Martin forces himself to wrest his eyes off her, even though he fears that, somehow, to let go is to lose her, for the second time. "Do you intend to play cards again?" he turns towards Behrnard. They are both standing between the rails, enclosed and protected by the magic of iron.

Suddenly it all strikes Behrnard as very funny. "No cards this time," he laughs and the laughter turns into a cough. He half-turns away from Martin and bends in a fit of hacking. He spits and straightens up again. "No cards this time," he repeats. "No cards left." He pulls something out of his breast pocket and throws it at Martin. Three pieces of paper, they fly half-way towards Martin, then stop in mid-air as if they'd struck a glass wall, and fall to the ground. Three pieces of paper, three cards, cracked and scorched at the edges, no, two of them half-consumed by flame and only one intact. A joker staring back at Martin, his mischievous grin trying to come through caked dirt. "No cards this time." There is a great sadness in his voice, as if for a lost friend.

"So what are we going to do?" asks Martin.

"I've spent years chasing you," Behrnard says. "I still don't know who you are, or why you did the things you did, but I know it was us who were supposed to be the new race of supermen. Himmler told us so." He nervously runs his hand through his unruly hair. The strands fall back onto his forehead the very moment he takes out his hand. "I still want to be a superman. I want out."

Martin closes his eyes and his body is shaken by a spasm of silent laughter. "Tell me who you think I am," he shouts. "Tell me!"

"You're a demon, a god! I don't know!" There is desperation in Behrnard's voice, a realization that perhaps there are no answers, there are no solutions, that this small, private house of cards will keep collapsing onto him, just as the big one is collapsing everywhere around. "You only come out at night," he adds, almost an afterthought, as if the answer lay somewhere in that one detail.

"Martin," her voice rattles him and he turns his head towards her. She is looking at him, raked by apprehension and concern. "I don't know ... what you're doing, but ... don't ..." her voice comes out haltingly, as if she had forgotten how to speak. Her dark eyes shine like precious stones from under the twisted mess of her hair. She has never looked so beautiful to him.

Martin turns towards Behrnard. "It is a great gift. A great prize," he says. There is now hardness in his voice and hardness in his eyes. The world around does not exist; there is only him, Behrnard, Katrina. And a bluff. There is nothing that can be bought but time.

Behrnard's eyes widen as the door starts to open.

But Martin speaks slowly, "After all you've done, how can you think you even deserve to escape?"

"It's not up to you to pass judgment on me," Behrnard half-turns and raises his head towards the sky. "Do you know what my life has been like? Do you have any idea? To escape all the shit, scraping my fingernails as I climbed the rock, until my fucking fingers bled. But however high I thought I'd climbed it was always only a few inches above where I'd started and the shit was still dropping down on me from up high ... all over me ... Nobody, from nowhere, going nowhere, that was me –"

Martin's face twists with contempt. "And that's the excuse for your life? 'Shit.' Is that what you've told all those people – children – whose eyes were asking you 'Why are you killing me?' – 'Shit' –"

"Damn you, Bittmann," Behrnard growls. "What do you care? I don't owe you any excuses ... I don't need any excuses. I need a way out." He pauses and then adds, "Take me with you. To wherever you go when you leave. We will all leave together and then once it's done you two can go your own way."

The offer.

The response. "Your black uniform, your shiny death's head on your cap didn't make you a superman, didn't give you a way out. Pumping bullets into screaming women and children didn't give you a way out. Killing von Schellendorff didn't give you a way out. What makes you think I will give you a way out –"

"I've got your woman!" Behrnard cuts in.

"What makes you think I will give you a way out?" Martin screams even louder. His voice sounds like the howling of a wounded animal. An angry animal, which only gets madder when gushed.

"I've got your woman," repeats Behrnard, his voice losing some of its force.

"Do you think I will work miracles for you? Make a little boy from some godforsaken shit hole of a village into a master among the master race?" Martin's angry yell echoes through the air. If anyone was listening ... But it is just two men, a woman and a burning tank, somewhere far, far away from the crowd, en route to nowhere. None of them see me, standing just outside the circle of light.

Behrnard pulls out his gun and points it at Katrina. He's had enough discussions, enough confessions.

"Take me with you or she dies. Now," he says.

Down the line, at the station that is not there any more, the train has now been filled to the last space and cannot take on any more people. For some unknown reason, as if to stir up memories, the engine driver signals to go. The mournful whistle pierces the night. It jolts Behrnard who looks around puzzled.

Martin reaches for his belt and pulls out the gun. Behrnard snaps out and his hand moves in an arc in Martin's direction.

I propel myself forward, out of the darkness. My body flies, so light, as if I have been a bird all my life and did not know it. Only to get between them. They do notice me, with the corners of their eyes, in a fraction of a second, but the whole eternity after it is too late.

The metal flashes and all I hear are two explosions that almost, almost, merge into one thunder.

I do not see what happens next. A blink of an eye, too fast. But I know.

It feels like somebody took a sledgehammer and pounded into my chest. When the impact throws me backwards, towards Martin, I see Behrnard spin around in a clumsy pirouette. Then his legs crumble underneath him and he is falling, too.

Only Martin is standing, the bullet aimed at his heart now resting somewhere inside me.

He seems to be in shock, frozen, the gun now dangling in his limp arm, by his side. I feel a great stone crushing my chest, pinning me to the ground. A moan escapes through my clenched teeth and then, suddenly, he snaps out of it. He drops down to his knees by my side and opens my blazer. The shirt has already lost its original color; a great beautiful river of red is now flowing through the middle of my chest.

"Who are you?" he asks. "Why did you do it?"

"Martin," I try to smile. "You always ask so many questions."

His hands stop in mid-movement and his mouth opens. He looks at me intently trying to decipher my face, superimpose one map onto another. There is disbelief in his eyes.

"I was young once, too," I say. "That is the way I want to stay."

"I –" he wants to say something, but I just shake my head. "Untie her," I whisper.

He hovers above me for a moment and then he runs down towards the tank and falls to his knees in front of Katrina. He is staring at her, almost uncertain what to do. And then he comes to life again, shaken and possessed, fumbling at her hands, ripping off the ropes, until her hands are free again, clasped between his. It is almost painful watching them, almost a sacrilege, but I see, I have no choice. I see even though my eyes are fixed on the skies above me.

There are no words. Speaking seems superfluous, banal. It will not go deep enough. There will be a time for words later. Much later.

They stand up and he is still holding her in his arms.

"Watch out," I say. I concentrated too closely on them to notice ...

Behrnard is looking up at them from between the rails where he is laying. His elbow is resting on the wood of a slipper and the gun trembles in his weakening hand, only centimeters off the ground. "You bastard," he winces and then he is silent again, for every breath is a red-hot pincer tearing at his lungs.

But even though I failed to see, Martin did not. In a fraction of a second before my warning he steps in front of Katrina and holds out his gun before him. A stalemate. Again.

"Run to the train," he tells her.

"No," she whispers behind him. "I'm not going to leave you again."

"Run," he raises his voice. His heart pounds against the ribs, like a caged bird desperate to get out. "Please," he whispers now. "Please, go. I'll be with you ..."

"Go," I say to her. She turns towards me. She does not recognize me. How could she? She only knows the same older me that Martin does.

"Please, go," Martin repeats. Katrina hesitates, then puts her hand on his shoulder and squeezes it lightly. A tremor runs through his hand at that moment, almost imperceptible.

"Don't make me wait," she pleads and turns away. She's remembering how to run again, slowly at first, then faster, as fast as she can. She sobs and she lets herself be carried away, leaving the memories bleeding on the rails by the burning tank.

Martin and Behrnard face each other across only a few meters of track, but the distance between them is greater than between here and the stars. I don't know how much time passes that way in silence and stillness. A few seconds? A minute?

Then Behrnard moans and his hand collapses to the ground. The gun slips out of his grip and tumbles onto the gravel. His head rolls from side to side in pain.

But Martin does not move.

The gun in his outstretched hand does not look like an alien object anymore, more like an extension of his arm. He really seems a god, a dark god of wrath, about to unleash lightning from the palm of his hand and smite the enemy stretched out before him.

"I have a way out for you," Martin whispers through clenched teeth. "So clean and simple. An answer to your prayer."

Behrnard makes an effort to shift his weight on the good shoulder and raises his head again.

"You wanted me to make you disappear? Your wish is my command. I will make you disappear. Forever," Martin says. There are beads of sweat rolling down his forehead, into his eyes, and the veins on his head throb madly. He bites his lip until he tastes the sweetness of his own blood.

"Kill him, and you will never be able to go back. With or without her," I say haltingly, pain squeezing my throat with its cold, steely hand. But he hears me anyway. "You might not exist there anymore."

Yes, he does hear me. "Maybe I don't want to anymore," he finally answers. It is no longer a consideration. For many reasons.

But all that is irrelevant anyway. There are no consequences when you cannot do the act. He cannot. He fired once, more out of instinct than intent. Now that there is consciousness there is no will. There is hatred but no animation. A man who has seen so much, a man who lost his friend to Behrnard, a man whose every sensibility is revolted by the existence of somebody like that. A man crazed with love. But still, his finger trembles on the little metal tongue, and there is no strength to pull it in just that little fraction more. Is it because the veneer of civilization suddenly and unexpectedly proves to be thicker around him than he would have expected? Or is it because, ever so mysteriously, he can hear Behrnard's blood calling out to him across the great chasm, and it is his own?

I can't, he thinks. God, I can't.

"Even if he has had her?" I whisper.

It is like an electric shock passing through him. He throws a glance at me, his nostrils flared, his mouth half-open, questions crowding on the tip of his tongue. In the end he does not say anything to me. Just as well; I was never very good at answering his questions.

"What did you do to her?" he asks Behrnard, the words struggling to get out.

Behrnard sighs. "Nothing." Even when he swallows saliva it seems to convulse his whole body.

"What did you do to her?" Martin repeats. Inside his mind there is nothing but red and black swirling together in a mad dance, drowning everything else.

Then the mask slips off Behrnard's face and he bursts out laughing. His whole body trembles and the laughter turns into grunts. He rolls on the side and his forehead rests on the ground. Blood drips from the corner of his mouth onto the gravel.

"So sweet, so sweet," he murmurs and yet again manages to balance himself on his side. Their eyes meet and his body is raked with a mute chuckle. "She loved every second of it," he says.

Martin closes his eyes and the whole scene becomes a snapshot frozen in time. Only the flames move, dancing out of the tank.

"Goodbye, grandfather." It is a dull, flat sound coming out of Martin. Behrnard strains to understand whether he's hearing correctly. In the end he thinks he is, and so the last thing that flashes through his eyes is incomprehension. Total and utter incomprehension. Not at his fate, because he knows he is about to die. But to die at the hands of someone who so obviously had lost his mind.

Then Martin pulls on the trigger. It echoes on forever.

After the forever is finally over he swings his arm and throws the gun into the night with a roar of pain. When he kneels down by my side I see tears starting to gather in the corners of his eyes.

"Why?" he whispers.

Because ... this is how it can end.

"Run," I say.

"I can't leave you here," he says. I know that his body is still here, leaning over me, but his mind has already started racing away. "Run," I repeat.

He is trembling, and his hand hovers above my forehead. He wants to touch me, as if his touch could heal me. But deep inside, he knows there is nothing he can do.

"Thank you," he whispers. "Thank you."

And then he explodes into motion, like a sprinter in an Olympic race.

There is a night sky above me and it looks like somebody has taken a fistful of little diamonds and strewn them across the dark canvas. I see the thin stream of my breath flow aloft and become one with the river of stars.

I see him running, like he has never run in his life. His feet barely touch the ground. He is flying now and nothing can stop him. The train is moving away, slowly at first, but it gains speed, like a giant cold-blooded lizard finally woken from slumber. She is standing in the door of the last carriage and screams out his name. He is getting closer, running past all the people who didn't find room onboard. Running as if it was not his own strength carrying him forward anymore – for there is almost none left – but some divine wind.

And I see myself, as I was not that long ago, as I do not want to see myself, as I will never be again. I see all the faces, hundreds and thousands of them, as they're driven onto the train – my train – and then I'm told to go, and I fire the engine and we travel until we reach the gate. *Arbeit Macht Frei*. Work makes you free. Again, and again, and again. Thank you, engine driver. Go back for the next load.

I cannot forget. I see them all, and I think how fitting – how good – it is for me to end it all only a few strokes of the clock before the whole monstrous time is no more. No, thank you, I think of Martin – and others – I do not think I have ever really had the chance to thank. For the gift of salvation. I know it has to be this way.

I see her hand stretched out to him, and I see his hand coming closer and closer as the engine inside him makes the last effort. Then their hands meet and grasp each other and he roars and his other hand flies towards the handrail. And as he clutches the cold metal with one hand and the warmth of her hand in the other, his feet leave the ground and he's flying.

I look at the sky and it seems that every star is somebody's face – their faces – looking down on the world at night, looking at me. There is no fear, no hatred, no pain anymore.

And then there is only peace.

* * *

? May 1945 ?

Dear T.J.,

We stopped by a country church, close to a small station the name of which I have already managed to forget. A Catholic priest married us. I haven't been inside a church in years, and it wasn't Katrina's church either ... But it seemed so right. The priest didn't ask any questions even though I can't help thinking that he knew – somehow knew – everything. It was all in his eyes, and his smile. Don't ask me to explain it.

And so I promised to have and to hold, until death do us part. God, how I mean it. I'm happy. I've never been so happy in my life.

I'm not sure how I'm going to send this postcard to you. I gave it to the station master and he assured me he will post it, when services resume. He's got an air of honesty about him, so I think he'll at least try.

Always your friend,

Martin

P.S. I forgot to tell you; it's a glorious day down here. We're travelling along the valley and there is no cloud in sight. The sun is so warm and the sky has turned almost orange ...